PRAISE FOR SALLY WRIGHT
AND HER BEN REESE

"Archivist and amateur detective Ben [...] far off the beaten path of fictional [...] delightful to get in on the ground floor with a mystery writer who, God willing, will be keeping us instructed, entertained, puzzled, and moved for many years to come."

LINDA BRIDGES, NATIONAL REVIEW

"Wright has given us intelligent, literate (and literary) adult...mysteries that follow in the tradition of G. K. Chesterton, C. S. Lewis, Dorothy Sayers, Flannery O'Connor, and Russell Kirk.... Wright succeeds well in avoiding the preachy and predictable, and—most of all—the trendy."

CHRONICLES

"If you like mysteries that are not cheap and tawdry, you'll enjoy the Ben Reese mysteries by Sally Wright."

CHRISTIAN LIBRARY JOURNAL

PURSUIT AND PERSUASION

"Involving and compelling...that rare combination of challenging classic mystery and compelling action novel."

THE DALLAS MORNING NEWS

"In *Pursuit and Persuasion,* Wright cements her position as a disciple of the conventions of the Golden Age of mysteries. Her style recalls the literary fluency of Dorothy L. Sayers and Ngaio Marsh."

CHICAGO SUN-TIMES

"There's an art to the academic mystery, and Sally S. Wright has it pretty much mastered in her Ben Reese series.... In *Pursuit and Persuasion,* Wright provides nice variations on the mainstays of the academic whodunit: a picturesque setting, bookish motives for murder, thick historical background, and an assortment of smart characters."

THE NEW YORK TIMES BOOK REVIEW

"If most mysteries seem too simple, with too few suspects, try *Pursuit and Persuasion.* This is the third Ben Reese mystery. We plan to find the first two."

THE ASSOCIATED PRESS

"Wright has created an intriguing character in Ben Reese, an intellectual who is also a man of action when necessary."

"*Pursuit and Persuasion* is a wonderful novel—evocative of Scotland, full of real, living characters, and backed by a solid plot. I highly recommend it."

BARBARA D'AMATO, AUTHOR OF THE CAT MARSALA MYSTERIES

"A very satisfying literary mystery. Wright gets to let herself go on such topics as microbiology, rubber, falconry and antiquarian books."

THE POISONED PEN

"Ben Reese is a most interestingly complex sleuth. He has a core of steel hidden by an intellectual curiosity that matches Wright's own."

AKRON BEACON JOURNAL

"If you'd like to spend time with genteel stalwarts whose love of Christ motivates sacrifices that are sermons in themselves, come on in. Sally Wright and Ben Reese are sophisticated, edifying friends."

ICHRISTIAN.COM

PRIDE AND PREDATOR

"This is quite a compelling story. Wright not only provides clever leads to challenge the readers, but she also has created a strong and interesting protagonist in Ben Reese."

PUBLISHERS WEEKLY

"Sally Wright shows us a good deal more about the mysteriousness of human existence than she tells. Beautifully written, compellingly told. A fine new writer has arrived."

RALPH MCINERNY, AUTHOR OF THE FATHER DOWLING MYSTERIES

"*Pride and Predator* is a suspenseful tale of good, evil, and greed. Fans of the stories of Ngaio Marsh, Dorothy Sayers, and other Golden Age detective novelists will find this just their cup of tea."

ROMANTIC TIMES

"An evocative storyteller, Wright's descriptions of the ancient land of Scotland and the family relationships of its inhabitants are as compelling as the mystery itself."

MOSTLY MURDER

"A welcome retreat to the Golden Age of mystery. Definitely a must for those who relish classic mystery authors."

THE SNOOPER

"If Sally S. Wright's budding mystery series doesn't get at least a little buzz out there in the book world, it won't be because she doesn't deserve it."

FT. WORTH STAR–TELEGRAM

PUBLISH AND PERISH

"Publish and Perish is put together with polish and precision. It echoes such classic writers as Dorothy Sayers and Ngaio Marsh without in any way imitating them."

THE WASHINGTON TIMES

"Wright has written a good mystery, and a morality tale as well."

INSIGHT

"In *Publish and Perish,* a disgruntled professor disparages the murder victim's attempt at fiction writing: 'He would never have been capable of creating rounded, realistic characters.' But Sally Wright is. Readers will not soon forget her protagonist, a much-wounded World War II veteran and now a famed academic archivist."

WILLIAM KIENZLE, AUTHOR OF NO GREATER LOVE

"Sally Wright has wrought a novel of exquisite wit and charm."

RALPH MCINERNY, AUTHOR OF THE FATHER DOWLING MYSTERIES

THE BEN REESE MYSTERY SERIES

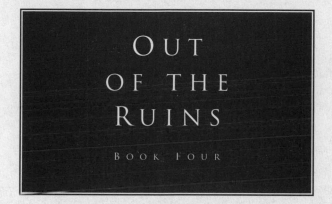

OUT OF THE RUINS

BOOK FOUR

SALLY S. WRIGHT

Multnomah® Publishers *Sisters, Oregon*

OUT OF THE RUINS
published by Multnomah Publishers, Inc.
© 2003 by Sally S. Wright

International Standard Book Number: 1-59052-031-9

Cover image by Raymond Gehman/Corbis

Multnomah is a trademark of Multnomah Publishers, Inc., and is registered in the U.S. Patent and Trademark Office. The colophon is a trademark of Multnomah Publishers, Inc.

Printed in the United States of America

For information:
MULTNOMAH PUBLISHERS, INC.
POST OFFICE BOX 1720
SISTERS, OREGON 97759

Library of Congress Cataloging-in-Publication Data
Wright, Sally S.
   Out of the ruins / Sally S. Wright.
      p. cm.
   ISBN 1-59052-031-9
   1. Cumberland Island (Ga.)--Fiction. 2. Inheritance and succes-sion--Fiction. 3. Multiple sclerosis--Patients--Fiction. 4. Aged women--Fiction. I. Title.
   PS3573.R5398 O98 2003
   813'.54--dc21   2002009317

03 04 05 06 07 08 09—10 9 8 7 6 5 4 3 2 1 0

Because of Joe
who, after half a lifetime,
still makes me want to get up in the morning
to hear what he's got to say.

In memory of C. too,
who faced the MS as well as Hannah does
for all the same reasons.

LIST OF CHARACTERS

Garrett Aiken:	Johanna Elliott's fiancé
Estelle Baxter:	Cook at Whitfield Inn
Roy Black:	Groundsman at Whitfield Inn
Adam Clark:	Captain, Whitfield Inn boat
Carrie Davis:	One of Hannah Hill's helpers
Johanna Elliott:	Hannah Hill's niece
Carl French:	Atlanta developer
Daniel Henderson:	Donor in Tryon, North Carolina
David Hill:	Hannah's deceased husband
Hannah Williams Hill:	MS sufferer on Cumberland
Mary Hill:	Hannah and David's daughter
Red Johnson:	Groundsman at Whitfield Inn
Mrs. Land:	Ship-to-shore phone operator
Kate Lindsay:	Writer, friend of Ben Reese
Charlotte Hill MacKinnon:	Owner of Whitfield Inn and most of Cumberland
Leah Louisa MacKinnon:	Daughter of Charlotte and Rafe
Rafe MacKinnon:	Charlotte's deceased husband
Reverend Douglas Michaels:	Hannah Hill's minister
George Milton:	Antiques dealer in Charleston
Edward Montgomery:	Real estate agent
Lucille Nightingale Montgomery:	Ed's mother, descendent of Nathanael Greene
Dr. Thomas Patterson:	Hannah Hill's doctor
Florence Rich:	Hannah Hill's nurse
Susanna Hill Smith:	Charlotte MacKinnon's sister

Dr. Will Smith: Susanna's husband

Hal Sutton: Owner of north end of Cumberland

Robert Sykes: Ben's lawyer friend in Charleston

Amelia Whiteford Walker: Ben's aunt, Whitfield's manager

Randall Wilkes: Nurseryman friend of Hannah and Johanna

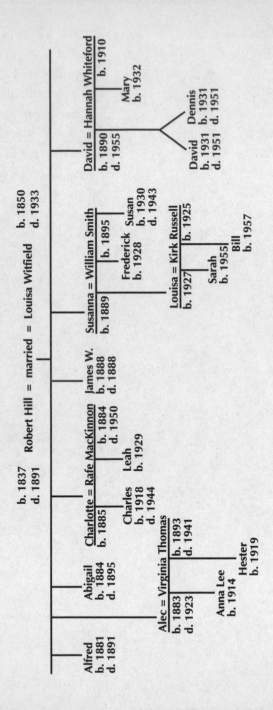

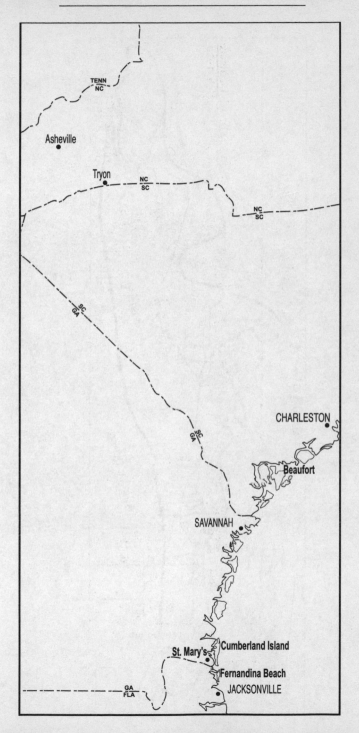

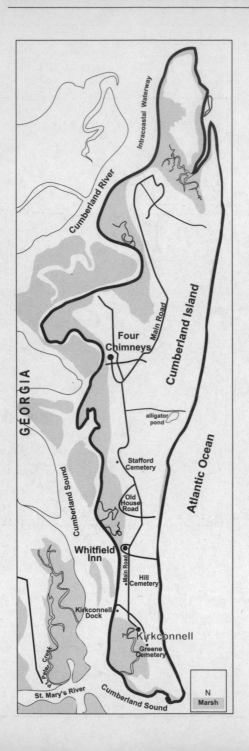

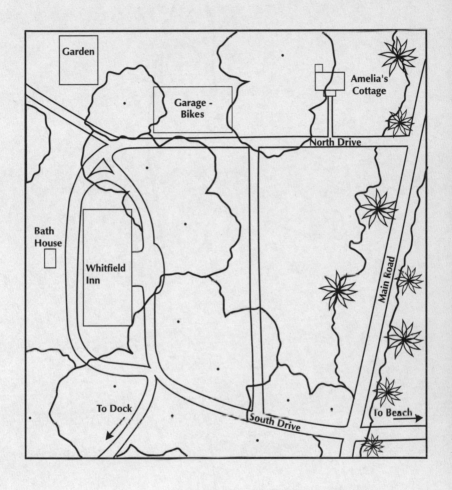

Garden

Garage - Bikes

Amelia's Cottage

North Drive

Bath House

Whitfield Inn

Main Road

To Dock

South Drive

To Beach

CHAPTER ONE

SUNDAY, JANUARY 10, 1960

CHARLOTTE HILL MACKINNON SHOVED her chair away from her desk and slapped a cloth-and-leather ledger shut before she stood up muttering hotly to herself about the price of food and upkeep and the cost of help on an island.

*Paying the lawyers what's killing me, and any fool can see that's what they're counting on. Me, running out of money. And I will too, in not too many years. If I keep having to fight the developer **and** the federal government.*

Charlotte tucked the last letter from the Atlanta lawyer inside the waistband of her skirt to take to Hannah. And then started looking for her car keys, shuffling papers and books and bones on the desk (one small flounder skeleton, the carapace of a horseshoe crab, three sun-bleached vertebrae—raccoon, squirrel and fox), while she felt her heart beating at her own bones and her face getting hot with irritation.

She was standing on a moth-eaten oriental rug rubbing an arthritic thumb knuckle with long bony fingers, glaring around at her office as though a trick had been played on her by a long-standing enemy she believed to be hiding nearby.

She looked past rocks and seashells, and gazed around the loggerhead skull, and the stuffed boar and antelope heads fixed to the dark paneled walls between snake skins, and the several stuffed birds she'd raised or shot.

She glanced at the African spears in a corner, and the photographs of friends in Kenya, next to maps of Cumberland Island from the sixteenth century to the middle of the twentieth.

She stared at the jumble behind the dirt and dust, at the thickets of unmatched family antiques shoved wherever there was room, without much noticing anything but what wasn't there—the keys to her old World War II Jeep.

Charlotte shouted the short Anglo-Saxon word she saved for special occasions (the one she never had said in front of Hannah, even when Kirkconnell was burning to the ground), as she threw her long silver braid behind her shoulder to get the itch of it off her neck.

She never carried a purse.

They weren't in the pockets of her old torn skirt.

And she couldn't think where else to look.

She'd put Rafe's set somewhere safe a week or so after he died, but she never had remembered where, and ten years had passed without them putting in an appearance.

So the only thing left was to search the backyard, on the route she'd walked from the paddocks to the house. And she picked up the sweater she'd thrown on the floor when she'd come in from feeding her horses—shouting, "About time!" in a harsh scratchy voice, when she felt the keys in the pocket.

Then she shot into the hall, grabbed her coat and hat off the rack of wooden pegs, stepped over two fat yellow labs—and blew through the back door on her way to feed the pheasants.

She scattered grain in their pen by the old wooden stables, then hand-fed the parrots and big macaws in the new winter cages she'd built in the garage, after she'd glanced at the clock on the wall and seen there was reason not to rush.

She didn't want to get to Whitfield when Hannah was eating dinner. It made her too uncomfortable to watch her being fed.

The Jeep started as soon as she turned the key, and she leaned forward and patted the star on the khaki hood, as she headed south to the north–south road on Four Chimneys's long tree-lined drive.

She'd lived under them for seventy-five years, the live oaks that covered Cumberland, and yet she still couldn't not look at them—the thick curling limbs a hundred feet long in every direction draped with gray Spanish moss, protecting the island from the east wind off the ocean and the mainland-side marsh from hot afternoon Georgia sun.

Many of the trees stretching above her had been there for three hundred years, shading the natives, the Spanish, the English, the pirates, the soldiers who'd fought there in three American wars, the family of General Nathanael Greene, when they'd owned the island and lived on the south end, and Charlotte's family since the late 1800s, once they'd come and bought Cumberland.

Although shade wasn't something Charlotte needed at that moment. It'd been chilly since morning, even for January, gray and damp after a week of rain. And Charlotte wished for half a minute that she'd put the top up on the Jeep—before she buttoned Rafe's Navy peacoat and told herself not to snivel.

She saw three wild pigs ten minutes south of Four

Chimneys—right where she eased the Jeep down a quick steep slope onto two parallel wooden tracks, just wider than a car tire, ten feet above a broad tidal creek. There she put it in neutral, and pulled on the emergency, and looked to her right toward the quick curve a hundred yards past, where the creek flowed west into the marsh.

There were no flocks of ibis. Which was no great surprise. The creek was too deep at high tide for them to feed. So she looked to her left, toward the center of Cumberland, hoping for egrets, or at least an alligator, while she listened to a Carolina wren.

Trees and vines hung over the water—emptying now toward the western marsh, running gray-green in the gray light—where a tall Great White Egret, its neck crooked in a painful-looking S, its tail feathers draped like a white lace train, stood fishing on one thin leg with silent concentration.

Charlotte grabbed her binoculars from the passenger seat, and watched the big bird catch a fingerling with awe-inspiring speed and swallow it with a shake of its head.

It gazed toward her, for several seconds, and then ignored her again—before silently spreading its wide white wings and sweeping up over the trees.

Charlotte smiled to herself as she put the Jeep in gear and climbed up the steep south hill.

When she came to the fork in the shady green tunnel (the narrow main road she kept hacked out of live oak and saw palmetto jungle), she hesitated, and then turned left—right where two armadillos were fizzing along like windup toys, tiny toes scurrying under the tank on top, oblivious apparently to the Jeep *and* the person, having very little brain with which to work.

Charlotte stopped on the way the way she always did on

Cumberland when something caught her attention—this time to watch Pretty Peggy crop frostbitten grass in a pine clearing, her chestnut coat thick now and matted, while her dark bay baby nursed. Peggy was wild like all the other horses on the island, except for Charlotte's two geldings, and ready to bolt if the Jeep got too close.

A quarter of a mile later, Charlotte pulled off, in a burned clearing between two ponds at White Branch where a few tall pines grew scattered near the marshy edge. She looked down at the patch of mud where she knew they liked to sun, without expecting to see any that late in the day, in that much cold and gray.

But there was one—a young alligator, maybe five feet long, his scaly snout half open, his eyes following Charlotte closely, the ridges on his head and back and tail the green of old moss and mud, his crooked short reptilian legs faster on land than you'd think.

Charlotte talked to him, as she got out of the car, and watched him from fifteen feet away, till he slid backwards into the water with hardly a ripple behind.

Then she backed the Jeep between two pines, shoved the gearshift into first, and looked at Rafe's last wristwatch.

It was quarter to six, so there was time to see what the crew had done at Stafford graveyard, but not stop anywhere else.

It was better than it had been, when she trekked in from the main road and opened the iron gate in the moss-covered stone and tabby wall. The weeds had been mowed. The cigarette wrappers were gone. But there were vines that needed cutting back, and breaks in the walls to be mended.

Charlotte planned the next talk she was going to have with Roy Black as she trotted a few feet on the path toward the car—then stopped and laid a hand on her heart. She told herself not to think about it then. That she'd find a doctor worth seeing next week when she went down to Jacksonville to talk to the lawyer there.

I ought to call the New York P.R. lady too, when I'm on the mainland. The one that Hal recommended. Because publicity's going to be crucial. Now, and in the future.

Why is it starting the first time I turn the key? Now if I could pad the springs in the seat, and keep my foot out of the hole by the clutch—

Oh, no.

It was the wild turkeys. The same two females from the afternoon before, hopping out into the road from the same stretch of saw palmetto, running south in front of the Jeep.

It was amusing, in a way. The two of them shuffling along as fast as they could, looking over their shoulders at Charlotte, their brown speckled feathers ruffling as they ran, swaying from side to side, kicking up a plume of sand.

She'd laughed at them the day before, to begin with. Till they'd kept it up for almost ten minutes at not more than five miles an hour.

She pulled up closer, hoping it would make them fly.

But it didn't. And Charlotte backed off the gas and waited. *I have to remember to tell Hannah about them. It's just the kind of thing to make her laugh.*

*Though how she can laugh at **anything** is more than I can understand. I wouldn't if I were her. I'd be a royal pain in the backside, and no one would darken my door.*

CCC

"It makes me want to spit! My family has cleared, and planted, and tended this island for eighty years. We've spent a fortune taking care of all the animals and plants that make it what it is. An absolute earthly paradise, without any of the commercial junk that's ruined the whole east coast. And what do my sniveling niece and nephew do? Sell to Eddie Montgomery so *he* can sell it to some snake of a developer! It's all I can do not to strangle all four of 'em!" Charlotte grabbed both sides of her head with her hands in half-serious desperation, and rushed away from the four-poster bed in the first-floor room that had been hers and Rafe's before she'd made Whitfield an inn.

"I don't reckon it'll do much good to ask you to stand still a minute so I can see your face while you talk."

"Do you care about what I just said?"

"Course I do, as you—"

"Well, then?"

"Don't know why I bothuh. You can't tell a Hill, born and raised, much of anything, any more than you can get 'em to change their ways." Hannah Hill's wide gray face, propped on a flat foam pillow and turned toward Charlotte's back, smiled as though she were trying not to laugh.

"*You* oughtta know, since you went and married the worst of us! Well, maybe not the worst. Papa was nothing to write home about either."

"What's Eddie Montgomery up to now?"

"Trying to talk Hal Sutton into selling to the big-shot Atlanta developer. Just the thought of a causeway's got Hal so upset he's about to call the park service back in and sell his land to them instead. Course, you know what *I* think of the park service and the way they're stickin' their nose in."

"Yes, I surely do. The next time you talk to Eddie, would you ask him to come see me?"

"Eddie and I don't talk, you know that. We holler at each other once in a great while from twenty feet away."

"Tell him I said it's impordunt. Ask Amelia to do it for me, if you wouldn't mind."

"What do you want to talk to *him* about? No, don't tell me. I know too much already about your pernicious little schemes."

"Now, wait—"

"I'll get her to do it first thing tomorrow."

"Thank you, Charlotte. I appreciate the help."

"I'm *not* going to turn my back on Cumberland." Charlotte was looking straight at Hannah, pulling her long silver braid forward across her narrow shoulder.

"I know you aren't, and you shouldn't."

"It's the last big barrier island that's still the way it ought to be, and I'm *not* going to let it happen, Hannah. I'm *not*. You hear me? I swear to you that there's *not* going to be a golf course on Cumberland, *or* a swimming pool, *or* a causeway over to St. Mary's. There's never going to be a string of tacky little vacation cottages, or some big pretentious development that caters to the nouveau riche."

"Nevuh's a long time, honey. Nevuh's not somethin' you and I control."

"The National Park's not going to take over either, I can tell you that, and they're working at it. They are. I talked to a woman in Bradley's office. I knew her mother during the war, and she said—"

"Congressman Bradley?"

Charlotte whipped her head around, her black eyes fierce,

deep-set and hawklike, as she said, "Who else would I be talking about?"

"Well, you might could be—"

"She said they're doing a 'long-term assessment,' and talking about bringing in seventeen hundred people a day. Twelve thousand a week, she said. Can you imagine what that'd do to the turtles? Loggerheads have been coming here to lay their eggs for nobody knows how many hundreds of years, and what would happen to *them*? *And* the wild horses, *and* the rare birds, and the woods full of deer and wild pig? Take the pig off the island, and you know they'd have to, if they brought all those idiots over here every day, and we'd have diamondbacks comin' out our ears. This is America, Hannah. How can the government take my land?"

"By right of eminent domain."

"If Rafe were still alive, or my Uncle Jim, either one, *they* wouldn't let it happen! Never in a million years." Charlotte MacKinnon stood glaring at Hannah, her fists on her narrow hips, her dark eyes hot in a broad-boned face that was cut in a complicated lace of lines by weather as much as time.

"Honey, you know I sympathize. I want you to fight this fight with every bone and blood vessel you got. But you still gotta take care of yourself. You went and got yourself so worked up you fainted Tuesday, and I don't think—"

"Who told you that! I told Roy—"

"I'm not gonna be sayin' who told me, so take you a good deep breath and don't even bothuh. Charlotte, honey, if you want to win this battle, you have to eat well, and get you some sleep, and not punish yourself more than you can stand. If you don't, your body's gonna give out on you before you can see it through." Hannah's wide pale eyes were holding Charlotte's hard.

And Charlotte turned her back on the bed and stared out at the night on Cumberland, black and blowing, through a tangle of ancient live oaks. "It makes me want to spit."

"You said that already. Could you toss you anothuh log on the fire? Would you mind? I'm feelin' kinda chizzly. You eaten today?"

"Don't start mothering me, Hannah. Don't you presume!"

"All right. I stand corrected. Well, no, I lie corrected." Hannah smiled to herself and turned her head toward the French doors. "Motherin's not somethin' I'm much good at." Hannah's voice had gotten dryer, and weaker, and she was licking at cracked lips.

"Mary may not be much to brag about, but you did a good job with Johanna. Better than I did with Leah, as anyone with eyes can see. Was it easier that Johanna wasn't yours?"

"I doubt it, honey, but I don't know."

Charlotte dropped two more pine logs on the dying fire, then straightened her back and looked at the hall door. "I'll tell Roy to bring you some more wood."

"It was hard for Leah, the way things were then. Bein' raised a Hill on Cumberland. Would you mind givin' me a drink of watuh? You don't have to touch me anywhere, just hold the glass and aim the straw at my mouth."

"Would you hush up? I'm perfectly willing to touch you! I don't know what you're talking about."

"There's nothing you hate more than nursin' people. You know that. Animals you do just fine. You gonna eat here at the inn?"

"Got to, I guess. Don't have a thing in the house. Need to get a list to Adam before he takes the boat in the morning." She was holding the straw for Hannah with an awkward self-conscious look on her face, like a dog who's thinking about sneaking out the door.

"I presume you're fixin' to change your clothes?" Hannah was smiling, looking up at Charlotte with half-mocking eyes.

"I am *not* gonna start worrying now about how I look. I'm seventy-five years old, it's my inn, and I haven't cared what anybody thinks since I was twenty-five!"

"Charlotte—"

"They're my antiques these 'guests' are setting their behinds on, and *my* oriental carpets they're tracking sand on, and I—"

"You're chargin' 'em a fair amount for the privilege, honey, and they don't expect you, the niece of James J. Hill, seen on society pages across the country, to be—"

"I haven't been on a society page since 1949!"

"—to be wearin' ten-year-old tennis shoes without laces, an old cotton skirt with holes in the back, and a sweater that's been eaten by moths and washed till the pills are the size of popcorn."

"Come on now, Hanny, it's not as bad as that."

Hannah didn't say anything. She lay without moving the way she always did—the way she had for two-and-a-half years, her arms tucked under the covers, the only life visible shining from her face—and smiled at the outrage, fading into irritation, on Charlotte Hill MacKinnon's.

"All right, Miss Smarty Pants, I'll put on my other clothes. You better be glad I'm a patient woman. I don't know anybody else who'd take that kind of bullying from an upstart poor relation!"

"Charlotte, honey, patient is *not* the word anyone in the whole wide world would use to describe you. We put your clothes in the armoire. My files are takin' ovuh the dressuh, and Amelia had to move your things."

"What do you keep in all those files?"

"Things I'm interested in. Stories 'bout people who puzzle me. Political decisions I want to ponduh. How the papers presented 'em years ago, and how they talk about 'em now, and how opinions get changed because of that. Now, that looks very nice. Your black ballet slippuhs should be there too, somewhere in the bottom. We threw away the white ones. One of the soles was fixin' to come off. You may have to make you a light."

Charlotte was tying a black-and-brown wraparound African batik skirt on one hip, having already buttoned a black cotton blouse. "Why are you such a meddler all of a sudden? You didn't use to be such a pain in the neck. It's only been since the MS got really bad. Every time I think about that chair—"

"Then don't. You knew that wasn't right. You knew it."

"That was my business, and it wasn't up to you to interfere. Hannah, I don't want to go out and talk to them."

"You'll do fine. You can be pleasant for a little while with folks you'll nevuh see again."

"They make me feel like an animal in a zoo, watching my every move. 'Robber baron's niece' right there on their faces. When they don't know *a thing* about Uncle Jim or how he ran his railroads. You know how ethical and hardworking he was."

"I know, but—"

"He built a fairly priced transcontinental railroad that supported itself when none of the government-subsidized ones could keep going."

"He was kind too, to the—"

"And having these people stare at me, and fawn all over

me, some of them, just because of Uncle Jim, makes me want to be really outrageous and give 'em a big thrill."

"I reckon that's the price you have to pay. If you turn Whitfield into an inn to make you some money, there're gonna be guests you have to talk to. Course, you also might meet someone who can help you fight for Cumberland. Lot of these people are somethin' impordunt. But I wouldn't try to be outrageous if I were you. You do that just fine on your own."

"I suppose you think that's funny." Charlotte grinned at Hannah as she opened the hall door. And then she said, "I'll send Carrie in to turn you over, and I'll come say good-bye before I go."

Charlotte took time for granted that night.

The way most of us do most days and nights.

Because forty-five minutes later, standing by the grand piano in the sitting room at Whitfield Inn, eating cold shrimp and drinking iced tea, talking about the developer who was trying to buy the island—Charlotte fell to her knees, rolled on her side, and died from an aortic aneurysm.

The crystal glass she was holding didn't break when she fell. Which was noticed at the time. And remarked upon later, after it had disappeared.

CHAPTER TWO

SATURDAY, SEPTEMBER 16, 1961

BEN REESE STOOD OUTSIDE THE WHITE wooden barn with his hands in the pockets of his old canvas barn coat listening to Journey tug hay out of a hay flake with his front teeth, then chew it slowly and quietly, while swishing his tail at a fly.

Ben waited, smelling the barn smells—the earth-and-animal scent of warm horse, the nutlike oats and corn, the hardwood sawdust bedding the stalls, the summer field smell of timothy and alfalfa carried on a fall breeze, cool and crisp and spiced with burning leaves.

He listened to Journey drink from his bucket—the long slow patient sucking in of water, the deep quiet swallows, the dribbling of drops off whiskers and muzzle that splashed back into the bucket when Journey picked his face up and looked for Ben, smelling him before Ben let him see him, watching with soft brown eyes, listening with his ears pricked forward.

Ben told himself to go in. But put it off again. Waiting behind the sliding end door, where he was only just able to see Journey pull at another bite of hay.

Journey rinsed that mouthful, dunking it in his bucket, then let it drip for a second before he tucked it up into his mouth and chewed on it thoughtfully, sliding his lower jaw from one side to the other.

Ben made himself remember the first time he'd seen Journey, and compare it to the life he'd had since—because then Journey had been standing in two feet of muck in a stall too small for him to turn around, getting fed corn to fatten him for the killers, who pay for horseflesh by the pound.

He was being sent to the rendering plant first thing the next morning, so Ben bought him that night. Even though the vet hadn't thought the old leg injury would hold up, or that he'd ever recover from having been starved down to seven hundred pounds.

But he did. And we had four more years of thundering around having a very good time together. Ben took a deep breath, and let it out slowly, then walked into the long wooden barn. "Hi, Journey, how you doing? How's your leg today? I know. I know it hurts, but you're a good boy anyway."

Journey stuck his nose over his door, his eyes on Ben's face, sniffing his coat for apples.

"You want to come out and get a bite?" Ben was holding Journey's lead rope and halter, while sliding open the bar bolt on the old stall door.

The copper-colored chestnut thoroughbred with a white blaze between his eyes managed to look both interested and resigned as he slipped his head in the halter and waited for Ben to fasten it.

He was limping badly on his left front leg as he followed Ben out of the barn. It wasn't the old jagged racing injury, the cut up the back and around to the front—the enlarged and scarred tendons he'd had when Ben bought him. No, now the hoof was hanging oddly, and there was a thick white bandage from his fetlock to his knee pressing a splint up the back—and his head shot straight-up every time he set that foot down as though the pain were almost too much for him.

"Here's a nice patch, right up here by the barn. Go ahead and get a bite." Ben lowered the lead rope. And Journey bit off a mouthful of grass in what seemed like less than a second.

"Want me to scratch your withers? Yes, I know, that feels good, doesn't it? I'm sorry about your leg, kiddo. I wish it hadn't happened. But remember when I first saw you? Life was pretty bad then, wasn't it? Which is why I took you home.

"And you've been a very good boy, haven't you? Except when you ran away with me. Remember that? The first time we went cross-country? You took off toward the woods when we must've been a mile away. We almost got there too, before I could circle you and get you stopped. But you got better. You just panic and act silly once in a while. And why wouldn't you, with what people have done to you?"

Ben was leaning against Journey's right side, his left arm lying across Journey's back, his own gray eyes looking hot and strained. "This time it's a lot worse, though. You've severed your big tendons and cut an artery, and cracked your cannon bone too. I still don't understand how you did it. I s'ppose you and Max were playing bitey face through the fence, and you caught your leg between the boards. The vet says there's nothing we can do about it. I wish there were. But there isn't."

Journey looked at Ben while he cropped the grass close— he actually picked up his head, curved his neck around, and looked Ben right in the eye.

"You're a very good boy, Journey, and I'm sorry it happened, and I'm trying to do what you'd do if you were me." Ben held Journey's head for a minute and kissed his muzzle right by the corner of his lips.

Journey snorted twice, a second or two later, trying to blow a wad of grass and saliva away from the other side of his nose—as a red pickup truck with a cap on the back pulled into the gravel driveway and stopped in front of the barn.

Ben led Journey around the corner toward the truck, to another thick patch of tall grass close to the edge of the drive. "Hi, Jack."

"I'm sorry, Ben."

"I know."

"You're doing the right thing."

"I don't see any alternative." Ben was patting Journey, rubbing him under his chin, scratching him behind his ears, with his own jaws clamped hard together and the muscles at the edges clenched. "He's a tough guy, though. Did I tell you about him being turned out in a field for three years without getting fed anything else? Even in the winter? Can you imagine? It's amazing he lived through it."

"Up north it is, definitely. How did it happen?" Jack Martin opened a drawer in a built-in stack of them at the back of his truck, took out a syringe that was six inches long and more than an inch in diameter, fitted in a broad needle, and filled the syringe with anesthetic from a large glass bottle.

"He hurt his leg on the track, either on the starting gate or on wire, probably, and the man who bought him just threw him out in a field. He sold him later in a group sale to the man I bought him from. This guy didn't know what to do with him, because of the old leg injury, except fatten him up for the killers."

"So it's a good thing you came along when you did. Where do you think we should do this?"

"Behind the barn, I guess. Let me give him an apple first." Ben took an apple out of his coat pocket, and when Journey saw him holding it in his hand, his head flew up and his ears pricked forward. "Here you go. You're such a good boy, I brought you another one too. Let's walk over here. I know, I know it hurts, but here's the other half. When you're done with that, I'll give you another whole apple."

Journey chewed the last piece of apple, drooling on Ben's hand as well as his own knee, sniffing the wind when he'd finished and turning his head toward Jack Martin. He ruffled his lips in a circle around Ben's palm, then tore off another bite of grass.

"I'm ready when you are, Ben." Jack was watching Ben's face while standing by Journey's bad leg, scratching the middle of Journey's chest.

Ben nodded, then pulled Journey's head up and kissed his cheek, stroking the right side of his nose, talking quietly close to his ear. "It's okay, Journey. Jack's not going to hurt you. You're just going to go to sleep."

Jack Martin popped the syringe off the needle, found the large vein on the left side of Journey's neck, stuck the needle in, and watched a trickle of blood drip out the open end before he attached the syringe again. He looked over at Ben one more time and then pushed the plunger.

Ben was holding the lead rope, still patting Journey's neck, talking to him, soft and slow, telling him what a good boy he was and that nothing would hurt anymore.

Journey's head dropped, and his front legs began to buckle, and Jack said, "Get back! He could thrash around when he falls."

Journey didn't. He fell on his left side and shuddered for a minute.

Jack Martin sat on his heels, his stethoscope on Journey's chest, listening to be sure the heart stopped, while Ben knelt down and stroked the velvet-soft skin around Journey's mouth, and worked at controlling his own throat.

"Thanks for coming, Ben. Sorry to cut into your Saturday, but there's something I need to talk to you about." Alderton University's new president, Dr. Frederick Allan Harper, leaned forward with his elbows on his desk and picked up his ball-point pen.

"It's good timing for me. I need to talk to you too."

"Oh? How can I help you?" Fred Harper was leaning sideways in his chair, studying Ben's face.

"I'd like to take three more weeks of the sabbatical I haven't had time to finish before it's up on November 30. I've got to write up the work I did in England and Scotland so I can try to get it published, and I want to make sure the timing's okay with you. If it is, then when I'm done with my own work, I'll run down to North Carolina and examine the artwork the donor there is offering us, and arrange to ship it back here. Assuming it's something the university would want, and that he and I can agree on the details."

"So you'd be away from your office all of November?" President Harper slid a forefinger inside his pale blue shirt collar, easing it away from his neck.

"Maybe even a few days in December. It depends on how long it takes to evaluate the donor's prints and paintings, and then work out the crating, the shipping, and the insurance. I've got to give a talk in Charleston in November, so I have to schedule around that. I sent you a memo a couple of weeks ago, but I've been so busy, I haven't had a chance to check back."

"I don't see any reason why not. Let me give you the authorization now before I forget." Fred Harper handwrote a note on presidential letterhead and slid it across the desk, while raising his sandy eyebrows and smiling carefully at Ben.

"Thanks, Fred. I appreciate it. So what can I do for you?" Ben folded the note and slipped it in the pocket of his corduroy shirt.

"Well, as I'm sure you would've anticipated, taking over Jim Cook's duties has not been an easy matter. Alumni gifts are way down, and though the country's certainly unsettled today, politically *and* economically, Jim's murder trial and conviction have undoubtedly played an even larger role in reducing donor gifts. We've got to reactivate our old donors, attract new ones, and learn to run Alderton in a much more efficient and disciplined manner if we hope to remain a private institution offering a fine liberal arts education."

"Right." Ben looked at the tall clock in the corner behind Fred Harper's desk, and wondered when the aspirin would move in and do something useful about his headache.

"I've appreciated your advice during this transition. You know several board members better than I, serving as secretary as you do. And as an archivist, unattached to an academic department, you have the perspective of a long-term faculty member who can take an independent view."

"I'm glad to help whatever way I can."

"As you may have heard, we've just learned this week that

we won't be able to use Harrison Hall for classroom space after the first of the year because of several stringent new building codes that have recently been enacted. We can't afford the requisite renovation, and it's my view that the time has come to sell Harrison Hall and put the money where we need it most, assuming the board—"

"We can't. Because of the Harrison will."

"What will?"

"Jedidiah Harrison's. He deeded the land and built the building with the stipulation that if the university should ever decide not to use the building for university purposes, the land and building couldn't be sold, but would revert to his family and their heirs."

"Then the will must be a hundred years old."

"Right, but what difference does that make?"

"We need to sell Harrison Hall, and use those funds to build a new girls' dorm on the untouched four acres behind Harrison."

"We can't, Fred. The will and deed are very specific. We could redo the building and use it ourselves for another purpose, but we can't sell it outright."

"We don't *have* the money to redo it. We *have* to sell the building." Fred Harper pushed his chair back, stood up slowly, and turned to the window behind him. He looked out at a maple tree, planted by an early Harrison, its leaves red now and wet with rain, and clasped his hands behind his back. "Who knows about the will besides you and me?"

"I have no idea." Ben was locking his fingers together on the top of his head, staring at Fred's broad back. "And I guess I don't see why that matters."

"Don't you?" Harper turned toward him and sat down

again. "This is an opportunity to do what's good for the school. Of course, it's nothing that has to be decided this minute. Think about it, and we'll talk later." President Harper smoothed one side of his thinning hair, then dropped his legal pad in his right-hand drawer. "Where is it, do you know?"

"What?"

"The will." His eyes were pale blue and watery looking and they were staring at the wall behind Ben.

"I don't know. Not offhand."

Fred Harper glanced at Ben then, before he looked at his watch. "It's after three-thirty. I guess I'd better get going. We're giving a dinner at our house tonight for a group of Ohio donors, and I need to help Suzanne arrange the place cards. I'm glad I could help you with your sabbatical. You going home too?" They were standing on plush green carpet, gazing at each other across polished mahogany.

"In a minute. I've got to stop by my office first."

They walked out together, down two flights of wooden stairs, talking about nothing the way they normally did, till they crossed the front walk and set off in different directions.

Twenty minutes later, Ben was back in the administration building taking the stairs to the basement. He turned right down the long hall and followed it to the end, where he unlocked a double wooden door on the left. All that could be seen through the small panes at the top was a tangle of heating pipes in a tiny room, but Ben followed the length of them to the right, behind the hall wall, toward an old iron door. He slid a five-inch black iron key out of his pocket and worked it into the lock.

The door swung open, grinding against its hinges, as Ben pulled a flashlight out of the jacket he'd grabbed when he'd gotten the key at his office.

There were no electric lights in that room, for it was one of the first, fitted out for storage in the early 1800s. It was eight feet wide and twelve feet long, and probably fifteen feet high, with deep shelves on three sides starting right at the door. A later set of shelves had been added above the original ones, and a handmade wooden ladder stood leaning against the far wall.

The shelves were mostly filled with the minutes of Alderton's Board of Trustees, from the earliest years of the nineteenth century to September 1961. But there were also boxes of wills and deeds and land grant information, along with other legal agreements and a handful of donor directives, most of them in Victorian bank files with labels on the ends.

Ben scanned dates and descriptions on the boxes on the bottom level. And then leaned the ladder against the upper shelves and climbed up to the top, thinking that if Harrison Hall was finished in 1841, the will and deed had probably been written late in the 1830s.

He was stirring up clouds of dust, opening files and sneezing, shining his light into musty cardboard interiors—while twenty or thirty minutes went by as he searched and found nothing he needed.

Then he found it.

And put the ladder back.

And locked the door behind him.

He'd already slipped the flashlight in a pocket, and the bundle of papers up a sleeve—asking himself where the closest Xerox was in Hillsdale, Ohio, that he could use on a Saturday afternoon.

ᴚᴚᴚ

Ben was standing on his lawn outside his study trying to take the flimsy metal-framed screen he'd been meaning to replace for at least three years off one of the sections of the bay window, while it fought him the whole time in the worst tradition of inanimate objects. The wooden window frame was wet and swollen, the metal track added later was bent, and one of the mechanisms on the screen was broken, so it wouldn't come out without bending. He wanted to get it out before it rained again, and then install the old storm window that didn't fit much better. The wind was beating at him too, blowing into him out of the west, whipping his thick straight wheat-colored hair in his eyes, which was getting more irritating by the minute.

He kept thinking about Journey, lying dead under a tarpaulin so the other two horses wouldn't panic when they saw him, hoping the farmer who owned the barn would call to say he'd found a backhoe they could borrow to bury him the following afternoon.

Ben was picking at it too, wondering if he'd done the right thing, second-guessing himself when it made no sense to do that.

And then he cut his hand on the corner of the metal screen. He watched blood run along the scar that sliced across his palm—till he tore the metal frame out of the window with both hands.

It broke, which was no surprise, and the screen ripped sideways, and he threw the pieces across the side yard toward one of the big blue spruce. He leaned his back against the thick Victorian brick wall, close up by the window, and was wrapping a handkerchief around his left hand, just as the phone rang inside.

He told himself to let it go. But didn't, at the last second.

He ran toward the front door. And grabbed the phone in the study.

"Hello?...This is a surprise. There's nothing wrong, is there?...Because *I* usually call you...No, Mom, I'm fine, why?...Dad's okay?...Yeah, I'll bet. Get him to take some time off...Yep, I'm still going to Charleston and North Carolina... Right, sometime in November. I have to be in Charleston on the, I don't know, the twelfth maybe. Why?...Is it that big a deal with Amelia? I've got writing to do here. I don't want to go all the way down to Cumberland. I mean I like Cumberland, but...

"Of course I remember Hannah. I like her too, I always have, but I don't know anything about legal stuff, and I don't...Wait a minute, you're saying that when Charlotte died a year and a half ago, she left the island to Hannah. Right? And now she...Nothing. No, I'm okay. You already asked me that...Maybe. I had to put Journey down today...No, you're right. As much as I like dogs, it's harder for me to put a horse down...

"Okay, so what you're saying is the park service is threatening to take the island, whether Hannah wants to sell or not, and Hannah doesn't want to, but doesn't know what to do, and Amelia has asked you if I would...I don't see what I can do, but I'll think about it...Right. I'll call you in the next couple days. Bye, Mom...You too."

Ben walked into the kitchen, washed the blood off his hand, and watched the rain blow across the back of his neighbor's cornfield. He drank a glass of water and set the glass in the sink, thinking, *It's pathetic. You know it is. At your age especially.*

Why didn't you just tell her you'd go to Cumberland and see what's up with her sister? Why'd you have to take it out on her? She's got enough to worry about already.

Because she's your mother. And you always have in your worst moments. And you don't know how to talk to her now as well as you once did.

Why did it change?

Why?

Not having much in common. Being gone all those years. Leaving college to go to war, and never going home again. Never having had a chance to get to know the young ones.

With Mom it was different.

Till you married Jessie. And started on your Ph.D.

Even when I try to talk about Granddad's farm, and working on old cars, I still make them uncomfortable.

So that makes it okay to act like a brat?

No. No, it doesn't.

It hasn't been the best couple weeks. Khrushchev builds a wall across Berlin, then shoots the East Berliners trying to escape. And what does Kennedy do? Next to nothing.

But. Four high schools in Atlanta were integrated this week without any trouble, and at least that's better than it could've been.

"Nuts." *My tools are out there getting rained on.*

CHAPTER THREE

GARRETT AIKEN SWITCHED THE RECEIVER to his other ear, while he brushed a flake of reddish clay off the toe of a polished loafer. He shook his head against the quiet voice on the other end of the phone, and said, "That's not true." And half-listened again.

"No. No, that's not the way it is. Listen to me, Johanna, please, it's not that I don't want you to sing, you have to understand that. It's that I want us to get married *now*. I can't wait anothuh year. I miss you. You know I do. We haven't seen each othuh since Easter, and then we had a stupid misunderstanding...If you'll move here and get a job while I finish law school, I'll take care of you...

"You don't actually think you're gonna make a livin' singin' opera?...I understand. I know you b'lieve that's what you're s'ppose to do, but that doesn't mean it'll put food on the table...You'd like Lexington. It's a beautiful town, and there're plenty of cheap places here in Chevy Chase. And while you work as a waitress or somethin', I can study without havin' a job like I do now...

"Soon as I'm done, I'll start makin' money. That's why I

chose estate law. And with the reputation I've built here in law school, I know I can get me an offuh from one of the big Charleston or Savannah firms as soon as I finish school…

"No, I *don't* understand…Then what you're sayin' is, it's not just the singin'. What you're really thinkin' is you don't want to marry me to begin with!…*No!*…What d'you mean by that?…You did not! Last April? When?…You never said that! You said you thought we should think about it some more, and not talk so often on the phone, but you didn't say…I *nevuh* heard you say that!…

"*What?*…Why? What is it that you don't like?…How could you think that? I don't brag!…When was that?…I don't con-siduh that bragging, that's…No, and you nevuh told me that eithuh…Oh, so what you're truly sayin' is you don't want to marry me eithuh way!…Come on, Johanna, please…That's not the way it was…Okay…Yeah…Think about it. Please. You know I love you, Johanna. You know I do. You and I are good for each othuh…Don't say it like there's no going back, honey…I'll call you again tomorruh…All right. I'll wait till the day aftuh."

Garrett Aiken had set his elbows on his knees, and was sitting with his head in his hands, when he heard the refrigerator door open and shut, and a bag of potato chips get ripped open. Garrett didn't look up, till Ted Grey said "Hey," as he walked through the arch from the kitchen.

"Hey."

"You got a call earlier. Not Johanna, the other one from there. She wants you to call her back."

Garrett didn't say anything. He stood up and nodded and

started toward his bedroom door.

"Why don't you come with us to Louisville tonight? Russ and I are meetin' a guy we knew in high school. He's just been stationed at Fort Knox, and we thought we'd play some pool and shoot the breeze. He's a smart guy and it'll be fun. You don't have to work tonight. I know you don't go out much, but I thought maybe—"

"Thanks. I think I will. Can I ask you somethin'?"

"Sure."

"Have you evuh heard me say anything that sounded like I was...Nevuh mind. It doesn't mattuh. It doesn't mattuh one bit."

"You wantta play a quick game of pool?"

"Now?"

"Practice up for tonight?"

"One game, I guess. Sure."

Garrett was leaning over Ted Grey's old family pool table in what would've been a dining room without it, in the house they shared with another law student named Russ Turner. Garrett was talking, while trying to make a corner shot that didn't look easy, and Ted was drinking Bud from a bottle, watching Garrett with a look on his face that was hard to read. Dubious, probably. Consciously polite. As though he were having to tell himself not to argue or interrupt.

Garrett's thick black hair was curling against the tan on the back of his neck, and you could see the muscles moving across his back under a blue button-down collar shirt, as he made the shot, his wide mouth and his brown eyes smiling as though it were important.

Ted said, "Good shot," and finished the Bud.

Garrett circled the table, his eyes on his options and his cue in his hands, till he looked at Ted as though there were something he was trying to get out and didn't know where to start. "You know what I was sayin' before?" He glanced at Ted for a second, as he braced his left hand on the table. "That we all of us have to take public stands. Well, when I was sixteen, and workin' in a sportin' goods store, I tore a dirty calendar off the wall and threw it in the garbage. I didn't know if I'd lose my job, but I knew it was the right thing to do, and I was willin' to take the risk."

"Well, I guess if you feel that way—"

"In high school, I was varsity quarterback when I was a sophomore. They never did that for any othuh sophomore, but even though it meant a lot to me, I saw I had to quit. The coach had a foul mouth. I mean he cussed all the time, and it wasn't the right example for a buncha high school kids. The rest of the team begged me not to leave, and a whole group of parents got involved too, and they had a talk with the coach, but I was ready to quit if nothin' changed, even though it was a tough decision. If you don't make that kinda hard decision, you won't be a good witness."

"I s'ppose—"

"It's because of my witness, and the work I've done with youth groups, that I've been able to influence as many as I have. That's why I don't go to bars, as a general rule, even though I don't drink when I do. I know I gotta think about the example I set." Garrett looked pleased with himself as he glanced at Ted, then irritated for a second when the six ball missed a side pocket.

Ted seemed to be considering Garrett out the edges of his

wide blue eyes as he leaned over the cue ball, sizing up his chances. "Lookin' self-righteous can be bad too. It can turn people away. And then the danger is—"

"Are you sayin' that I'm self-righteous?" Garrett grinned his most disarming grin as he stood his cue on end. "Nobody's ever said I'm self-righteous. I set an example, and I take a stand when I have to."

"I'm not sayin' you intend to be, but if it looks—"

"You don't think I'm self-righteous, do you?"

Ted made the shot and reached for the chalk on the edge of the table. "Everything okay with Johanna?"

"Oh, yeah. Sure. Fine. It's even harduh on her bein' away from me than it is for me to be here without her. We're both gettin' frustrated. You know what I mean. You and Carol too, it's the same thing for you. Long engagements get old fast. You want to come with me to church tomorruh? You said you would one of these weeks, so why not—"

"I don't think so. I've got work to do at the library. Anyway, about tonight, Russ should be back before four, and he told me we'd leave for Louisville about five. Is that okay with you?"

"Sure. It'll do me good to get outta here for a while. I think I been workin' too hard. I'll get at it again tomorruh."

Garrett took time for granted that day.

The way Charlotte had a year and a half earlier.

Because as Russ drove them home from Louisville that night, two miles east of Frankfort, he decided to pass a pickup truck that kept speeding up and slowing down.

Russ pulled out before he realized they were starting up a low hill, and hit another pickup loaded with hay head-on.

Russ was killed.

The truck driver was killed.

Garrett was killed too.

Ted was hurt, but lived through it. His face was cut up and he fractured a shoulder on his way out a side window in the back.

Then he got to call Russ's parents *and* Garrett's, and Johanna Elliott too, to keep them from hearing from someone else that Garrett and Russ were dead.

MONDAY, SEPTEMBER 18, 1961

"It's mighty fine of you to have your cook fix me up a good lunch like this." Randall Wilkes was sitting on a chair by Hannah Hill's bed eating a piece of banana cream pie and drinking a glass of iced tea, having already finished a chicken salad sandwich and a big bowl of fried potatoes.

"I appreciate you comin' ovuh here and seein' to the prunin'. I don't trust anybody else with the flowerin' shrubs, and it does me good to see you." Hannah Hill was watching Randall, her face pale and her eyes smiling, as he swallowed the last of the pie. "I owe you a good bit more than lunch when you're ovuh here workin'."

"Miz Hannah, you don't owe me nothin'. You wouldda done what I done, and you know I'm proud to help you out."

"I'm grateful to you, Randall. You know I am. You've been a good friend for a good many years."

"I enjoy bein' on Cumberland. Makes a change for me from St. Mary's, and I take me some time to fish the creeks before I go on home. 'Member how I called Miss Johanna 'Little Skeeter' when she was small? She used to smile so fine, then look at me real shy and serious."

"She still asks about you when we talk. How's your youngest boy? Willie. He still in school?"

"Yes ma'am, he is. Third year up to Atlanta University. Gonna quit awhile, aftuh Christmas, make him some money till next fall, but he'll be right back there as quick as he can. He's tryin' to decide if he's got a call. Says it's eithuh that, or the law. Lord's sure been good to that boy, but makin' them decisions's real hard. Bein' that age and all."

"I wouldn't be young again for all the tea in China."

"Me neithuh, Miz Hannah. Not 'less the Lord Himself spoke to me from a burnin' bush and told me that's what He wanted."

Hannah and Randall both laughed, while he mopped his lined black face with a faded red bandanna. "Sure was sorry to hear 'bout young Mr. Aiken. Cain't say I thought he'd be right for Miss Johanna, but I sure feel real sorry for her, and for his folks. Not much worse than losin' your own child."

"No. We both know that firsthand."

"We surely do. Yes, ma'am, we surely do. How's Miss Johanna takin' it?"

Hannah choked, and was trying not to cough, and he held the straw from her ice water up close to her lips. She sipped a little. And finally swallowed. And said, "She's fixin' to blame herself for his death. You know how she is. She'd decided on her own not to marry him, and now she says if she hadn't told him that the day he died, he wouldn't've gone out with his friends like he did, and he'd be safe up there in Lexington. *I* nevuh thought he was good for her eithuh. He wanted to do right, but he didn't seem to know himself very well. Not well enough for her to marry, in my opinion. But I nevuh did say that to Johanna. You gotta make that decision yourself. And I don't have

49

any room to talk. Not with my marriage the way it was."

"We gotta lay Miss Johanna in the Lord's hands."

"I know. I know we do. How's your church doin'? You still preachin'?"

"We're doin' fine. Lord's been good to us, but I don't b'lieve I'm gonna take on anothuh year. It's time to pass the ministry on to somebody younguh."

"You takin' care of yourself since Miz Myrtle passed away? You got somebody to cook for you and all?"

"Ruthie looks after me real good. I eat down to her place reguluh, and try not to get to meddlin' with the grandkids so much she won't ask me ovuh evuh again. Miz Hannah is you feelin' all right? You ain't lookin' as good as sometimes. Lookin' like there's a weight bearin' down on ya, and I wantta know how to pray."

Hannah's pale face had been turned toward Randall, but there'd been a set distant look in her eyes. And she sighed and smiled before she looked right at him. "I'm fine. I'm just thinking about Miss Johanna."

Randall nodded and laid his plate on the table beside Hannah's bed. "Once you take to raisin' up young folks, you feel for 'em till the day you die. I bettuh get on back to work. Reckon I'll be done by the end of the day."

"Amelia'll give you a check when you're finished. Oh, I know what I forgot. The envelope there on the table? That's for Willie. It'll help him out with school some."

"Bless your heart, Miz Hannah, I ain't gonna let you do that again. You ain't got much yourself, and with—"

"I want to do this, Randall. You have to let me. Please. It's been laid on me to do. We both know what you've done for me, and I wish you'd give me the pleasure of this."

Randall stood with his straw hat in his hand and stared at the envelope on the table, his soft brown eyes fighting hard for control. "You done too much already."

"No, I haven't. It's 'bout all I got left to me, handin' out a little handful of cash. You take that, please. You just tell your Willie to do the same thing for somebody else when he can."

"Thank you, Miz Hannah. You been good to me since the day we met. You tell Miss Johanna I hope she's doin' well and I surely would like to see her the next time she gets home."

"I will."

"You need anything?"

"You might could ask Carrie to come in when she can."

Carrie came in right then, to tell Miz Hannah she had a ship-to-shore call from Miss Johanna. And while she turned the dials on the radio console, Hannah asked Randall if he wanted to talk to Johanna.

Randall nodded and waited for Carrie to hand him the microphone and show him the button to push. "Miss Johanna? This is Randall, suguh. Want you to know how sorry I is 'bout your young man. Ovuh."

"Hey, Randall. Thank you. I wish I could've kept it from happening somehow. You okay? Over."

"You couldn't, sugar. It ain't in your hands. I'm fine. I'm getting old, but I'm fine. Child, y'all talkin' like a northernuh. Ovuh."

"I know. I have to. I get trained to because of my singing. Over."

"That's all right, honey. Sacrifices come with every kind of work, and I know you'll make out just fine. I'll let you talk to Miz Hannah. God bless you, sugar. You take care o' yourself, ya hear?"

Randall handed the microphone to Carrie and she pushed the button for Hannah and held it close to her mouth. Hannah smiled at Randall as he waved from the door, and said, "I'm here, sweetie. How you doin'? Ovuh."

"I'm in Tryon. I'm staying with Aunt Susanna and Uncle Will. I drove down without stopping from New York and I'm pretty tired at the moment. I'll be there tomorrow night. Probably nine or ten. Want me to stay in St. Mary's for the night, or you want to send the boat over? I'll have to get back to St. Mary's the next morning in time for Garrett's funeral. Over."

"I'll send Adam. He'll be there at nine. You're sure you're all right? You must be worn out. Ovuh."

"I'd be better if I could take back what I said to Garrett."

"Honey, what you said was true and kind. You'd told him before what was in your mind, and he wouldn't listen. He didn't want to hear it in the spring, and he didn't want to hear it now. But it wouldn't've been right *or* honest if you hadn't told him the truth. It won't do you any good to wish things were different. You just get yourself home to me and we'll talk about it some more. I love you, honey, and it'll be all right. You drive carefully, and we'll talk tomorruh night. Ovuh."

"I will. I love you too."

TUESDAY, SEPTEMBER 26TH

It was after midnight. High winds beat at the house. Lashing the windows. Rattling the glass. As rain pelted the sheet-metal roof, clattering like marbles scattered from the sky.

Telephone wires whipped and whined. Thunder shook the

roots of the world, and old oaks and tall palms and high-rigged boats bent against the blow.

It was dark in the big bath. Except when lightning ripped the sky. Coming quicker and closer as the storm moved west. The outside door wasn't curtained. The shades on the windows weren't drawn. And lightning flashed on the black marble floor, as rain rolled in sheets down black glass.

A short broad hand turned a dial on a hi-fi, then dropped a needle on a well-worn groove, and the wail and thunder at the end of Wagner's *Götterdämmerung* fought the night and the storm.

A candle was lit. Then another. And another. Then twenty or thirty or more. Till the cold black room guttered with flickering tongues reflected in glass and mirror and marble, rows and clusters of fiery tongues, shivering in shifting air.

The tap was turned off in the big tub.

A razor blade was laid on the marble ledge.

Five sandalwood and mother-of-pearl boxes were arranged carefully on the narrow ledge so the insides faced the tub.

A shivering body slid into water and lay against the slanted back.

Then it started, low and soft. Like an animal caught in a trap, ripping and gagging on its own pain. Swelling and breaking. Tighter and higher. Twisting into a groan. That ground down to a sob. A stream of sobs.

That stopped. Then shrank slowly to a whimper.

The contents of each box were taken out. They were touched and turned over. Licked, some of them. And put back.

Before the razor blade was picked up.

It was looked at in candlelight, shimmering across the water. One edge. And then the other.

A fingernail split, sliding down the long side.

A wrist turned to catch the light.

The razor blade tapped against the ledge for half a minute. Before it was put down.

The hot water was turned back on.

A rolling, boiling, waterfall of steam in cold air.

A cool voice, low, deep, dead, said, "Not this time.

"No.

"Not after this.

"Not you. Not with what you've been through.

"Don't turn your back on this.

"Not now. Not ever again."

CHAPTER FOUR

SATURDAY, OCTOBER 28TH

BEN REESE STOOD ON THE SHADY front porch of a small Victorian house in the old part of Fernandina Beach, Florida, arranging his camera in his briefcase and listening to a shrunken, white-haired, faded looking gentleman with black-framed glasses hanging on a cord around his neck, as he talked in a thin wavery voice about the history of Fernandina.

He'd started with William Bartram, the colonial naturalist (who "visited all of Amelia Island in the 1770s and recorded our flora and fauna"), before sliding into earlier ages in Fernandina's four hundred years of trying to survive under eight flags.

Ben was interested, but late. He'd been talking to Dr. Butler since before noon, and he had to meet the boat from Cumberland at two-thirty, which was less than ten minutes, and six or seven blocks away. He'd been trying to extricate himself without seeming to, but was finally reduced to saying, "Dr. Butler, I've got to catch the boat to Cumberland, but I'll phone you from Ohio when I get back. Thanks for letting me photograph your Bartram papers."

"One *could* say that without John and William Bartram, *and* Bernard McMahon, the veruh impordunt colonial horticulturalist who first wrote about—"

"I have to run, Dr. Butler. Literally. Or I won't catch my boat. I'll be in touch." Ben was down the white porch stairs, a suitcase in one hand, his briefcase in his other, his canvas dispatch case slung across a shoulder, sprinting north on Broome Street toward the town wharves, his corduroy sport coat flapping behind him as he ran.

"We'll discuss Robert Stafford of Cumberland then. He made a fine livin' on the island when none of the Greenes could. *If* you're interested. Some folks aren't, though I—"

"I am. THANK YOU." Ben had turned his head to shout without slowing down, and he could see Dr. Butler's disappointed shoulders and his desolate face and his frail fingers fumbling with his glasses as he watched Ben run away from him.

Ben could feel life at Alderton melting away on the boat ride to Cumberland, standing in the wind and the sun, the sound of water splashing on the hull, the engine throbbing at his feet.

He'd stayed in the back on the open deck of the *Charlotte MacKinnon,* Whitfield Inn's thirty-five-foot Maine lobster boat, where the captain couldn't hear him humming "Old Blue" to the rumble and whine of the engine, which sounded to Ben like the drone of a bagpipe and made him want to make music.

He didn't think about the Harrison will and the confrontation coming with Fred Harper. He didn't worry about how to write up his research, or how well he'd be able to put a speech together for Charleston, or what, if anything, he could do to help Hannah.

He watched the Amelia River slide by as they cruised north toward Cumberland Sound and looked at what lived along it— the albatross, the pelicans, the seagulls feeding and sunning, the shrimp boats, the freighters, the sailboats, the almost-not-seaworthy of several descriptions docked at Fernandina.

He stared off on his right, at the west coast of Cumberland, when they came to it ten minutes later, as they worked their way north through Cumberland Sound along Cumberland's long intercoastal side. Most of it was fringed with saltwater marsh, with twisting creeks in marsh grass, golden then instead of green, growing low in front of live oaks and widely spaced spikes of tall palm.

Ben started to watch the water, bottle green and grass green and blue where the sky lay shining on its rippling skin, but he couldn't keep his eyes off Cumberland—where whole flocks of white ibis, their four-inch beaks curling in toward their chests, stood feeding in grassy shallows and meandering low tide creeks. The boat ran close enough to shore in places to see oyster beds and mussels in the mud, while the smell of iodine and sand and salt made Ben grin almost uncontrollably and ask himself how he could stand to live as far from the sea as he did.

That made him think of how Butler lived. Alone his whole adult life. Desperate for someone who'd listen—to who he was, to what he did, to what he knew, to what he loved about a long dead world more real to him than the one he walked in every day.

It made Ben wince for him. Stranded on his porch. For a life lived on paper. Without family. Without friends to speak of. A secondhand life lived twice removed. At a distance, at least, from risk and pain. A life of the brain, but not the blood.

They'd been trading information on herbalists and botanists and pioneer medicinal practices for several years, but seeing him had been unsettling. Unexpectedly. In an oddly personal way. Partly because of a book Ben had been reading about Robert E. Lee's family.

He stepped into the cockpit, to the left of the tall cylindrical metal heater, and hollered, "Adam?" loud enough to be heard over the noise of the engine.

Adam Clark, the captain of the *Charlotte MacKinnon*, was a large quiet man, six-foot-four probably, broadly built and strong looking inside skin toughened by wind and sun—and he looked at Ben inquiringly while he steadied the wheel with one hand.

"Is there still a dock by Kirkconnell?"

"Yes sir."

"Is it usable?"

"Sure."

"Could you put in there without it being inconvenient?"

"It'd be no trouble at all."

"I'd like to see the Greene family graveyard and walk up to Whitfield from there."

"Leave your things on board when we dock, and I'll haul 'em up yonduh to Miz Amelia's."

"Thank you. I appreciate it."

Neither of them said anything else after that. Even after they'd turned into the narrow channel east of Drum Point Island and were slowing toward a long wooden jetty jutting out from shore on their right.

Adam docked like he'd been handling boats since the day he was born, then jumped onto the weathered boards of the old Kirkconnell wharf and wrapped the bowline around a piling, as Ben climbed onto the dock.

"Thanks, Adam."

"I'll tell Miz Amelia you'll be up aftuh while."

"How do I find the graveyard?"

"Walk straight-on on the path from the dock, then take you a right when you come to the main road. Bear left at the ruins, and walk on past the old stables into the woods. Then look for a trail on your right."

"How far is it from Kirkconnell up to Whitfield?"

"Two miles, straight north up the main road."

"Then I should be there in an hour and a half or so. Thanks for making a special trip to get me in Fernandina."

"No trouble at all. I had to come ovuh anyhow to pick up a compressuh for the freezuh."

Ben walked to the north-south road under live oaks and magnolias, past wild muscadine vines climbing on everything around them, between cedars and holly trees and saw palmetto—thinking about Robert E. Lee.

Lee as a little boy. Caught up in the idea of his father. Light Horse Harry Lee. Military hero of the Revolution. The first and probably the best of Washington's cavalry leaders. Whose grave was right there on Cumberland.

Ben turned right onto the main road, where it curved slightly on its way to Kirkconnell, passing between two sets of square stone pillars a quarter of a mile apart, the second set ornamented by a high black filigreed arch.

He walked down a long allée of tall palms that led straight to Kirkconnell across a huge stretch of open lawn, staring at the broken stone and brick skeleton of what the house had once been—the torn stairs and gaping doorways, the strips of wall under straight brick chimneys, the towers of granite and crumbling tabby surrounded by piles of stone and brick covered in tangled vines.

There wasn't time then to see Kirkconnell the way Ben wanted to see it. And he turned left between the third pair of stone pillars into the side drive up by the ruin's wide stairs, and walked east into woods a hundred yards later, wondering how old Robert Lee would've been when his father was almost killed.

Six maybe? When Harry was attacked by the mob for nothing. For defending a Baltimore publisher who opposed the War of 1812.

All Robert ever had of his father after that were letters. Written to his wild older brother from somewhere in the Caribbean.

Why did they think that at the time? That living in the islands would cure disease? I can see it if it were a lung condition. I know Washington, when he was—

That must be the stables up ahead.

Ben took the sand track on the left side of the wide white stuccoed building toward a row of rusting cars, most of them from the twenties and thirties, and then began to look for a path into the woods on the right.

Why has it stuck in my mind the way it has? That's a question worth asking.

Because what you went through was similar. Obviously. Even though your father lived.

Ben had turned right into a very narrow overgrown path, and he bent under and climbed over live oak limbs and knotted vines, pushing fronds of saw palmetto out of his face and chest, till he stepped out into a shady clearing surrounding the stone walls of the Greene family cemetery, and looked down over the broad sweep of the big south marsh.

It's interesting. To me at least. That Robert E. Lee would've stood right here. In a gray uniform the first time. Before he had the Army of Northern Virginia. When he was still called "Granny Lee." By the dim, the dull and the demented.

The next time was after the war. When he knew he was dying and wore himself out coming back. Largely because of the crowds on the way that wouldn't leave him alone.

Celebrity. Being what it is.

Hard on the body.

Bad for the soul.

Nothing I'd want to live through.

Ben opened the rusting black iron gate and stepped inside the waist-high walls, where he read the words on Caty Greene's grave first (the raised stone box built like a coffin with the epitaph cut on the top) and deciphered what he could of the other Greene inscriptions—before he walked to the southwest corner.

It was a plain thin upright rectangular gravestone that read, "Sacred To the Memory of GEN. HENRY LEE of Virginia. Obiit— 25 March, 1818 AEtat 63."

At least he died among friends. That must've been some kind of consolation. For him and his family too.

What was Robert then, eleven? With nothing much to remember him by. Except the words he wrote.

Ben took a small blue hardbound book out his coat pocket and turned to the excerpts from Harry Lee's letters.

"Fame in arms or art, however conspicuous, is naught unless bottomed on virtue."

"You know my abhorrence of lying, and you have been often told by me that it led to every vice and cancelled every tendency to virtue. Never forget this truth and disdain this mean and infamous practice."

"A man ought not only to be virtuous in reality, but he must always appear so—thus said to me the great Washington."

Ben smiled and waved a gnat away from the back of his neck, as he slid the book in his pocket, thinking about Robert's older brothers, who paid no attention to their father's letters. *While Robert read them over and over. And took Harry's principles as a way of life.*

It still couldn't have been easy later. When Robert faced the tough decision. He opposed secession. Hated slavery. Saw nothing worse than the dissolution of the union. Believed absolutely in the Republic of the Founding Fathers. Spent twenty-five years serving that Union in the army. Only to decide that his first obligation was still to Virginia, the land his family had settled and loved, when Lincoln offered him the whole federal army before he offered it to anyone else.

What must the war have been like for Lee?

Terrible. Either way.

No matter what happened.

Ben was looking around the cemetery, smelling the smells and listening to the marsh, when he noticed a broken corner piece of Caty Greene's tomb had fallen off on the ground.

He picked it up and was starting to fit it into place when he saw a small oval crudely carved stone lying inside the raised tomb.

He brushed off the sand, and worked at reading the uneven carving.

Your heirs
will be repaid
everything that they are owed.
E. G. M.—1941

Ben was asking himself what it meant, as he replaced it and refitted the corner, and if it looked like a child had carved it.

He closed the gate behind him and climbed down the bank above the marsh, then stood by the edge of a tidal creek watching egrets and ibis pick dinner out of mud. Seeing his own father lying for weeks in a hospital—fighting to breathe, fighting to work, fighting to raise his family—with lungs almost ruined in World War I.

Dad never had words like Harry Lee's. But he did set a good example. And now he sees me the way I see Butler. And there's nothing I can say to make that change.

Course, maybe he's right. Maybe you'll look back on your own life and think the same thing.

Ben's hands were on his hips—his brown-blond hair blowing in an east wind ripping in off the ocean, his strong-boned face stretched tight and still.

Look at that. Look at the marsh and the dunes. Cumberland's a lot more incredible than I understood as a kid.

Which leads me to helping Hannah. And what I don't know about eminent domain.

You can learn, though. You've got the Xeroxes of the legal stuff. The congressional papers on Yellowstone. And the old Yosemite case that went to the Supreme Court. Whatever you can do will be better than nothing. If that's not too dangerous an assumption.

Anyway, walking up Cumberland won't be boring. Not if it's still what it used to be, because you never know what you'll run into.

He ran into four white-tailed deer, a largish bay stallion (who didn't look any too pleased at seeing Ben while he herded three mares and three babies south down the main road), several armadillos, two pheasants, five or six turkey vultures, one wild turkey, and the rear end of a small wild pig—just on the north-south road.

WEDNESDAY, NOVEMBER 1ST

Estelle Baxter was sitting on the sofa in her room by the Whitfield office, rolling her stockings down and scratching her calves as though her legs were itchy and sore, thinking, *There's somethin' 'bout this Ben Reese fella that makes me real uneasy.*

Way he looks at you's the worst, when he doesn't think you're watchin'. Like he's seein' inside your head.

Carrie says he's talkin' to Miz Hannah. And you know where that could go. Course, it won't. Not for no reason. Not 'less you lose your head.

Estelle kneaded the bottoms of both feet with her thumbs, thinking about Ben in the front drive watching her walk from the dock after she'd finished cooking for the night and had come back to see if the cleanup crew had left the kitchen in order. It was after eleven, and she'd been strolling along, remembering Orlando in the good days—when she'd seen Ben Reese in the shadows following her face in the light from the porch.

He doesn't know nothin'. There's no way in the world he could. You're just feelin' skittish again 'cause Amelia set you off. Talkin' 'bout him tracking some fella who killed his friend up north.

Estelle picked up her worn brown shoes, then loosened the laces and pulled the insoles out so she could reach the paper in each—the small color photo of a plump young man with a stethoscope around his neck in one, the torn and creased newspaper clipping folded to fit the other.

She looked first at the man with the stethoscope. Then laid him on the table. And read the yellowed clipping, holding it close to the lamp.

She rested her head against the back of the sofa, and smoothed the newsprint against her chest, pondering how she'd made it this long. And if she had the courage she'd had then.

Miz Hannah's laying there wracked with pain. Legs and arms and body burnin' everywhere, every minute.

When it wouldn't take much. Not at night. Not if you don't give out, and you do what oughtta be done.

THURSDAY, NOVEMBER 9TH

Four years this week.

I wonder if Johanna remembers.

No, why would she? Her life's bigguh than this bed, thank the good Lord. And so is mine, and I wouldn't want her hindered by my MS. I surely wouldn't. Not like the rest of the family.

Is that Betsy out there with her new foal, or is it Fleet? Almost gettin' too dark to see. Just this last week seems like the sun's sinkin' earliuh, and a good bit fastuh, once it starts.

Been good talkin' to Ben Reese. 'Bout his mama, and Amelia, and visitin' here when he was little, 'bout the kind of work he does now too. Seems like he's grown up sensible, thank God, when some folks don't. Not when they've got his kind of education.

It surely will do my old heart good to have Johanna home again. It's time I got to see with my own two eyes how she's gettin' on. I can still hear her hurryin' to blame herself for Garrett dyin', right there in her voice when I ask her how she's doin'. Course, not one single soul there in all Atlanta will tell her any different. And it's time for me to say it again, fixin' my eyes on hers.

That must be Fleet. Back's too long to be Betsy. 'Less she's standin' there at some funny angle.

The wide pale face on the pillow was turned toward the screens in the open French doors, dark eyes straining, squinting to make out something more than the bare black outline of two bony wild horses quietly cropping Bermuda grass under a wide spreading live oak.

"You need anything special tonight, Miz Hill?" It was a blond-headed girl who was asking, twenty maybe or a little older, as she felt for the light switch by the bedroom door.

"I'm fine, honey. You sure you have to make you a light?"

The girl laughed and said, "If you want me to brush your teeth I do," as she set a pitcher of ice water on Hannah's bedside table. "Course, I can come back latuh."

"No, you go right ahead, honey. Whatevuh you gotta do."

"If you'd rathuh I came back, I could."

"Nope. I'm not goin' anywhere. Just watchin' the world settle in for the night." The breath rasped through the dry throat, weak and thin, cut by consonants she had to work at.

"It's real pretty out now, but Miz Walker says it's gonna turn real cool. I brought you a new straw."

"Thank you, Carrie, I could do with one. See the mare and foal, out there past the side porch? Can't tell if it's Betsy or old Fleet."

"I nevuh *can* tell any of 'em apart myself. Less they're speckled or something like that."

Hannah Hill coughed and couldn't get her breath for a second, but then she turned her face toward the small thin girl and smiled. "If you watch 'em long enough you will. You still fixin' to go back to school?"

"I hope to. If Miz Walker has work enough for me to help out here some on the weekends."

"Sit Amelia down and talk to her. You know she'll help you any way she can. The inn's gettin' busiuh all the time, 'specially on the weekends. Maybe not so much right then, right in the cold of wintuh, but she'll try to find a way to help. I'll talk to her too. Course, I don't tell her who to hire here at Whitfield, but I do give her my opinion."

"Thank you, Miz Hannah, for thinkin' of it."

"Bettuh turn me on my side, honey, to clean my teeth. I don't want to choke and die right tonight, not with Miss Johanna comin' home. Would you turn me to face the winduhs this time too? I do love to watch the night comin' down on Cumberland." Hannah laughed a tight dry laugh.

And Carrie smiled at her and patted her arm, as she pulled and pushed and settled Hannah Hill on her left side in the high mahogany four-poster bed. She checked the catheter, while she talked about what the guests had for dinner, and then she plumped the pillows, and tucked the sheets and comforter tightly under the mattress. "Does that feel all right? Your bed-sore's not botherin' you?"

"Fine, honey. You're gettin' pretty good at this."

"Thank you, ma'am, I hope to. You like me to spoon you some chopped ice?"

"I would, yes."

"Want me to read awhile too?"

"Not tonight, honey. Amelia read to me aftuh dinnuh, and I'm feelin' kinda tired. You might could make sure the pencil string's where I can get to it with my mouth, though, so I can pull down the paper if I take a notion."

"It's right here on your pillow. Course the camera's pushed

way up. Is that all right, or do you want it lowuh?"

"Don't think I'll be photographin' much out there in the dark."

"No, I don't s'pose you will. I like that new picture you took. The one of the five deer in the mist by the porch. You should get you that one blown up real big, and send it out with your Christmas cards."

"Thank you. That's very kind."

"I'm gonna go get me a cup of hot chocolate, and then I'll sit out at the desk and read. Lizbeth'll come on at two. But you call me if you need me before that, ya hear?"

"I will. Thank you, Carrie. How's your muthuh doin'?"

"Bettuh, I guess. She's s'pposed to go home tomorruh."

"You give her my love, ya hear? Surgery like she's had, it takes a while to get your strength back."

"Yes ma'am, it surely does. I'll be back to turn you ovuh again in a little bit. You want me to close the winduh?"

"Not right now, honey. Latuh when it turns cool."

Time passed, predictably. Slowly. With the sound of footsteps on floors and stairs, the clatter of cups and saucers, a wisp or two of conversation drifting down the wide halls, a whiff of wood smoke from the inn's big sitting room, the slap of the front screen, the rocking on the porch settling into silence sometime before eleven o'clock. Hannah was turned every two hours, one side and then the other, till sometime after mid-night, when she found herself in the dark, lying on her back, trying not to choke on the phlegm in her throat.

Her mouth was even drier than normal, and her lips were more cracked and chapped, and crushed ice would've felt good, melting in her mouth, sliding down the back of her throat.

She didn't want to call anyone, though, and wake herself up all the way. And she told herself to keep her eyes closed and listen to the hiss of the sea.

She tried to clear her throat, but the phlegm stayed stuck where it was, drainage from sinuses she couldn't empty on her own. She opened her eyes for a second, but closed them again right away, then turned her head toward the French doors and tried to breathe through her nose.

She couldn't, of course. She knew better. She also knew she wouldn't mind if she could just slip off to sleep again, where the air came in without her worrying at it, and the burning in her legs settled down.

There's no light shinin' from the hall desk. Close your eyes now and go to sleep. Carrie must've shut the door to keep it from wakin' me up. Winduhs must be closed too. Can't feel any breeze on my face from anywhere. Got cool, pro'bly, and she must've come back while I was sleepin'.

This is not the time to start thinkin', Miz Hannah. You just quiet yourself down now. And make yourself breathe like a butterfly. Just as light. And just as slow. Like dust settlin' on a dresser.

You could try to imagine the moonlight.

Sweepin' the porch clean.

Bleachin' the bones of the big oaks.

Whitenin' the dunes into high waves.

Curved waves like rolling foam.

Bringin' the deer onto the beach. Littlest ones with their mamas. Twitchin' their noses and turnin' their ears to the sea.

'Membuh the smell of confederate jasmine, way back in the yard when you were little? Mothuh sewin' in the shade, maybe workin' in the beds in the early mornin'? You should try to breathe it

in again. Real soft and real slow. Just like you did then.

You could picture yourself here, walkin' to the beach. Out the front door.

'Cross the porch floor.

Sixteen steps to the sand.

Takin' the drive off to the right between the two rows of live oaks.

Never could take those trees for granted. Never will as long as I live. Hundred feet high. Two hundred feet wide. Rough old arms curlin' right down to the sand.

Who was it first said they take "a hundred years to grow, a hundred years to live, and a hundred years to die?" Nathanael Greene's widow? Or old Robert Stafford?

Go on and walk unduh 'em. Feelin' like a child in a stand of giants, just like you used to do. Then cross the north-south road.

Most of the old oaks are behind you then. New ones, startin' to get smalluh aftuh that, above the saw palmetto.

That's where there'll be a spiduh web. Breakin' cool and sticky on your skin.

And somethin' thrashin' through the underbrush. The squeal of a wild boar, maybe. Horses, gettin' startled. The scurry of somethin'...

*What is **that** that I keep hearin'? Like a hissin' sound from somewhere. Can't be the sea slidin' on the beach. What was I thinkin' of when I said that before? Doors and winduhs are all shut tight. And it's too far away besides. Sounds like somebody sprayin' something. Spritzin' the laundry, to get to ironin'. Course, that makes no sense at all. Silly, what you come up with. Driftin' off in the dark.*

*Now, **that** was a door opening. No question. The door out to the hall.*

Hannah coughed, and half-opened her eyes, and was just

70

turning her face from the outside wall toward the center of the room, and it looked to her like someone in coveralls, wearing a gas mask, of all things, with a spray bottle in a gloved hand, had slipped through the hall door closing it quick behind.

Hannah smiled to herself, and said, "Idiot," under her breath. Before she actually coughed up phlegm for a second, and closed her eyes again.

Mothuh always said my imagination would be the death of me, and here it is makin' a fool of me again. Must be Carrie. Or 'Lizbeth, if it's after two. Lookin' in on me like they do, tryin' not to wake me up.

Now, Miz Hannah Hill, it's time for you to close your eyes again and go to sleep!

Carrie's head was down on her desk, the light was off, her right hand was folded under her chin, the mug with a scum of hot chocolate in the bottom was knocked on its side near her elbow.

Broad hands in surgical gloves picked up the mug and set another down. Its inside covered by the same sort of slick of cold mud-colored chocolate.

CHAPTER FIVE

FRIDAY, NOVEMBER 10TH

BEN LAID HIS PEN DOWN BESIDE Amelia's typewriter and pushed his chair away from the big walnut desk. He walked to the back windows that looked out on a swath of lawn and marsh, and stretched his arms over his head as he watched one of the Whitfield guests come out of the new cedar bathhouse.

Whitfield plumbing fixtures were old and infirm, period pieces, picturesque at best, most of them shared between rooms. Which inspired a large number of Whitfield guests to slip out to the cedar house to enjoy more modern conveniences.

Ben told himself not to watch the short plump middle-aged man slinking back to the inn, even though he found it marginally amusing the way most fully clothed guests looked embarrassed, as though it were indelicate to let themselves be seen walking to, or from.

Ben stared instead at the library where he'd been working—the dark dusty usually abandoned room, its high heavy shelves stuffed with brittle unopened books, its two Victorian tufted chairs covered with claret-colored velvet, its old maps of Cumberland, its faded sepia photographs of long-deceased Hills taking tea on porches, caught dead in their tracks in high buttoned shoes in rows of self-conscious strained looking faces, above tight collars and tighter waists.

He wondered if they'd had time to clean his room at Amelia's cottage, and decided probably not, as his eyes stuck on a bottom bookshelf where three large volumes lay on their sides under a short stack of smaller books.

Ben read *Rafinesque* on the spine of the leatherbound book on top, and squatted in front of the shelf.

Two journals of Constantine Rafinesque. One on ants. The other on a collecting trip along the Ohio River. Written in his own hand when most of his papers have been lost.

Why here, I wonder? No name on the flyleaf. No sign of provenance at all.

*I s'ppose one of the Hills could've been a botanist. An enthusiast at least. Educated enthusiasts **were** the scientists of earlier ages. James J. Hill maybe. He was interested in almost everything, and he knew a lot about plants.*

Ben laid the journals carefully on the carpet, and picked up the next book in the stack—a larger volume that almost made his hand shake. Printed on linen. Covered in leather. Usually found in rare book departments in well-endowed libraries.

Bernard McMahon. First edition. 1806. The American Gardener's Calendar.

The landscape designer Jefferson consulted. The nurseryman he bought plants from for Monticello. The botanist he gave most of Lewis and Clark's specimens. The first—

No, that can't be—

Ben set the Rafinesque and the McMahon on a velvet chair.

And laid another leather-bound book on the center of the old desk. It was two feet tall and almost as wide. And he sat fast, and reminded himself to breathe, before he opened the front cover.

Mark Catesby. The Natural History of Carolina, Florida, and the Bahama Islands.

The first illustrated work on the flora and fauna of North America. One of the greatest accomplishments of eighteenth-century science. Here. When I'm writing my speech for Charleston.

Ben brought the other books over to the big desk and dusted them off with his handkerchief.

Then looked back at the bottom shelf, and the shelf to the left of it too, where there were thirteen matched volumes, clothbound and faded, with the name *Wilson* readable, from where he sat, on the one closest to him.

He went over and picked it up.

And then lost track of the next four hours.

Wind was shifting the beach on the east coast, the whole length of the island, wrinkling water in shallow tide pools, ruffling sheets of wet reflected sky, ripping at ribbons of hard wet sand wavering in rows like ribs along the beach, whipping dry sand into spears and scourges that scoured the beach and the dunes, as seabirds hunted at the waterline (sanderlings, sandpipers, oystercatchers, gulls) hopping, scooting, strutting, waddling, swooping from the sky too, to pick the beach clean—while Ben Reese watched.

He'd been walking the beach for more than an hour, away from the wind and back into it, running two miles at least and maybe more, waiting too, for minutes at a time, to watch clouds and birds and grasses blow.

When he got back to the break in the high dunes that led to the path to Whitfield, he sat on a driftwood log and pulled a small notepad out of his canvas hunting jacket. He wrote for almost an hour, crossing out words and making notes in the margins, holding the pad hard against the wind. He stared out at the sea, as he slipped it back in a pocket, watching a shrimp boat troll south as clouds rolled around it, turning darker and denser in uncountable shades of gray, thinking, *Why do I have to get my blood moving when I work? And why is it easier to write outside?*

Then he remembered Hannah, and said, "Nuts." *I should've started back by five.*

Ben walked fast through deep drifting sand, high dunes on both sides, rows of them like earthworks, speared by spikes of sea oats—till he climbed the last dune before the live oak forest, and watched what was left of the sunset staining the sky above the trees.

He ran down the sand hill where the path fell away forty feet to the forest floor, then ran the mile to Whitfield through the black-lace tunnel of snaking branches, through gathering dark and rustling palmetto and the thrash and scurry of large and small animals running from the sound of man.

"Honey, I don't worry 'bout much of anything. And why that is, you don't have time to hear now. I oughtta go. Somebody's here. I'm sorry it's asthma, but I'm glad you're both okay. Give my love to her daddy. Ovuh." Hannah's voice was cracked and weak and she coughed while she looked at Ben, who'd just walked in from the hall.

"I apologize, Hannah. I meant to be here by six, but I lost track of time."

"Good. You need to relax. That's why folks come to Cumberland."

"Your dinnuh tray's right here, Mr. Reese."

"Thanks for bringing it, Carrie." Ben had stopped just inside the door, his hands in his pockets, pinning his navy wool shirt back behind his elbows.

"You missed all the excitement. Miz Hannah was talkin' to a friend of hers on the ship-to-shore this afternoon, and the friend's daughtuh started chokin' and turnin' blue, and then the mothuh almost fainted, so Miz Hannah talked her into puttin' her head down, and then got the police to send the rescue squad."

"That's not exactly right." Hannah was coughing and looking embarrassed.

"'Mounts to the same thing, though, 'cause you got Miz Land." Carrie smiled at Hannah, as she closed the door behind her.

Ben moved a small caned chair close to the head of Hannah's bed, and sat with the tray on his lap. "So what *did* you do?"

"It was the operatuh who connects the ship-to-shore calls from up in Brunswick, she's the one who got the police. She listens to everybody's conversations, always has, just goes from one to the othuh, so I had Carrie get the operatuh, and she got the police to send an ambulance. Miz Land got on right quick, and I reckon she'd been listenin'. You remembuh Charlotte's husband? Rafe MacKinnon? He used to just get fit to be tied ovuh Miz Land, 'cause if she heard *any* cussin' or swearin' when she was listenin' in, she'd cut you off right then." Hannah chuckled, before she coughed, and her soft green eyes smiled.

And then Ben could see for one split second what Hannah must've looked like before she'd gotten sick. "We had an operator like that when I was a kid."

"Did your writin' go well, honey?"

"Nope. It never does. I fight over every word. Have you eaten?"

"Good long while ago. You go right ahead. What are you writin' about? You told me 'bout bein' an archivist, but not what you're workin' on now."

"Early English and American medicine. The way seventeenth and eighteenth-century herbals came from England and Scotland with the settlers, and influenced treatment here. They were family herbals usually, books full of recipes that got passed down for using medicinal plants to treat all sorts of ailments. I'm writing articles from a couple of different perspectives hoping to publish them in different kinds of journals."

"My mothuh made her own medicines. Used cherry bark for cough syrup that tasted wonderful, and worked as well as anything. Made mustard plasters for sprains too that fixed you up fastuh than any store-bought liniment I evuh used."

"Most of that kind of knowledge is long gone, and it's a shame."

"It is."

"I'm also working on early American naturalists and illustrators, mostly botanists, people who collected plants in the New World, then drew or painted them, usually for the English."

"How early would that've been?"

"Seventeenth, eighteenth, early nineteenth century. They must've been almost fearless when you think about it. Catesby came over here from England in the early seventeen hundreds, and tramped, mostly alone, across South Carolina, Florida, and the Bahamas, painting what he saw, and sending plants and seeds back to England."

"I've nevuh even heard his name."

"Most people haven't today, and yet his work influenced Linnaeus and every other botanist back then. I got to see his original watercolors in Windsor Castle this summer. George III bought them after Catesby died, and they're there in the family library. I was given special access, which I hadn't expected at all, and I shot slides of every one of them for our library. The amazing thing is that here in the Whitfield library *you've* got a first edition of the book he published using his engravings of those paintings."

"It would've belonged to a Hill, but I don't know which one."

"It's valuable. And before I go, I'll clean it up a little and give you some ideas about how to take care of it. There're others here too that are worth something and need to be preserved."

"I'd be grateful for whatevuh you can do."

"Would you mind if I photographed parts of Catesby's book? And a couple of other books too?"

"You go right ahead, honey, and use 'em whatevuh way you want."

"Thanks, Hannah. I appreciate it."

"The only illustratuh I know about is Audubon."

"There were others. Bartram. Rafinesque. *He* was a wild man, believe me. Mrs. Delaney was wonderful too. She was later, and she worked in England. She made absolutely realistic paper collages of almost a thousand flowers before she went blind, and they've got them all in the British Museum. There are a lot of early illustrators who are interesting to me, and I *hope* they will be to people in Charleston. I'm talking about illustrators there tomorrow to a preservation organization and a bunch of art groups, even though I'd rather be boiled in oil."

"You don't like speakin' in public?"

"That would be an understatement."

"So what do you reckon I oughtta do about Cumberland?"

"It's not an easy situation, is it? Would you mind if I ran through what I know and see if I've got it straight?"

"Course not. I'm not goin' anywhere."

"You say things like that just to watch the rest of us squirm." Ben smiled and popped a forkful of green beans and bacon in his mouth.

"I have to amuse myself somehow." Hannah laughed softly and looked away from Ben, out toward the French doors.

"Yes, and I'm glad you do. So this real estate guy—"

"Ed Montgomery."

"—bought two parcels of Cumberland land from Hill relatives of Charlotte's, and brought in a developer who tried to buy up the rest of the island too, with the intention of putting in a causeway and making Cumberland into a ritzy community like Sea Island or Hilton Head."

"Eddie bought the land the year before Charlotte died."

"So while the negotiations were going on with the developer, the National Park Service got interested, spurred on by your local congressman, and they started pushing all the owners on the island, of which there weren't many, to sell their land to the government."

"Charlotte had the biggest parcel of Hill land. She'd bought my husband's piece years ago, when he was short of money.

And Alec's too, the only othuh brothuh who lived on to maturity. He died of tuberculosis in the twenties, and Charlotte bought his portion from his widow round 1930. Charlotte's sistuh, Susanna, she divided her parcel between her son and daughtuh ten years or more ago."

"Why? She didn't like Cumberland?"

"She'd gone to boardin' school up north, and nevuh spent much time here. She didn't want to spend money caring for the Grange. That's the house she inherited here. Her husband's a surgeon, and they live near Asheville, North Carolina."

"And *her* kids sold to Eddie Montgomery. There's the Sutton land too. Right? Up on the north end of the island?"

"Yep. There'd been a small summer hotel there from the 1880s on, and the owners sold to the Suttons 'bout 1920. The Hills bought the rest of the island in 1888. Ninety-some percent of it."

"So the developer talked to Charlotte—"

"And she sent him packin'. She was a hard-headed woman."

"That's what Aunt Amelia says."

"She evuh told you 'bout the first time she met Charlotte?"

"No."

"Amelia was eight or ten years old, standin' in the hardware store in St. Mary's where her daddy worked, and Charlotte came in wearing lace-up English riding boots with a pistol stuck in the belt of her skirt, complainin' 'bout the price of seed."

"I met Charlotte myself, the one time I was here as a kid, and she made an impression on *me*." Ben laughed as he put his tray on the dresser near the hall door, then stopped and read one of the greeting cards Hannah'd had tacked to the wall. "So the park service made overtures to Charlotte too, but nothing definite had been done when she died and left you Cumberland?"

"The park people told her they'd get it one way or the othuh. No one thought she'd leave it to me, land *and* money to pay the taxes and take care of the island, when it should've gone to her daughtuh, Leah. Charlotte left Leah a third of her investments, and gave her the use of her own house here for her lifetime. Four Chimneys. Robert Stafford's home place."

"But that, and the rest of Cumberland, she left to you lock, stock and barrel?"

"Made me feel terrible. I told Leah I'd deed it right ovuh to her, but she said she didn't want it. That she has her daddy's houses—one in Charleston, one in Beaufort—and land in New England as well, and Cumberland would be nothin' but a legal and financial burden."

"Leah was her only child?"

"No. Charlotte's son was killed in the Pacific in World War II. Course, Charlotte explained why she gave me Cumberland in a lettuh the lawyuh read with the will. That I was a Hill by marriage, that Leah'd nevuh cared for Cumberland, and Charlotte wanted me to fight the developuhs and the park and keep Cumberland the way it is. Leah nevuh liked bein' here. Never liked the animals, *or* the troubles of living on an island, or having to use a boat to get back and forth."

"Why?"

"Leah's scared to death of watuh. Her brothuh, Charlie, when he was sixteen and she was five, took her out in a sail-boat and nearly drowned 'em both, and Leah's nevuh been the same since. Won't even use the boat that takes folks back and forth to the inn. Hires an old gentleman from St. Mary's who worked for her parents when she was a child to ferry her when she comes to visit. And that's very infrequent." Hannah was coughing and beginning to choke.

And Ben grabbed her glass and held the straw to her lips. "You want me to put some Chap Stick on you too?"

"No, I'm fine, honey. Thank you." The skin around her wide green eyes looked swollen and sore and her eyes were watering.

And Ben wiped around them with a Kleenex. "So after you inherited her land, the family at the north of the island, the Suttons, started negotiating some kind of agreement with the park service?"

"Hal Sutton's the owner. The son of the founduh of a very large furniture makuh in North Carolina."

"Tell me something about the history of the island. Whatever might help when I read the legal papers."

"I reckon the first thing you'd need to know is that General Nathanael Greene was given the island aftuh the Revolution to pay a debt he was owed. He intended to harvest live oak here for ship buildin', but died very suddenly of sunstroke. His widow, Caty Greene, was left two or three pennies to rub togethuh, and a big plantation up rivuh of Savannah that was deep in debt. She spent what she had helpin' Eli Whitney get his cotton gin perfected, hopin' to turn it to a money makin' business, but...Would you mind giving me some chips of ice?"

"Of course not." Ben grabbed the spoon and the glass and slid a few slivers in her mouth. "Whitney never made any money on the cotton gin. Right? Everybody and his brother infringed on his patents, and he couldn't make a living till he'd invented interchangeable parts, and used them to mass-produce guns for the army."

"He nevuh took out anothuh patent eithuh. Not as long as he lived. Caty Greene lost money too, with the legal suits defendin' the patents. And she came here with her second husband, aftuh she sold the Savannah plantation, and built her a big old house that some say she couldn't afford to finish. Planted orange groves and gardens all round it, down on the southern end, and made it self-sufficient. Called it Dungeness, after the hunting lodge Oglethorpe had built right there."

"Did she die before Light Horse Harry?"

"Three or four years before. Her children cared for Harry Lee when the ship dropped him on Cumberland. Caty'd had a hard time of it here, and aftuh she died, her children couldn't make a go of it eithuh. They sold the land off, piece by piece, to Robert Stafford, the son of Nathanael Greene's overseer.

"Stafford was a clevuh man. Very frugal and farseeing, and he did just fine for himself. He'd already settled his own family up north, before the War between the States. His common-law mulatto wife and their children. And they did right well in society, nobody realizin' their muthuh was colored. One daughtuh married a European prince."

"Stafford must've irritated a few folks."

"Oh, he did that, yes. Sometime aftuh he died in the 1870s, one of the Greene heirs, who'd been scrimpin' and savin', tried to buy him up the parcel of land where Caty's Dungeness had stood, before it burned years before. That was right when the Hills got interested, in the 1880s, and they bought up the whole island, all but the summer-camp hotel up on the north end. The Greene descendent couldn't pay what the Hills could pay, and I know they took it to heart. The Hills built them a big house down where Dungeness had been and called it Kirkconnell."

"Which is the ruin that's there now."

"Yep. Somebody burned it down in 1950. They say it was a poachuh set it on fire. Revenge for havin' been shot in the leg here while poachin' deer. Course no one evuh admitted to havin' been shot here, or shootin' anyone eithuh. It was all rumuh. But it could've been a caretakuh or a yardman patrollin' the house, takin' a shot at a trespassuh. Could've been Charlotte, to tell you the whole truth. But we'll talk about that anothuh time. Nobody'd lived in Kirkconnell in years. Not after Charlotte's mother died. Once income taxes came in, it was too expensive to keep up, and it was sittin' there rottin' away."

"And now Eddie Montgomery has sold the park service the parcels he bought from the Hills."

"Yep. And they've given him the right to stay at the Grange till they use the house for somethin' else. He comes ovuh from time to time and docks at Kirkconnell."

"The development man decamped, once he saw Sutton wouldn't sell to him. And now the federal government's pushing hard, trying to scare you *and* Sutton. Saying, 'If you won't sell, we'll condemn your land and take it by right of eminent domain.' Is that accurate?"

"It surely is. And I just heard this mornin' that Hal Sutton signed with the park last week. They say they'll let him keep the land for his own use for his lifetime *and* his children's, but at the death of his last child, the government'll take it all."

"Great."

"The park's talkin' 'bout bringin' in close to two thousand folks a day. Startin' gradually. Startin' in the south end, where they bought the land from Eddie. Reckon it could be as soon as the spring. They're sayin' they'll bring 'em in just north of the ruins of Kirkconnell, on the west side here, then direct 'em to paths that take 'em ovuh to the Atlantic side and let 'em use the beach there. They aren't s'pposed to go down to Kirkconnell, or into the cemetery where Caty Greene's buried. Course how you keep 'em away from our land I don't rightly know."

"And you think all those people will affect the land and the animals?"

"You know they will. I'm sittin' here between park land on the south, and what's gonna be park land on the north, and I've gotta figure out a way to keep 'em from forcin' me out."

"What's your lawyer say?"

"I don't think he wants to be bothered. Says make a deal for the rest of my life, and Johanna's life too, like the Suttons, and don't lose any sleep ovuh it. I don't sleep real well anyway, and I don't mind losin' a little more. Speakin' of sleep, I oughtta tell you what happened last night. You'll get a chuckle out of it, like I did."

"Oh?" Ben leaned back in his chair and locked his hands behind his head.

"I was driftin' off and wakin' up, like I do, and I was telling myself to keep my eyes shut and not let myself get to thinking too much. Tryin' to calm my mind by tryin' to remembuh the walk to the beach, and watchin' everything like I used to, and I thought I heard somethin' like a spray bottle being squirted. I opened my eyes halfway, and I imagined somebody. It was probably just the tail end of a dream, but I saw someone in a zipped up coverall wearin' a gas mask and rubbuh gloves sneakin' out my door into the hall carryin' a spray bottle! Can you imagine me doin' that? What kind of mind pictures somethin' that outlandish so real you think it happened? I reckon it was one of the girls, Carrie or the other one, coming in to check on me, and I just pictured the rest."

"Dreams are strange things. I still dream about the war once in a while. And those dreams always end with two specific events that actually happened to me. Which seems weirder to me than anything else. Anyway, why don't you let me talk to a friend of mine who's a lawyer in Charleston, and then we'll discuss it when I get back? I'll be gone a week or ten days. I've got to go up to Tryon, North Carolina, too, and meet with a man who's offered to donate some paintings to my university."

"Honey, anythin' you can do I'll be grateful for. Ask Amelia to give you the legal files, and then you'll know where we stand."

"What's the book on the bedside table, the handmade one tied with the leather thong?"

"Little bits from George MacDonald. Parts I 'specially like that people copy down for me."

"May I ask you something personal?"

"Course you can."

"How do you handle the MS so well? I couldn't do it the way you do."

"You don't have limitations?"

"Sure, some, but nothing like—"

"We all have limitations, honey. You have scars you carry. Inside and out. And your life's not ovuh yet."

"True."

"None of us knows how we'd do ahead of time. I lost twin sons in Korea. That was a good deal harduh than this. Lyin' here's made me a whole lot more patient. I used to be in such a rush, runnin' the hotel in St. Mary's, worryin' about it when I wasn't there. Watchin' every little thing the children did every second, sometimes when I shouldda turned loose. Worryin' over 'em, and what David was doin'."

"Ah, yes. Life interfering with how you'd like to live."

"Didn't talk to people like I do now. Didn't even see the world around me. Clouds. Stars. Birds in the yard. Lizards on the front walk. Now I've got time and I watch. I listen to people too. Lotta folks don't have time anymore. Used to be grand-parents talked to grandchildren. Did for 'em. Paid attention. Families are gettin' farthuh apart today. Lot a folks need some-one to talk to."

"Yeah, I think that's true."

"All these girls who've helped me ovuh the years, most of 'em from a girls college outside St. Mary's. Three shifts of 'em now, every day. They got troubles. School. Boys. Family. Money. I get 'em to talk when othuh folks can't, and sometimes I can see some way to help."

"You still cope with a lot of pain and misery."

"It's not gonna last much longuh. It's gettin' hard to swal-low, and when I can't, I'll go fast. God allowed this for a reason, honey, and if the rest of us leave Him alone, He'll end it the right way."

"I admire the way you're handling it."

"Not seein' my daughter's the worst of it." Hannah coughed and looked away from Ben for a second. "Mary hasn't called or come to visit in six years, and I don't rightly know why. I know she blames me for makin' David leave. When I was brought home from the hospital one time, I found him in bed with one of my nurses."

"Geez."

"I'm not judgin' him. I don't have the right. But I wasn't gonna live with him anymore. We nevuh divorced, but he went off with her. And then aftuh she left him, he died of lung cancer two years latuh. I've told Mary I love her. And Johanna'll tell her too, after I'm gone, that I loved her till the day I died, if she still hasn't come to see me."

"And you don't know why she won't?"

"No, honey, I don't. Some folks can't stand to see imperfection. Someone in a wheelchair, or missin' an arm. I knew a woman who had a mangled foot who couldn't look at a hare-lipped dog I had. Said horrible things about him. But Johanna calls all the time, and she comes to Cumberland as often as she can. She's an opera singer, just gettin' started, so her time's not her own. But she's takin' next summer off and stayin' here the whole time. She's comin' for Thanksgivin' too, and it does my heart good to think about it."

"It's odd, really, when you think about it. You're isolated here, away from the world on an island, stuck in a bed in your own room, and yet it doesn't protect you at all from what goes on out there, does it?"

"Nope. We're none of us protected till we're dead and gone. But there's good comin' out of me lyin' here. Look at all those cards and lettuhs on the walls. Folks goin' out of their way to remembuh me, to do somethin' to say they care what happens. That's as good for them as it is me. I don't know, you never do, but maybe seein' me will help someone else with somethin' in their lives."

"I suspect it has already."

"I used to have a vicious tempuh. Terrible. Got it from my daddy. I don't anymore. I take more time to think 'fore I open my mouth. I didn't change that in myself. It came from what I'm livin' through. Still can't stand liars, though. If somebody lies to you 'bout one thing, they'll lie to you 'bout anothuh, and

I have no patience with that. That doesn't mean I've nevuh lied. I hate it in me too."

"I feel the same way." Ben had picked up the book of quotes, most of them in his Aunt Amelia's handwriting, and read where the ribbon marked a page. "'Half the misery in the world comes from trying to look, instead of trying to be, what one is not.'"

"Isn't that the truth?"

"'When we begin to do something we know we ought to do, we cease being the poor slave of circumstances.'"

"You know, one thing I reckon I oughtta tell you is that I'm leavin' Cumberland to Johanna. Leavin' her Charlotte's money too, so she can fight for it. You need to know for when you're talkin' to your lawyuh friend. Johanna loves it like Charlotte and me, and she'll try her best to take care of it. Whatevuh else there is goes to Mary. I sold my house in St. Mary's when I came here, and whatevuh's left of that is hers. Mary doesn't like Cumberland. Never has. It's too wild for her. Too natural. No stores, or restaurants, or theaters."

"Does she live in St. Mary's?"

"No. Savannah. You help Johanna with Cumberland, y'hear? You and Amelia. Help Johanna decide what to do."

"I will. I'll read the paperwork you gave me and talk to your lawyer, and mine too. But you're not going to die any time soon."

"None of us 'knows the hour of our passing.' And I do b'lieve that's a very good thing."

SUNDAY, NOVEMBER 19TH

A TALL WOMAN, WITH LONG LEGS and narrow hips and a
stomach that noticeably preceded her, was standing by
Hannah's bed, holding a Kleenex against her nose. Her chin
was trembling and her thin plucked eyebrows were crushed
against small green-eye-shadowed eyes half-hidden behind
almond-shaped glasses. She sighed loudly and fluffed the back
of her thin permed hair, before Hannah turned her head
toward her and opened her eyes. "Hey, Miz Hannah. I didn't
mean to wake y'all up. I just come to see how you're feelin'
tonight."

"I'm doin' all right."

"It don't seem right you'd get pneumonia again, it surely
don't." Estelle Baxter blew her nose before she shook her head.

"That's what happens with lungs like mine, honey. You get
pneumonia at the drop of a hat."

"With all you've had to go through, I just *hate* to see you
lying there, sufferin' like you do."

"Tell me what you fixed for dinnuh."

"I cain't hardly think about that, not now. All those rich folks eatin' their fine food, and you here—"

"I know how you feel about me. And you know what I think about it."

"I didn't mean—"

"Didn't you?"

"Miz Hannah needs to rest." Florence Rich had opened the door from the hall, and she was standing just inside it in her pristine white uniform and starched white cap holding a bottle of skin lotion, staring purposefully at Whitfield's cook.

"I only been in here a minute." Estelle Baxter started toward the hall, walking awkwardly and self-consciously with her head held high and her eyes straight ahead.

"I'm not sayin' you don't mean well, but we can't let Miz Hannah get tired out."

Estelle didn't argue or defend herself. She just looked past Florence Rich and stepped through the hall door.

"The massage felt good." Hannah shivered with her face and neck, after the thermometer was taken from her mouth, then closed her eyes and sighed. "Course, it's makin' me feel sleepy."

"That's just what you need, Miz Hannah. Get you some rest to fight the infection."

"Rest is all I *been* gettin' the last four years."

"Now, Miz Hannah—"

"It was a joke, Florence. I'm doin' fine."

"Reverend Tate called today. He'd like to come see you tomorruh."

"I'm not ready for him, honey. I'm too worn out to do right by him."

Florence Rich looked at Hannah with a faintly alarmed expression on her no-nonsense face.

And Hannah smiled before she tried to swallow. "He and I are just gettin' acquainted, and I know I gotta hold my tongue, but I keep wantin' to ask him why he'd go and become a preachuh when he doesn't believe for one minute that Jesus Christ rose from the dead. If Jesus *didn't*, honey, we're a pretty sad bunch, and sittin' in a pew's beside the point." Hannah started coughing, and then asked for a spoonful of ice.

"Reverend Michaels is comin' over Tuesday. You want Miz Amelia to postpone his visit?"

"No. No, Douglas has been teachin' me a good long while, and he does my old heart good. We're workin' togethuh on how the church can help shut-ins too, and I'm hopin' knowin' that will keep Reverend Tate from feelin' hurt."

"I'll go ask Miz Amelia to give him a call in the mornin'. I'll make me a cup of tea, and run to the potty too. Can I get you anything?" Florence had slid the thermometer in its stainless steel holder and was smiling at Hannah Hill with a gentle, pleasant-looking expression on her smooth, round, middle-aged face.

Hannah shook her head slowly, her face drawn and her eyes sunken, and said, "No, thank you, honey. I don't need a thing."

"Your temperature's stayin' down, and your color's bettuh tonight. Course, you still got you some congestion, and I'll be thumpin' on your back again to loosen it when I come back. Dr. Patterson said you were doin' bettuh today too. Course he nevuh would've let you out of the hospital if he was all that concerned."

"I didn't give him much say in the mattuh." Hannah licked

her lips and swallowed like her throat hurt, before she spoke again in a quiet raspy voice. "I told Tom I was comin' home to Cumberland to live or die, eithuh one, and I didn't much care what he thought about it."

"He still wouldn't've let you come home if he'd been real worried. He'd taken away the oxygen by then, and that was a good sign. Anyway, you try to get you some sleep, and I'll be back as quick as I can."

"Would you mind stirrin' up the fire some before you go? I feel kinda cold. Like it's takin' the starch right outta me."

"I'll turn the thermostat up too, and bring you some consommé when I come. I'll get you anothuh comfortuh soon as I get back, if you're still chilly then. I hate to lay more weight on you if we can warm you up without it." Florence started toward the hall door, then turned and looked back at Hannah. "Did I do right with Estelle? Makes my skin crawl to see her in here, starin' at you with her chin wobblin', sayin' she 'cain't bear to see you suffuh.' She's done it every night since you've been home, and I—"

"You did fine, honey. It'll be all right." Hannah coughed, slowly and painfully, till it almost sounded like a lung was ripping, after she'd watched the hall door close behind Florence.

She turned her head then, half a minute later, to face the French doors. She'd heard a handle turn, unexpectedly. And she could see the right-hand door opening toward the bed.

The room was dark now, except for the smoldering fire, and yet Hannah saw clearly what she'd never expected to see again— someone in dark brown coveralls zipped up to a gas mask that hid the face and head. "Who *are* you? What'd'you want here?"

There was no direct answer—but a gloved hand reached up and adjusted the rubber mask.

"Why're you here in the dark of night?" Hannah tried to raise her head, every hair standing on end, thinking, *Dear Jesus, I can feel it. Evil and hate, cracklin' in the air like lightnin'.*

There were no words spoken that time either— as the person in coveralls locked the hall door and walked toward the head of the bed.

"That's what you *would* do, isn't it? 'This is the condemnation, that light is come into the world, and men loved darkness rathuh than light, because their deeds were evil.'" The breath caught in Hannah's throat as she finished the last of the quote, and she coughed again, staring at the eyes behind the mask, coming close now above her own, as the figure in coveralls and knit cap bent across her to pick up the pillow beyond her head.

"Why you want to kill me? I can see who you are now." Hannah choked, and shook her head, and strained to catch her breath. "I'm ready to go. It's not gonna bothuh *me* any. No, you're the one to feel sorry for. You're destroyin' yourself, and bein' cowardly too, don't y'think? Suffocatin' a sittin' duck?" Hannah smiled as she said it. Till the pillow was pushed against her face. *Comfort Johanna, Lord. Don't let her despair when I'm gone. Direct and guide her, and help turn my—*

Hannah could've whipped her head from side to side.

But she didn't.

Dignity was better than nothing.

Dignity was all she had left.

MONDAY, NOVEMBER 20TH

Johanna Elliott opened the door to the practice room and set her music case and purse on a chair, and her thermos on the table by the upright piano.

She shook her thick brown hair out behind her back, combed her fingers through it from just above the temples, telling herself to look for tension and release it, especially in the neck and jaw—to feel for it with her fingers, while she closed her eyes and focused her mind.

She took a sip from the thermos, then walked around the room, humming quietly for a minute or more. She stopped and stood very straight, concentrating on her breathing, reminding herself to direct up and feel the top of her head, to release her shoulders, and widen her chest, and try to feel the bottoms of her feet.

When she was ready, she began to speak, very slowly, very fluidly, saying, "Huminuh-huminuh-huminuh," descending the scale from the first word to the last, repeating the phrase over and over, starting each new phrase a half-step higher—till she'd climbed an entire octave. She worked her way down the scale again—checking her jaw, her neck, her shoulders for signs of tension, concentrating her mind on her body.

Then she sang, "mee-may-mah-moh-moo" on a single note, drawing out the "oo" sound in "moo" first, finding the pure vowel and holding it, before moving up a half step and repeating the whole phrase. She held the rest of the vowels the same way, starting with the "ee" in "mee," climbing the scale and coming down again, while weaving one of her hands in the air to visually pull the sounds out—using her fingers to paint sound in space, to help make the vowels more expressive.

She did sirens after that, starting with the "ee" sound, singing it low, sliding it much higher, making a long keening whine like a fire siren, imagining the sound as a glowing disk of light that had to be thrown across a field and brought down as smoothly as a boomerang.

She sang five or six more sirens, feeling for tension in her throat and jaw, her shoulders wide, her chest high and open, consciously relaxing her head on her neck.

She did two new exercises to work on her high notes, and then stacked her music on the music stand, debating which aria to work on first, worrying too, that at nine in the morning, working too hard could tire the voice.

Eric Allen was tough, and she knew he was going to push her. She wanted him to, that's why she paid him. To give her the perspective of a vocal perfectionist who also knew the business side of opera. But singing was grueling that early in the morning. Hard on her vocal cords and her throat.

Of course, there wasn't much choice at that moment. All four arias had to be ready for auditions in New York with companies from around the country ten days after Thanksgiving. So she had to keep from over-singing before Eric got there, and yet work the arias into her voice enough that she was able to do what he asked.

She told herself one last time to stick to what she'd decided too—to not do the *Roméo and Juliette*, or the *Cosi*, either one. Just one Mozart. "Cherubino." Plus the Massenet, the Rossini, and the Johann Strauss. All of them were right for her, at that moment in time. For a mezzo-soprano with a voice like hers, who looked like she did—tallish and thin—and wasn't quite twenty-seven. There were pants roles and roles in female costume, and there was contrast and breadth in musicality and language. And that was what she needed.

She was checking her watch to see how much time she had before Eric arrived, thinking, *Two more days, and I'll be talking to Hannah on Cumberland, and boy will that feel good*—when the door opened and the security guard told her she had a phone call and that the lady said it was important.

Johanna thanked him, with a cold hard clot in her own heart—worrying already, as she had been for days every time the phone rang, that the call had to do with Hannah and that the news was anything but good.

Johanna closed the hall door to the practice room and walked across the squeaky parquet floor to the folding metal chair by the piano.

She was shaking when she sat, and there were tears streaming down her face. Her nose was running hard, and the lids that hid her dark blue eyes were pink and puffy. Her face and throat were red and mottled looking, as her hands fluttered onto her knees, resting there for not much more than a second, before they reached for her purse and pulled out a package of Kleenex.

Lord, please, I…Sweet Hannah. Why didn't I do what I knew I ought to do? I should've gone when—

The door opened then, and Eric Allen walked in, tall and cadaverous, looking down at her through thick tortoiseshell glasses, his gray-streaked hair slicked tight against his scalp, his black silk shirt open at the throat, a black-and-red handkerchief in the pocket of his charcoal jacket.

He stared at her silently for a second with his arms hanging at his sides, before he said, "If you weren't able to work, you should've phoned."

"I'm very sorry, Mr. Allen, I just now got a call saying that my aunt—"

"As I told you on Monday, I can't work with you any other time before you go. It's a shame, under the circumstances. We both know how much work you have to do before you'll be ready for New York."

Mary Hill opened the French doors at the back of her studio apartment in Savannah and congratulated herself for the fifth time that morning on having unearthed the black wrought-iron table and chairs in a cluttered back corner of "Yesterday, Today and Tomorrow"—and *then* managing to talk the price down to something she could justify, if not afford.

They still had to be painted (and she was hoping she wouldn't have to do that herself, that she could talk Earley at the shop into doing it for her as a favor), but they were exactly the right look for her cubbyhole niche of the back garden. Once she found four urns with the right pedestals, and filled them with tall ferns, the terrace would begin to work the way she'd always wanted it to.

Mary took the silver tray that had come from her father's mother and set it on the terrace table, even though the air was damp and a little too chilly for eating outdoors. She wanted to use her table. And she wouldn't let the weather interfere.

She arranged the English sterling and the lace-edged napkin at the chair with the best view of the bougainvillea, then sat and poured herself a cup of tea from her father's silver teapot.

She tied the butterfly-embroidered yellow silk dressing gown more tightly around her waist and slowly sipped her Earl Grey tea, as she slid one finger down the teapot's ebony handle, wondering why Amelia hadn't called. *You'd think she would've by this time, when she knows I have to leave for work.*

There wasn't much breakfast on the tray in front of Mary— half a crystal champagne flute of freshly squeezed orange juice, a half-slice of dry whole-wheat toast carefully cut in three long strips, four slivers of Baldwin apple artfully arranged on pink-and-white porcelain—yet Mary sat and stared at the tray, telling herself it was much too much, and to leave the juice for dessert at dinner.

She slowly nibbled a slice of apple, telling herself he'd been more right than she'd known then to suggest she call Hannah at the hospital. *He knew they wouldn't let me talk to her. Not with her in an oxygen tent. But they told her I'd called, which is what we wanted.*

He's been right about calling Amelia too, to make her think I'm interested, and I think that's one of his most valuable traits. That cool, calculating business sense that makes him postpone ease and comfort today for greater benefits in the future.

It's not one of **my** *strengths, which is why I'm in trouble with the bank all the time. But I do complement him. Culturally. Being at ease in sophisticated society. He never had the background I had, visiting the Hills on the Cape.*

"Mary?" A young woman wearing a trench coat over her bathrobe appeared around a corner of the house.

"Hey, Jane. Come get a cup of tea."

"If you're sure you have enough. I wanted to see how the table looks."

"Make yourself at home while I get another cup."

When Mary came back, Jane Peters touched the top of the silver teapot. "This is absolutely gorgeous. Where'd you evuh find it?"

"It's a family piece. Daddy let me use it on my birthday to pour tea for my dolls." Mary shook her bangs away from her face and folded her linen napkin. "There is *that* advantage of Mother not caring how things look. I could take Daddy's family pieces without her fighting over a solitary thing. Mother has no understanding of family pride."

"No?"

"And no conception at all of the appearance she presents. May I offer you something to eat?"

"Thank you, but I've already eaten." Jane Peters played with the belt of her trench coat and glanced shyly at Mary.

"I s'ppose there's no way she *would* know better. The daughter of a pig and lettuce farmer who failed at both. Who had to beg for a job in a post office the size of a postage stamp. In a town without a future or a past."

"Why d'you reckon your daddy married her?"

"He was reeling from the Crash of '29. He was back in St. Mary's, feeling completely cut off after he left New York, and I don't s'ppose there were many choices."

"And if he *had* found an heiress on Jekyll, her family would've expected—" Jane Peters looked appalled by what she'd almost said.

And Mary Hill looked irritated for half a second. "Course, if he hadn't married Mother I wouldn't be here, so far be it from me to say he shouldn't have. She was beautiful when she was young. And that would've been important to Daddy."

"From what you've said, she must've been hard working."

"She was. She ordered his life for him. And she did have a house. I suppose that was important during the Depression. Even *her* father's ugly Victorian. But she never had taste. Not in any sense in which Daddy and I would mean that. And once she came down with multiple sclerosis all her worst traits were amplified."

"It must be awful, bein' paralyzed and all."

"I'm sure it is. Suffering is all I can think the minute I hear her name. Dying and death. And what she did to Daddy. When *I* want a normal life. That's not too much to ask, is it? Someone in my position?"

"No, suguh, it's not. Unless——"

"She has people taking care of her. Telling her how admirable she's been. Mother's always enjoyed that, the attention you get for not complaining."

"I know just what you mean. My grandmothuh's just like that. Heavens! I've got to get ready for work. You want to have dinnuh some night this week?"

"I might. Give me a call later."

Mary listened to Jane's footsteps climbing the back outside stairs—seeing Hannah in a wheelchair, the way she had seen her six years before, struggling to pull her feet onto the footrest with weak unsteady hands.

I'm young. I'm healthy. I'm finally beginning to live life on my own terms. I've got work I like and am suited for. I've got a fiancé who loves me, who's brilliant, and ambitious, who won't sit and wait for life to drag him along. Someone who makes his own luck, and creates the life he wants.

I don't want to spend my time tied to someone with no time left. Whose life revolves around catheters and urinary infections and trying not to choke on phlegm.

She doesn't have any room to talk either. She threw Daddy out. She made him die all alone. She never did try to understand, back when he had his affair. And why wouldn't he? With her that sick. Anyone would understand.

I couldn't have taken him in myself. Not in a studio apartment. And I couldn't move to Atlanta either, not and keep the job I have.

It's quarter after eight. You'd think Amelia would've phoned.

Except you know she would've called Johanna first. Johanna always has come first with anyone who listens to Hannah.

Johanna never had to diet. Johanna never had thin hair, or short legs, or stubby fat fingers. Johanna never made a fool of herself trying to learn to play tennis. And she never had to worry that no one would fall in love with her. Everyone fell for Johanna. Even Garrett. Who turned his back on me and everybody else he ever saw after he took one look at her.

She's had more than she deserves from everyone since the day she came to St. Mary's. And I had my fill of that a good long time ago.

The phone rang as Mary set the silver tea service on the counter in the kitchen. And it was Amelia. Calling to tell her Hannah had died in the night.

Amelia Walker stared out the back window of her office at Whitfield toward a long triangular streak of sun slicing down on an angle, lighting a wood swing in a tall oak.

Amelia didn't see the trees, or the swing, or the light glittering across the river-marsh. She sat shut up inside herself, clicking a ballpoint pen, without hearing the clatter and clink in the kitchen, or the gossip by the pickup truck parked by the back door.

But the worst was over.

And she said it out loud for the second time.

She'd stopped crying. And having to try not to. Her throat wasn't clenched around itself. She could sit behind the scheduling desk, blowing her nose and wiping her eyes, and almost breathe with her mouth closed again. And now, if someone did walk in, she could force herself to talk.

Telling Johanna couldn't've been any harduh, with Garrett's death and all. Course, if Hannah had died tomorruh night, 'stead of last night the way she did, Johanna would've been here talkin' to Hannah, and sayin' good-bye, and knowin' she'd done what she could.

Can't think what else I could've said. 'Cept Hannah was ready to go. That we know. And I did say it, I think.

Same way I said, like the fool I am, that Hannah would've wanted more than anything else to see Johanna one last time.

Why didn't I think before I opened my mouth? Makes me want to cut my tongue out.

Johanna couldn't have known Hannah would die. We all thought she was doing fine. Dr. Tom himself, he told Johanna not to come home. Hannah too. Said to wait till this week when her opera was done.

But that won't make much difference to Johanna.

Papa used to say, "Guilt grows on death like moss on a wet stump." And I reckon he had it about right.

I oughtta tell her 'bout Taylor. Waitin' for him in the hurricane. Listenin' for his truck, and his key, and the sound of his voice in the hall. When I couldn't hear a thing in that storm, but wind and blowin' rain.

I knew right then that he wouldn't've taken the boat out on a chartuh if it hadn't been for me. Wantin' to buy our first sofa and get to paintin' the house.

Taylor Walker was the finest husband I could evuh have had. And he's been gone all these years because of me.

Amelia Walker twisted a strand of hair around her finger the same way she had since she was three. She swallowed the last of her coffee, then turned a metal dial on the Simplex box and pushed the microphone button.

"Where's Amelia? The manager, is she here? Oh, there you are." She was from New York, the plump dark-haired woman in the doorway, short and narrow shouldered and very broad in the hips, wearing a leopard-spotted skin-tight blouse that showed every crease and roll, over equally skimpy toreador pants, and sandals with jewels on the heels. "The water's ice cold, and whatta you do? Nothin'! I'm not puttin' up with it, not with what you're charging!"

"I'm sorry, Mrs.—"

"Horse droppings everywhere! Deer jumpin' out of bushes. But no hot water, no TV, no telephones, nothin' to do—"

"I'm sorry, Mrs. Lorenzen. I know it's an inconvenience, but one of the watuh heatuhs broke and the brand new spare turned out to be defective. We've sent the boat ovuh to bring back two new bigguh ones, and we'll have hot watuh by this afternoon. You could use the bathhouse till then. That has a separate heatuh, and it's workin' fine."

"Traipsing across the backyard to use a bathroom is *not* my idea of a good time! My husband'll be down to see you later. If you think we're payin' for this, you got another think comin'!"

She flapped through the door to the back hall.

And Amelia took a deep breath, and touched two fingers to her forehead, before she pushed the button on the ship-to-shore. "Cumberland 8 callin' Brunswick. Ovuh...Cumberland 8 callin' Brunswick."

"Cumberland 8, this is Brunswick. I wantta tell you one more time how sorry I am 'bout Miz Hannah. Everyone I've talked to this mornin' is just as sick as I am. Ovuh."

"Thank you, Miz Land, that's very kind. You still can't get through to Leah? Ovuh."

"No, Ma'am, I cain't. There's a big storm up by Beaufort, and the lines're all out. Blew real hard last night. May be ovuh now, but it won't be till nighttime they get the lines fixed. I called Walt MacCaffrey down to the telephone company, and told him about Miz Hannah, and he said they cain't get done any soonuh. Ovuh."

"Then I need to try to reach Ben Reese in Charleston. He's stayin' at the residence of Mr. Robert Sykes. It's just north of Broad. Could be King Street, or Meeting, or it might could be Archdale, but it's right close around there somewhere. Could I impose on you to get the numbuh from the long distance operatuh, and place the call and patch me in? I'd be grateful to you. Ovuh."

"I'd be happy to, you know I would. Is that your sistuh's boy? I reckon I placed a call for him last week. Ovuh."

"Yes, Miz Land, it is. Did you reach Dr. Patterson. Ovuh?"

"Got him at the hospital an hour or so ago. He'll be ovuh on the noon boat. I told him you said you'd have Adam run him and Miz Hannah right back to St. Mary's. Will the burial be on the island? A lotta folks are askin'. Ovuh."

"It will, but there'll be a public memorial service at the Presbyterian Church in St. Mary's. Thank you for bein' so helpful. Ovuh."

"Will Hannah's daughtuh, Mary, be comin' to the funeral? I know there's been real hard feelings there, and I know you phoned her this mornin', and I—"

"I don't know, Miz Land. Thank you again. Ovuh and out."

CHAPTER SEVEN

BEN WAS WALKING NORTH ON KING STREET, a block or so up from Broad, looking at the short sides of long narrow houses, brick and stone and stucco, built high and turned to catch the sea breeze, with long verandas on upper floors made to keep the sun out. He looked through iron gates toward deep slender gardens soft with ivy—at boxwood and azalea and waxy-leafed magnolia, at statuary and sundials and splashing fountains, at high stone walls smothered in bougainvillea, at small garden tables and curlicued chairs—at cool private worlds made to smooth and shade a sweltering summer city.

A lot of houses needed to be worked on, but it was better than the last time he'd been there. More history being saved. Less waste. Less ruin. A timelessness, still, in human proportions most American cities had lost to the wrecking ball and concrete blocks and flashing signs made of neon.

There were new shops now in eighteenth-century ones, and in a handful of old houses too. And as he walked past an art gallery, he thought, *It ought to be around here somewhere. East side of the street, probably, though… This could be it. With the kitchen stuff in the window.*

It was a wide white Palladian window in a narrow brick end wall where baskets and silver and antique copper pots had been arranged by someone who saw things most people don't.

Ben walked on toward an open wrought-iron gate, where he read, "Board and Beeton Antiques" on a small polished brass plate—and turned into the courtyard garden that stretched down the long side of the house.

It was paved with brick and edged with lush green plants. And he studied a fern he'd never seen before as he opened the right half of a wide white door and stepped onto heart pine floors that must've been two hundred years old.

The whole first floor was one open room, separated into smaller spaces by tall furniture and freestanding screens and a whitewashed brick double fireplace that narrowed to meet a tall chimney exposed to the second floor.

Between Ben and the fireplace stood an old simple tavern table, and on it lay an open book, propped on a carved mahogany stand. It was *Mrs. Beeton's Book of Household Management,* Victorian England's housewife's Bible. And Ben stooped and read the "Proper Procedure for Making Tea"— until a deep voice, from the deep South, called from the front room on his right, from behind a louvered screen.

"If I can be of any service whatevuh, please don't hesitate to ask."

Ben said, "I think maybe you can," and walked toward the disembodied voice, passing humble butter crocks and blue-and-white checks arranged around Chinese porcelain plates, and a Georgian mahogany Irish sideboard, with lion faces carved on the apron, that was covered with antique baskets of every time and place. "You've got a lot of really great things."

"Thank you, sir, you're veruh kind." He was a tall man, sitting stooped in a slipper chair, crumpling his white linen suit, a lorgnette hanging from a ribbon around his neck, his dark hair smoothed from his forehead, his hands folded across his well-rounded vest. "Has it turned cool? I haven't been out yet this mornin'."

"No, it's great. Sunny and somewhere around seventy."

The phone rang. And while the large man in white talked, Ben walked to the fireplace and looked at the antique cooking utensils in and around the hearth—the copper molds, the braziers, the kettles on the oven cranes, the honey-colored maple bread shovel, the Elizabethan wooden mousetrap on the floor under the baking oven.

"It's chastenin', isn't it, the way our ancestors combined beauty with utility? The wrought-iron bastin' spoon with the horsehead handle is one my favorite pieces. I can almost see the blacksmith makin' it, and the women enjoyin' it as they cooked."

"Now we use paper napkins and plastic forks and throw everything away. I guess some families don't even talk at dinner. They watch TV and eat on folding trays."

"American culture is dyin', sir, witherin' as we speak. Imagine such a repast as you describe. No discussion or laugh-tuh or care taken togethuh. No thought given to smoothin' away the strain of life. 'Dine we must,' as the immortal Isabella Beeton wrote, 'and we may as well dine elegantly as whole-somely.'"

"Or as Oscar Wilde put it, 'After a good dinner one can forgive anybody, even one's relations.'"

"*That* is a witticism I shall remembuh. My name is George Milton, sir."

"Mine is Ben Reese."

"Why is it we avail ourselves so rarely of the leisurely pursuits which once ennobled life?"

"I don't know. I guess it depends on what—"

"The writin' of crafted letters. The pleasant rituals of talk and table. We live on the way to somewhere else." He'd stood up by then and was wiping his forehead with a fine embroidered handkerchief, gazing across his desk at Ben. "We open our boxes, our mixes, our freezer bags. We savor little, and eat much, often of the artificial. Hence, the creation of Board and Beeton. If you've nevuh tasted homemade bread, how would you divine the difference? If you've nevuh drunk from a finely wrought cup, why would you think to look for one? One must teach. One must show. One must share the possibilities. Still, *De gustibus non disputandum.*'"

"True. There's no accounting for taste. *I* can't cook at all, but I appreciate it when someone else does. Your wrought-iron gate's a work of art, by the way."

"Thank you, sir. We commissioned it from Philip Simmons. He's a mastuh blacksmith, and very well respected in Charleston."

"I can see why he would be. But the reason I'm here is I need to find Leah MacKinnon."

"She's at her home in Beaufort."

"My aunt is Amelia Walker. She manages Whitfield Inn on Cumberland, and—"

"Then you know Miz Hannah Hill?"

"I do, yes. Actually—"

"My wife and I have stayed on Cumberland several times, and we enjoy her veruh much."

"I do too. Watching her cope is an education. Anyway, I need to talk to Leah right away, but the phones are out in Beaufort."

"There was a storm down there last night. That's the difficulty here in the low country, we're sittin' a foot or two above sea level, and we get waterlogged at the least provocation. Leah had a dental appointment in Beaufort at seven-thirty this mornin', and she was plannin' to work at her store there durin' the day, then come up here tonight."

"I'm on my way back to Cumberland. I s'ppose I could stop in Beaufort on the way."

"It's a lovely town, right on the water, that was used as a northern naval port durin' the War between the States. It wasn't bombarded, as a result, unlike Charleston and Savannah. And it's largely in its antebellum state. It has wonderful architecture, sadly in need of repair, like most of the South. Though Leah's helpin' with that. Fixin' up her house and openin' a shop, and encouragin' others to preserve the town."

"Would you mind giving me her address in Beaufort?"

"It would be a pleasure, sir." George Milton pressed his lorgnette on his large nose as he pulled a cracked leatherbound book from a deep desk drawer. "I shall draw you a map as well."

"Thank you. I appreciate it. How long will it take me to get to Beaufort?"

"An hour perhaps. Possibly a good deal more. Depends on trucks and traffic."

"So you and Leah are in business together?"

"No, sir. No, Leah owns the building. Inherited it from her fathuh. My wife and I have an apartment on the third floor, and we share the cost of the shop with Leah. She specializes in French furniture and culinary objects, I in English and Irish, as well as Southern and Colonial American. Our businesses are separate. It's as though our pieces were on consignment."

"You've arranged them really well."

"My wife is the artist. I'm a reformed professuh, sir. A student of history. A lovuh of household objects. One who learned many years ago to recognize his own deficiencies. Veronique designs and arranges the store. I do the heavy lifting."

"Spoken like a wise man. Anyway, thanks for the help." Ben turned toward the door. And then turned back again. "Maybe I ought to give you a message for Leah, in case she comes in unexpectedly. Or I miss her somehow down in Beaufort. It's bad news, I'm sorry to say. Her Aunt Hannah died of pneumonia last night. Which was a real surprise for everybody."

"Gracious! I'm sorry to hear that. I truly am. Hannah Hill was a remarkable woman."

"She was. I wish there'd been time to know her better."

"A benevolent spiduh, I've always thought. Watchin' the world from the centuh of her web."

"I'm not sure I know what you mean by that."

"A kindly spiduh, sir. Feelin' the tiniest emotional vibrations, as they travel along silken threads. Threads tied to a collection of delicate and damaged souls."

"Oh? I guess I thought—"

"She involved herself in othuh folks' lives, Mr. Reese, with veruh high-minded intentions. Giving a gentle nudge. A judicious warnin'. Decidin' what strings to pull, to extend the metaphor, to help. Or reform. Or inspire. Unlike true female arachnids who follow the tremblings across their web in orduh to eat their victims."

"That's an interesting perspective. Although—"

"Hannah was an observunt woman. A *veruh* observunt woman, sir. And she didn't shy away from responsibility."

"No, I'm sure that's true."

r r r

Ben found the Carter House without too much trouble, once he'd driven through the new part of Beaufort, past the carry-outs and the grocers and the motels that catered to the Marine Air Station on the northwest edge of town.

He slowed in streets with standing water and waited for other cars to pass. Till he found a place to park by the Carter House, a block away from the bay, in the old historic district at the corner of Craven and Newcastle.

It was a three-story white clapboard house with long white pillared porches, its rows of black shuttered floor-to-ceiling windows shining with new paint and polished glass.

Ben climbed the wide curving stone steps to the first floor veranda, and found the double doors to the shop standing open. He waited for a minute, gazing at what he could see of the waterfront, and the small white inn across Newcastle.

Then he stepped into a wide center hall, where black-and-white photographs in gold-leaf frames hung on yellow walls above a French half-round table that probably cost more than he made in a year. He called, "Is anyone here?" in a loud low voice.

But no one answered. So he looked into the living room off the right of the hall, and the dining room on the left (both filled with fine antiques, displayed and tagged for sale), before walking down the hall between the upper and lower staircases, into the kitchen in back. He called again, and looked out across the lawn toward a small white clapboard cottage.

Then he turned back the way he came, and saw a young woman climbing the right-hand stairway from the floor below, looking directly at him, asking if she could help.

She was solid and stocky and maybe five-foot-four with

short legs and broad bones and a flat looking slightly fleshy face. She was elegantly dressed in a well-cut suit and country-club gold and pearl jewelry.

"I'm Ben Reese, and I'm trying to find Leah MacKinnon."

"I'm Leah MacKinnon. Is there something particular you're looking for?"

"No. Not exactly. Amelia Walker is my aunt, and I got a call from her this morning. She's been trying to reach you—"

"But the phones have been out since last night."

"Yes. And since I was driving down from Charleston, she asked me to see if I could find you. It's not good news, I'm sorry to say. Your Aunt Hannah died last night. Everyone thought she was getting better, but she couldn't fight off the pneumonia."

Leah Hill MacKinnon didn't say anything. Her small brown eyes pulled away from him, and her eyebrows pinched together in a look as much puzzled as grieved. She'd been carrying a sheaf of papers in one hand, and she held on to them as though she'd forgotten them, while she eased herself slowly onto a Chippendale chair backed against the upstairs stairs. "I don't understand. Dr. Patterson said she was doing well."

"I don't know what happened. He was surprised too, I guess."

"I thought Hannah would live a long time."

"Did you?"

"No, I didn't express that very well. We all knew the MS would be terminal eventually, but I didn't think it would be soon. Hannah was so strong. As a person. Almost everyone who knew her leaned on her in some way."

"The MS had damaged her lungs, apparently."

"I knew that, but…"

Ben couldn't think of anything else to say, except, "I wish I'd known her better."

"This will be terribly hard on Johanna. First her fiancé, and now Hannah."

"Doesn't sound easy, does it?"

"It won't be. Hannah raised her after her parents were killed, and helped keep her stable all these years. Johanna's...how should I put it? Johanna's a fragile person. I don't like to think what this might do."

Ben didn't say anything else. He put his hands in his pants pockets and stared at the banister above Leah's head.

"She raised me too. Hannah did. As much as I *was* raised. And I'll always be grateful for what she did for me." She shook her head and sighed and laid her papers on the floor. Leah's eyes had filled with tears, but she didn't act as though she'd noticed. She swallowed and looked down at her hands lying still in her lap. "At least Hannah's not suffering anymore. That's a good thing."

"Yes."

"I don't know why I'm talking so much. You'll have to forgive me. I don't normally, to strangers."

"I don't think you're saying too much."

"I'll call Amelia as soon as the phones are fixed. I'll make arrangements here, and in Charleston, and I'll come down to Cumberland as quickly as I can. By Wednesday anyhow. Possibly even tomorrow."

THURSDAY, NOVEMBER, 23RD

Ben was sitting in the dark in a chair at a kitchen table in a house in France, his hatchet lying on the tabletop, his arms crossed across it, his right cheek lying on cold steel.

He hadn't been asleep long, half an hour, maybe, in a safe town, invited in by a French family, as he'd worked his way back from behind the German lines. Somebody else was with him. Ben wasn't sure who. A new scout he'd gone out with who'd handled himself well.

They'd intended to stay till morning, and Ben was just beginning to wake up, his eyes gazing mistily around the room, his head still lying on the table, seeing the first streak of gray out the east window. Asking himself if there'd been some sound, something soft and indistinct that had called to him and prickled the skin on his neck.

He heard a woman's voice a few seconds later, as the gray began turning salmon, whispering in another room.

Ben told himself to wake up before it happened again.

But then he heard something he didn't expect. The hiss of something being sprayed. Something pungent. Acrid. Sickening.

Then he was clawing his face, choking, gagging, trying to dig the acid out of his own skin.

He was lying on a snowdrift a second later, in the evergreen woods near Trier, looking down on his own dead body, the same way he had in real life in January of '45. When he'd been sent back inside himself to dream about it till the day he died.

Then he was screaming, strapped in a stretcher under a Piper Cub, flying through treetops under the ack-ack fire, so cold it made him cry. Exactly the way it had happened when they flew him to the railhead in France.

Ben threw the covers off and sat up shivering, sucking in air like a diver who's been down too long—or a long-distance runner gagging a breath at the finish.

He sat for a second, staring at the dark places in the room. At the shadows. And the corners.

And then he stood up beside the bed, his skin a white slick of sweat. Quicksilver shining in the moonlight.

There was no one there. Watching.

No one coming after him.

Nothing he had to fight, right then.

No one to talk to. Or listen to. Or watch.

No one to touch. Or hold in the dark.

With Jessie dead and gone.

He was on Cumberland.

He was in his room in Amelia's cottage.

And Hannah was being buried in the morning.

He told himself to breathe. Slowly. Deeply. To let his shoulders drop. And relax his stomach while he made himself exhale. Then find the towel on the chair.

There was a quiet knock on his bedroom door, and a soft southern voice asked if he was all right.

"I'm fine, Amelia. Go back to bed. Sorry I woke you up."

"You sure, sweetie?"

"I'm sure."

Ben waited till she walked away. Then wiped his chest and his back and his thighs—the jagged gash around his left ribs, the lopsided round indentions spattered on his legs and upper body, the longest and deepest incision running through the muscles of his left arm up around his shoulder and across his back (all of it healed now and faded)—before he pulled on a pair of sweatpants and dug out a rumpled sweatshirt. He stuck his feet into tennis shoes. And opened a drawer in the desk.

Weird, seeing my hatchet. The blade Dad made. His curved pick on the other side. Why are the dreams like that? Fact and fiction mixed?

He took out a plastic bag and pulled out his pack of Camels, then stuck his arms in his hunting coat and stepped out on the back porch.

He leaned against the post above the two stairs to the lawn and lit a cigarette with a kitchen match.

He told himself not to think, while he inhaled the first time. And then he inhaled again, and braced against the quick burst of dizziness that hits your brain when you don't smoke often. He waited for it to pass. Telling himself not to poke into any of it. Or look for the face of the French girl.

He still couldn't touch it and stay calm.

Rage. Weighted down by years. He could feel it taking over, rushing at his heart, pounding at his chest, even when he told himself to push it back and forget.

Yeah, our friends the French. America's loyal allies. Grateful cheering recipients of American liberation.

He told himself not to do it. To let go of it then. To not waste any more time. *Because you know there were French you could trust. That was one family.*

Except it wasn't just that family. There were others. Plenty of them. Making money off the Germans. Informing on the Jews. Taking their businesses. Turning us in. Setting us up with the Nazis.

There were lots of them who didn't, though. You know there were. Plenty who were trustworthy. And it makes no sense to drag it out now and wallow in it.

He couldn't stop himself. Not after the dream had dredged it up. He was hearing her on the phone, whispering to her

German boyfriend, calling in firepower to flush out the town while Ben and his buddies slept.

He heard the shells coming in again. The earsplitting scream coming closer and closer. And he felt the earth shake—in front, and beside, and behind him and the others—obliterating the backyard, as he looked back on it at a dead run, Hal limping beside him, Bernie and Sax blown to pieces. To pulp. To tiny wet red shreds of bone and gristle. Mostly a mist. A shower. A vapor. Blown in front of his eyes.

This is doing you a lot of good. Letting it get to you and make you nuts.

Do something constructive. Make a move that makes sense.

Figure out what to tell people who ask why you haven't gone back to France since the Second World War.

Ben laughed a quick cryptic laugh and French-inhaled his Camel.

A mist.

A vapor.

A spray.

Which brings me to the sound of spraying.

The spray bottle in the dream. Full of acid.

For who knows what reason.

Nothing like that ever happened to me, but it makes me think of Hannah. Hearing something being sprayed. Seeing someone in coveralls and a gas mask, carrying a spray bottle in her room.

If you can spray perfume, and you can spray bug killer, and you can spray all kinds of other things like disinfectants, why couldn't you spray a solution of pneumonia bacteria?

You'd have to know what you were doing. But that wouldn't be hard to find out. I presume.

And yet why would anyone, in their wildest dreams, want to kill Hannah Hill?

Dreams.

Dreams are strange things.

Smoke one more cigarette. And go back to bed.

CHAPTER EIGHT

THURSDAY, NOVEMBER 23RD

THE FAMILY THOUGHT IT WOULD BE a small service on Cumberland, after the memorial service in St. Mary's. But boats kept anchoring by the Whitfield dock, from Fernandina Beach and St. Mary's, tying up to it when there was still room, anchoring in the channel and pulling dinghies up on shore when there wasn't, using the old Kirkconnell dock too, and walking up from there.

Everyone who came had to walk, a mile south from Whitfield or a mile north from Kirkconnell, along the main road the crews had scraped smooth that morning. The cemetery track was on the west side, like Whitfield—a switchback trail, a hundred yards long, that hid the Hill graveyard from the road.

When Ben got there with Amelia, a crowd had already gathered outside the iron fence—some white, some black, standing in separate groups, some crying, some dry-eyed, most of them looking shaken.

The wrought-iron gates stood open between stone pillars, and inside those gates family and close friends were moving into the open ground around the center grave—the joined graves of Charlotte Hill MacKinnon's parents, flanked by the tombstones of three infant children.

Family and friends stood quietly, shifting from one foot to the other, nodding silently to friends and acquaintances, facing the sandy hole in the back right corner where Reverend Douglas Michaels stood holding a Bible in his hands.

Ben and Amelia moved over behind Charlotte's grave, in the front right corner of the cemetery, and watched Leah and Johanna walk past to the chairs by Hannah's casket.

Leah MacKinnon looked prepared for the worst as she sat in a green folding chair, stiff and controlled, solid and stoical, her mouth tight and her eyes fixed on the ground, her black-gloved hands clasped in the lap of her black Chanel suit.

Johanna Elliott looked like a waif beside her. Young, thin, nervous, fragile, tears at the surface, shoulders limp but tense too, fingers fiddling with each other, pushing the ponytail of thick dark hair off her shoulder, tightening the tortoiseshell clip, smoothing the skirt of a fitted navy suit that was carefully pressed but worn.

She gazed over at the minister and tried to smile at him, after he'd smiled and nodded at her. Then she glanced away to her right toward the crowd behind the fence. Her eyes widened, suddenly, and she stood up and stepped to the side fence in front of Ben, where she reached over the wrought-iron pickets for the hand of an old bent black man who'd been wiping his eyes with a handkerchief.

"I'm so sorry, Miss Johanna. You know I am. But Miz Hannah's sufferin's past now, and she's with the Lord."

"I know. I'm just going to miss her every day of my life. It's so good to see you, Randall. Thank you for coming."

"Wild horses couldn't've kept me away, you know that. And if you need me, you call on me any time of the day or night, y'hear?"

Johanna nodded, as tears started down her face, and she pulled a handkerchief out of her jacket pocket and turned back toward her chair.

She nodded to a young woman in a chair at the end of the row behind hers—a well-dressed young woman who'd been watching Johanna with a closed, still, mildly contemptuous look on her face. Johanna motioned her to the chair she'd been sitting in herself. But the young woman shook her head, crossed her arms across her black silk dress, and looked away toward a statue by the back fence of a tall aristocratic angel with his hand on the head of a small robed child.

Ben leaned over to Amelia and asked her who the woman was, and had just heard Amelia whisper, "Mary Hill," as the minister said, "Good morning."

Ben watched Johanna through a lot of the service—Johanna and Leah and Mary—while he listened to the minister standing just past them. Douglas Michaels (who was gray haired and tall, but stooped and twisted by a painful-looking spinal condition) smiled as he remembered Hannah as a small cantankerous child. He'd known her too as a hotel manager, as well as a wife and a mother, and finally as an MS sufferer who'd turned toward those around her.

"Now Miz Hannah didn't always mince words." There were twitters among the crowd and more than one nodding head. "But you nevuh had to wonduh what she said behind your back. Whatevuh she thought, she said to your face. She was wise. She was kind. And she grew to understand a good deal over the years about how we all carry on.

"She took life as a gift from God. She took it as it came without whinin' about it. She b'lieved it to be an intended business, and she did her best to make the best of it." Michaels turned his whole body as he talked, moving his feet to face both sides of his audience, as though he couldn't swivel his neck or twist at the waist or the shoulders. "She found joy in it, *and* pleasure. And she was a fine example for me in her latuh years, takin' up her cross the way she did. With humor. With grace. With patience she'd nevuh had before she took sick.

"When I'd say somethin' about that, 'bout her handlin' the MS well, she'd quote me somethin' from George MacDonald. 'To trust God when no need is pressing, when things seem going right of themselves, may be harduh than when things seem to be goin' wrong.'

"I would like to read you anothuh excerpt from his writings that Hannah took to heart. This was the passage she had hung beside her bed after she became bedridden four years ago. 'By actively willing the will of God, a man takes the share offered him in his own making, his own becoming. In willing actively and operatively to become what he was made to be, he becomes creative—so far as a man may. In this way also he becomes like his Father in heaven.'

"Hannah Williams Hill was the child of our Lord and Savior and she let those words into her heart, those and othuhs like them. Those of us who knew her, and were helped by her, could see the ways she was strengthened by them.

"Now we've come togethuh, in our own grief, but in thankfulness that she's been released from the sufferin' that must've been a burden.

"The Lord giveth. The Lord taketh away. Blessed be the name of the Lord.

"Let us pray…"

Ben listened and said, "Amen," when the time came.

And then watched Johanna try not to cry, asking himself why it was different this time. Than Richard West's funeral, or Jonathan MacLean's, or others he'd been to since Jessie died.

It hasn't been as hard for some reason. And I find it oddly disconcerting.

Is it because Hannah was in misery and must've wanted to get out of it? Or because there wasn't a husband or wife left behind the way you were?

Maybe it's just time. Wearing away at memory. Dulling what ought to be felt.

Though I hope it's not that. Not this soon.

Not when Jessie deserves better.

Ben watched the friends and relatives trying to express the inexpressible. Waiting in line to talk to Johanna before walking back to their boats. Waiting for Leah too. And Mary, a few of them. Though most didn't make the attempt. And Mary turned on her heel, her short dark hair swinging across her face, and stalked out through the gate.

It was then that a heavyset elderly Negro woman hobbled up to Johanna like her feet and legs were killing her, sobbing the same way she had been ever since Michaels spoke. Johanna looked half-panicked. As though she didn't know her well, and had no idea what to say.

Amelia was standing next to Johanna, and Ben could hear her talking to both of them about all the years Rhoda had cooked at Whitfield, for the Hill family first and then the inn, as she patted Rhoda's shoulder and gave her another Kleenex. Amelia said something to Randall when he came up to them too. And Randall put his arm around Rhoda and led her away toward the gate.

Ben was waiting for Amelia.

Who was waiting for Johanna.

So he looked around the graveyard at the standing stones, carefully situated in family groups—the obelisks and gothic arches growing out of sandy ground like pieces arranged on a chessboard.

Speaking of chess pieces, Michaels looks like a wounded bishop. Consoling the ones who need it. While Dr. Thomas Patterson reminds me of a medieval knight. Tall. Stiff. Sure of himself. A little too combative. Which leads me to the well-dressed Leah, holding herself together. Looking dignified and subtly imperious. A queen used to deference, with enough good taste to hide it while she talks to the Whitfield cook. Estelle? Is that right? Smiling nervously like a displaced pawn who wishes she could get away.

Why are you doing this? Speculating on who people are based on how they look? Whatever this is, it isn't a game, and I shouldn't be playing with people like that.

I do need to talk to the doctor. Hopefully before he leaves.

"So what can I do for you, Mr. Reese?" Dr. Tom Patterson leaned back in one of the velvet chairs in the library at Whitfield, pressed his fingers together under his double chin, and looked at Ben with a half-condescending expression.

"I want to ask you something that's going to sound peculiar, especially without a context. But would it be possible to make a solution of pneumonia bacteria, and put it in a spray bottle, and spray it in a closed room so that someone who had to stay in that room would become infected?"

"What?" Tom Patterson didn't say it as though he expected Ben to answer. He shook his head and raised his eyebrows, then snorted as though he prided himself on humoring next to no one.

"What if the person with the spray bottle wore a gas mask? What if he shut all the doors and windows in a small room, sprayed the pneumonia solution, and aired the place out later so nobody else got sick, except for the person who lives in that room and can't get away? What are the chances of someone who never left that room coming down with pneumonia?"

"You're not talkin' 'bout Miz Hannah?"

Ben told Patterson about the last conversation he'd had with Hannah. About her hearing the sound of spraying and seeing someone in a gas mask carrying what looked like a spray bottle. "She'd been trying to get back to sleep, and she assumed it was a dream, but—"

"You prefuh to jump to thoroughly irrational conclusions." Patterson crossed his arms across his rumpled tan suit and cocked his head away from Ben.

"Did you do an autopsy?" Ben leaned back in his chair, and told himself not to say anything he'd live to regret later.

"Why would I do an autopsy? She died of asphyxia caused by pneumonia."

"Florence Rich thought she was much better. She couldn't understand why she died when she did."

Patterson smiled like a middle-aged college boy listening to advice from his mother. "So you'd bet a cup of coffee on what a nurse thinks, would you?"

"She told me *you* said Hannah was much better too, and that you said it in front of Amelia."

"I *also* told 'em the congestion was still a very serious concern as well. Have you been worryin' othuh folks here with this nonsense?"

127

"I haven't said anything about what Hannah saw to anyone but you, if that's what you mean. What do they call it when the pneumonia becomes systemic, when it's growing right in the blood and there's almost nothing you can do?"

"Septicemia. Being septicemic."

"Had she become septicemic?"

"No. We did blood work that mornin'."

"So, aside from whether it's unlikely, could someone make a solution of pneumonia bacteria—"

"*Streptococcus pneumoniae.*"

"Could you spray it in a closed room, if you're wearing a gas mask, a military gas mask maybe, and infect someone stuck in that room, but not infect anyone else if you aired the room out afterwards? Also, would someone with MS be more susceptible to the pneumonia bug than the rest of us?"

"An MS patient would be more susceptible. They come down with it as a mattuh of course. As to your othuh…supposition, I s'ppose such a thing would be theoretically possible. An isotonic salt solution could be made. I'm a veruh openminded thinkuh, sir. I enjoy a reputation for it, in and around St. Mary's. But I see no reason whatevuh to assume that's what happened. Hannah succumbed to pneumonia for the third time this year and died of asphyxia. She couldn't get up her own sputum. Not from her lungs or her throat. Now, if there's nothin' else I can do for you, I want to catch the launch to St. Mary's."

"That's all I wanted. Thanks for being so patient."

Neither of them said another word, but Patterson looked at Ben to see if there was a barb buried in that last remark, as they both got up and walked out.

Ben followed Patterson to the front porch and watched him

walk down the wide wooden steps, and off to the right toward the dock.

Then he sat on the top step, thinking about what to do next.

It was a beautiful night, still and warm, and there were conversations going on behind him, the whole length of the veranda—guests who couldn't be turned away because of a family death.

A well-dressed sixtyish woman in a high-backed rocker at the south end, said, "Oh, my deah, I knew her *verruh* well! Her muthuh was a verruh deah friend of my muthuh's younguh sistuh. Now, if y'all are from Macon, then you must know Miz Winthrop. Miz Edgar Winthrop? She used to be verruh active in the women's club theruh, though I do believe she hasn't been well this wintuh. Now, my husband…Could I offer you a cigarette? No, you go right ahead and help yourself, honey, I brought two whole cartons in my suitcase. Now…"

A gentleman on the north end, swinging on the big swing, lighting a good-size cigar, said, "I do b'lieve, sir, you'll become enamored of Cumberland soon as you've seen it in the light of day. I've been comin' here for close to ten years, and soon as I get here, I forget business, I forget my aches and pains. I stroll that beach for hours on end watchin' the birds and the shore.

"You nevuh would believe the animals you see if you sit yourself down on a log and listen to the forest. And if you ask someone here in the inn to take you out in the truck, you'll see how very different the land is on the north end. And with the history at the south end, with the Greene cemetery and all, there's nevuh a dull moment. Where did you say you were from, sir…?"

Another man's voice from right behind Ben, higher and less

melodic, said, "I still have me an orange grove or two in central Florida, but I declare, sir, with the cold snaps this year, and the cost of fightin' disease, I reckon it makes bettuh sense to turn your land to development. All these folks retirin'…"

"Now, when Miz Winthrop was quite a young woman, I remembuh hearin' that one Sunday, at the old Methodist church, the sermon had referred to the Medes and the Persians, and when everyone was greetin' the ministuh at the door, Miz Winthrop heard anothuh woman, whose name shall remain unmentioned between us, say to that preachuh, with a sweet sweet smile on her kind ole face, 'I can't tell you how much I enjoyed your sermon. I don't recollect if you know, Reverend, but my muthuh was a Meade. One of the Meades from Richmond.' I declare, when my aunt told me what Miz Winthrop told her, I thought if someone doesn't tie me down…"

"Sittin' on a sand dune in the dark of the night, watchin' the turtles diggin' out their nests and laying their eggs, you can feel yourself turn loose of every trouble and worry you evuh had, even 'bout your own children. And that, sir, is sayin' somethin'.

"You pay hard-earned money to send 'em to college and what do they learn? Not Greek. Nor Latin. Not like we did. They won't have read Aristotle's *Politics*, even in translation. Or Caesar's *Commentaries on Warfare*. Or Pliny's depiction of Hannibal crossin' the Alps. And I don't b'lieve they can begin to understand what we're livin' through today when they don't have the faintest notion what went before.

"They don't study the Foundin' Fathuhs as we did. They don't contemplate the intentions of the Constitution. It's gettin' to be just the fads of the moment. Our republican form of government is becomin' a mattuh of contempt, though the Soviet system is whitewashed in the papers. And when you considuh the Berlin situation today, with this new wall, denying the citizens of Berlin any pretense of freedom, and the cold-blooded murduh of those poor souls tryin' to escape. If you take you a long hard look at the Soviet presence in Cuba, and President Kennedy sending our boys to Southeast Asia, to this…"

"Now, my husband's people have been farmin' ovuh neah Marietta more generations than I can count, plantin' peanuts and tobaccuh mostly in recent yeahs. After his daddy died, we moved to the old house on the home farm to look aftuh his muthuh. She bore seven children and raised up three. That was veruh common at that time, though my mama, she bore twelve, and all but…"

Ben smiled to himself. Then turned toward the door and went to look for Johanna.

CHAPTER NINE

FRIDAY, NOVEMBER 24TH

BEN WAS STANDING WITH HIS HANDS on his hips looking at Hannah's room. He'd already pulled down the camera above her bed and put the exposed film in his pocket. And he'd looked at Hannah's pad of notepaper without finding anything, even indentions from earlier words, that seemed remotely useful.

He lay down on the big four-poster bed and looked out the French doors past the side porch at the trees and lawn beyond, trying to see what Hannah had seen every day of all the years she'd lain there.

He stared out the south window on his right, past the bedside table and the chest beyond, then glanced at the fireplace to the left of that window, and the floor-to-ceiling bookcase beyond that just his side of the door. He turned his head to the opposite wall and stared at the armoire beyond the French doors, then looked over the sofa that faced the four-poster, at the dresser by the front wall between the two tall windows.

The cards and letters tacked to the walls made the

strongest impression, and the number of hand-carved wooden animals from people who knew Hannah liked them.

He felt the polished smoothness of a ten-inch ebony elephant, while he read one of Hannah's birthday cards tacked on the wall above the chest.

Then he moved on to the bedside tables, and worked his way around the room, not finding much that caught his attention till he got to the files in the dresser drawers between the two front windows. Those took him by surprise—the number *and* the range of the newspaper and magazine articles Hannah had seen reason to keep.

There were files on all presidential elections in the twentieth century, as well as dog training, turkey hunting, and the raising of quail and pheasant (the last three with notes saying "copy these for Charlotte"). The two thickest files were "Good News" and "Bad News"—the first filled with articles on acts of kindness and fortuitous events, the second on tragedy and vindictiveness. The "Euthanasia" file was larger than most of the others, and Ben looked at it carefully before he wrote a note to himself in his pocket-size leatherbound notebook.

There were files on household, inn, and legal matters, as well as the usual bills paid and receipts kept. There were two files on Johanna—her legal papers and family information, and another of personal memorabilia since she'd first come to live with Hannah. There were files on Mary, identical in type to Johanna's, and one for each of Hannah's twin sons who'd been killed within weeks in Korea. There was a file on Hannah's husband, David. There was one about land being saved from development by landowners working together, and another on land conservation on estates in England and Scotland. There were clippings on cooking, landscaping, and interior decoration with notes that applied to the inn.

It was all interesting to Ben, but nothing gave him the hope of a hint that here was a motive for murder.

There were very few clothes in the walnut armoire (three nightgowns, two pantsuits, one dress, two pairs of shoes). It was mostly filled with her nature photography, stacked on shelves that had been built on the right side, next to the family albums Ben took out to look at later. Recent cards and letters were tacked inside too, and Ben glanced at all of them before he shut the doors.

He stood for a minute with his hands on his hips, staring out the front windows, wondering why she'd kept so many cards. *I s'ppose there must've been comfort in them. Some measurable sign that people still remembered her lying here. Though it might've been ego too, maybe. 'Look how many people have written to me.' Which makes me a valuable person.*

I s'ppose it could've been done for those who'd sent them, as much as anything. 'You've all gone out of your way for me, and I want you, and everyone else, to see how much I appreciate it.'

It could've been all that. Or something else entirely. But I can't leave a stone unturned. Wonder why she had tacks put in all four corners of every single card?

He started with the cards between the armoire and the French doors, reading every word and writing a list of senders' names to show Amelia and Johanna.

A lot of the cards were funny, some were well-meaning but gushy, most included a poem of some sort that Ben (as a person who loved words) found generally painful. Almost all had handwritten notes thanking Hannah for help she'd given and remembering time spent together.

One card was a work of art—a simple, spare, handmade

pen-and-ink drawing of an egret in the Whitfield marsh drawn by the person sending the card, who'd also written the one well-phrased line. There was a smear of something on the signature, and Ben picked at it with his nail—at what looked like pizza sauce with a speck of dried cheese—and began to think, as he worked at it, that there was something stiff attached to the back.

He took out the tacks and turned the card over, and found a small white envelope glued to the paper.

He opened the flap and pulled out a black-and-white wallet-size photograph of four men standing with drinks in their hands in a backyard of a small frame house with an air conditioning truck parked in a side drive.

Ben read the developer's printed date on the back—June 12, 1958—and said, "That's interesting." *Yes.*

Hannah would've had a reason.

Which leads me to wonder what else she might've put under the rest of the cards.

"Who would want Hannah dead?" Amelia Walker had stopped in her tracks, and turned around in the drive, looking hard at Ben.

"You'd know a lot better than I would. But it seems like we've got to look into it."

"Course we do. I couldn't rest if we didn't."

"I may be wrong. We both have to remember that. She could've just dreamed the person with the gas mask. But I keep waking up in the middle of the night thinking, 'Yes, but what if she didn't?'"

"She nevuh told me about anyone with a spray bottle, and

it makes me feel bad. I thought I was Hannah's closest friend, and had been for a good many years."

"I'm sure you were. I don't think she thought the gas mask thing was important. Not then anyway, if she ever did. No, she and I were talking about dreaming, and I think she just thought it was amusing."

"How could anyone kill Hannah?" Amelia's dimples came and went as she talked, and her soft gentle eyes looked stunned, as though she were focusing on something in the distance that looked more dangerous the closer it came.

"There's the conflict over Cumberland. Although where there's an obvious suspect there I don't know. I have a hard time imagining a park service bureaucrat doing her in in cold blood. *Or* a congressman either. Though with politics the way it is—"

"You can't be any too sure. Isn't the baby pretty?" Amelia stopped halfway between Whitfield's front steps and her own cottage (just past the north edge of Whitfield's front lawn), looking at a wild bay mare and her gray filly cropping Bermuda grass twenty feet away.

"They're also so dirty it makes you want to brush 'em off."

"You won't be doin' it, honey, I can tell you that. They won't let you even come close."

They walked on in hot sun and silence toward Amelia's small white cottage, till she said, "Why don't you make yourself comfortable on the porch, and I'll get us a glass of iced tea."

"That'd be great, thanks. But if you do have time, I'd like you to look at Hannah's things."

"Course I will. I won't go back to work till one. You don't take sugar?"

"No."

"I don't know about you northernuhs." Amelia smiled as she opened the door.

"I don't know about us either."

Ben sat on the porch step listening to a mockingbird and looking at the converted stables (the three guests getting bicycles, the yardmen working on equipment), at the horses shambling toward a moth-eaten mare, at Adam Clark on the far side of Whitfield walking up from the dock—while he thought about what to do next.

He had his chin on his fists and his elbows on his knees when Amelia came up to the screen door, and she watched him for a minute, wondering about blood traits, and brains getting passed down, and his childhood up north. And how it was that this strong lean face—a hunter's face, maybe, or a fisherman's—how those straightforward quiet watching features could have the look of her own daddy's face as soon as Ben asked her a question.

It made her feel shivery when she thought about it. That look that came from her daddy—who'd been real outgoing and talkative, who couldn't hardly stay alone a whole afternoon once her mama died—could be sittin' on a solitary man who studied quiet things of the mind and the soul that her daddy wouldn't have cared to know. Who could half-close his gray eyes and look amused the way his mother had when she was a child, and still be a total stranger who'd scream out loud in the middle of the night out of some pain she couldn't imagine.

Her own flesh and blood and a stranger too. It wasn't right. It wasn't the way it ought to be. It gnawed at her like a puzzle with a piece missing. A sister with a grown boy she hadn't seen raised. Who could've died in Germany. Who almost did, the way Mernie told it. Who would've died with a grown man's face his aunt had never seen.

It's not the way it used to be. It's not the way it should be. And it's long past time I got to know him.

"Here, let me get the door." Ben held the screen while Amelia carried the tray to the table between two wicker chairs.

"I brought you out some cookies too, in case you might could use some. Now," Amelia offered Ben the plate, and then sat down before he did. "What can I do for you, suguh?"

"First of all—"

"I still remembuh you lookin' embarrassed when I'd call you 'suguh' when you were little. The one time I saw you. How old were you, twelve?"

"Yep. Right around there somewhere."

"I reckon you didn't hear 'suguh' a whole lot, living way up in Michigan."

"No, and I was probably worrying about my dignity and trying to look like a man. Anyway, here's a list of the people who wrote cards to Hannah. When you get a second, would you write a quick note beside each name telling me who they are?"

"Course I will. I'll be happy to."

"And can you tell me who these people are?" Ben handed her the wallet-size photograph. "It's one of those things I told you about I found behind the cards."

"Well, first off, it's a view from Hannah's bedroom in her old house in St. Mary's. You're lookin' at Eddie Montgomery's house next door. He bought it to fix up and sell, once he got up the gumption to move away from his mothuh. That's Eddie there, the one on the far right."

"I can't see him very well, with the drink in front of his face."

"Bein' a black-and-white doesn't help eithuh, with him in the shade. When it's such a small picture."

"True."

"Eddie's not real tall. Maybe five-foot-nine or so. He's got dishwatuh-blond hair, and kind of a baby face, and he always dresses like he's stepped right out of a bandbox. Always has. Even as a little child. Now, the one next to him, he's from the park service. He's the one fightin' for Cumberland. Shucks, I can't remembuh his name. I will, though, if you give me time. That's the developuh there, right next to him, the one who tried to buy Cumberland first. Carl French. From Atlanta."

"That's interesting. The developer *and* the park people together that long ago."

"The one on the left, that's Benton Clay Bradley our illustrious—"

"Congressman Bradley."

"Yep. I went all through school with his sister, May."

"Look at the date on the back."

Amelia did, and said, "That can't be right. How can that be? June 1958?" Amelia looked up at Ben with a startled expression on her face, that turned shrewd after she'd thought about it. "That's before any of us heard about the developuh."

"That's interesting, isn't it?"

"He hadn't talked to Charlotte, or Hal Sutton, or Eddie Montgomery eithuh. That's what we were led to b'lieve. But this must've been taken two or three months or more before he made himself known. So this is tellin' us they all could've been in cahoots."

"I didn't know who they were, except Bradley. But yeah, it makes you wonder."

"It must've been that March or April when Charlotte's niece and nephew sold their land to Ed."

"So does that mean Eddie Montgomery bought the land from them, and then he got the congressman and the park people together with the developer? Why would he do that? Did *he* want Cumberland to become a park? Course, we don't know that Montgomery initiated it. It could've been one of the others."

"I don't understand it at all."

"What seems to make sense?" Ben leaned back in his chair with his feet out in front of him and stared at the porch's ceiling. "They could've brought the developer in to scare Charlotte and the Suttons. Hoping they'd be willing to sell to the park service without there being a nasty public fight. Right? I guess they'd have to pay the developer. To spend the time, and go through the motions, and keep his mouth shut. That's one possibility I guess."

"There's a donor involved too. Did I tell you that? Someone who's given the park service money to buy land here and convert it into a park. He's not given 'em all they need, but some. I can't remembuh all the details. Can't recall his name right now, but he's from New England. Connecticut, I think. Somewhere like that."

"So they could've used the developer to scare him too, to get him to give the money?"

"Can't you just see all the lyin' and cheatin' that would've had to go on? Makes you sick to think about it. I just heard the othuh day too that Eddie's tryin' to start a construction company. Maybe he's plannin' to build for the park service."

"Maybe. Seems like he could've made more money with a developer. With the real estate and construction both.

Assuming that money's the main thing he cares about. I don't know anything about him. Did Hannah ever talk to Eddie? Once she moved to Cumberland, and the developer put in an appearance?"

"He sure hasn't come to Whitfield, and I don't remembuh her talkin' to him on the ship-to-shore, but that doesn't mean she didn't. She asked me to call him for her, to ask him to come to Cumberland right about when Charlotte died, but he never did come ovuh. She went to St. Mary's two or three times last year. And once, I think, this summuh. Got herself strapped in the chair and carried ovuh. Johanna went with her every time she went, so she might know. But Hannah nevuh said she'd seen Eddie to me. Did you know Eddie's a Greene? His mothuh is General Nathanael's descendent, and she's none too fond of the Hills. She blames 'em for buyin' Cumberland away from her family. A grandfather who was tryin' to buy Kirkconnell back from Robert Stafford's family."

"Do you happen to know what Ed's middle initial is?"

"I could find out for you. Why do you want to know?"

"Don't worry about it. I can do it if I need to. What can you tell me about this?" Ben took out a photograph of Leah MacKinnon putting a round Chinese table into the passenger seat of a World War II jeep. "Handwritten on the back it says, 'This photograph was taken July 4, 1961. I put new film in the camera the morning of the fourth and removed the same roll that evening, and got it developed in St. Mary's.' It's signed by someone named Teresa Wayne and dated July 7."

"Well, I declare. I never would've thought that." Amelia sat staring at the photograph, half-shaking her head. "Teresa worked for Hannah this summuh, while she was home from college. Don't see why Leah would've taken the root table.

Hannah inherited it from Charlotte with everythin' else in Whitfield, but she'd have given it to Leah right quick if she'd asked. Hannah offered her Whitfield and everything in it, but Leah didn't want anything 'cept a portrait of her grandmothuh and two antique chairs. She got everythin' at her mothuh's house, and said that was all she wanted."

"What do you know about the table?"

"It came up missin' this summuh aftuh we'd closed the inn on the Fourth of July. We take off the whole week. We don't get as many guests in summuh. July and August 'specially. It's real hot and sultry, and the bugs are terrible, and we don't have air conditionin', 'cept for Hannah's room. So we use that time to work on the house. We had workmen ovuh from the mainland re-stuccoin' the south side, and building the bathhouse out back, but we all took off the Fourth of July. We cooked up a big dinnuh, and all of us on the staff had a picnic down behind Kirkconnell. Spent the whole day. 'Cept for Hannah. She said it was too hot for her to go to the trouble of gettin' carried down there. Teresa came to the picnic for an hour or two, and then went back to Hannah."

"The workmen were at the picnic?"

"No, they left the island the night before, then came to work again on the fifth. Nobody realized the table was gone till latuh the next week. It was back in a corner in the library. Staff people don't go in there much. Not when we don't have guests. It was valuable. Carved from the roots of some special tree."

"Could Hannah have given Leah the table?"

"She would've explained when it came up missin'. Some folks thought it was one of the workmen, but Hannah said no, it wouldn't have been them, that we've all known 'em all our lives, that it was pro'bly someone comin' ovuh here to look at the inn like they do, or lookin' for work, or eatin' dinner at the inn. Someone comin' in their own boat. There aren't lots who do that, but some. We nevuh lock the place up. Nevuh had to. I'm sure Hannah would've told us if she knew Leah had taken it."

"I s'ppose if she—"

"I know Leah was here on the fourth. She was packin' up some things from Charlotte's house while we were at Kirkconnell. We invited her to the picnic, but old Mr. Terry, Mr. John Terry, the gentleman who ferries her ovuh, had to get back to St. Mary's at a certain time."

"Why would she do it? Why not just ask for the table?"

"I don't know, suguh. It doesn't make sense to me."

Neither one of them said anything else for a minute. They sipped their tea and watched the wild horses trot toward the north-south road.

"What can you tell me about Hannah's MS? When did she move here, when was she paralyzed, that sort of thing?"

"She was bedridden for four years, but she could still use her hands the first two. Less over time, of course, but some. She only lived here at Whitfield a little over two years. Before that she had her house in St. Mary's. She gave up workin' at the hotel six or seven years ago. She was in a chair then, the last couple of years while she was workin'. I worked for her there for ten years."

"How'd the two of you get here?"

"When Charlotte started the inn, she tried to manage it herself the first three or four years, but she wasn't good at it, and it irritated her to have to do it, so I came to work for her when Hannah left the hotel. Three years latuh, Charlotte asked Hannah to move in here, to help me with the plannin' and some of the trainin', and because Charlotte wanted to help

Hannah out. She never said that, but I b'lieve that's true. And Miz Hannah was glad to come."

"How long ago was she diagnosed with MS?"

"Twenty years at least. Maybe a little bit longuh."

"What do you make of this?" Ben pulled a newspaper clipping out of his pants pocket and handed it to Amelia.

Amelia stopped pulling on her pearls and took the clipping from Ben. Her dimples appeared as she concentrated, as she wrapped a curl in front of her ear around her finger. "I don't recall a thing about this. I pro'bly nevuh knew. It happened right aftuh my husband's boat went missin', and I wasn't noticin' a thing. Why would Hannah have kept this?"

"Your husband's name was Taylor?"

Amelia nodded and handed Ben the clipping.

"That must've been hard. Losing him at sea."

"Couldn't've been as bad as what he went through." Amelia didn't look at Ben. She sat and sipped her tea.

"No. No, of course not. So the kid jailed in the brawl in Jacksonville twenty years ago is the Adam Clark who's captain of the Whitfield boat?"

"Look at the face. It must be. Don't know what he was like when he was eighteen, but he's been dependable as can be for us."

"Adam said in the article that he'd picked the fight with a descendent of Nathanael Greene's because—"

"It wasn't a Greene from anywhere round here. This was some college boy from Rhode Island, according to the caption. I've heard the name before. He's Eddie Montgomery's distant cousin."

"Right. It's interesting that Adam said one of his own ancestors helped Eli Whitney and Caty Greene invent the cotton gin.

That this great-grandfather of his had actually invented it himself, and that the Greenes and Whitney cheated him out of the money that should've been his."

"I know that's not what happened. And how's this for a wild statement? 'The Greenes are all liars and cheats and they bettuh watch out down here.' Doesn't sound like Adam. Not to me."

"You haven't had any trouble with him?"

"No. Nothin' to speak of. Reckon he's grown up since then. Once in a while he yells at one of the fellas, but nothin' alarmin'. Course…" Amelia didn't say anything else. She just stared across the lawn, past the live oaks and the mounting blocks, at Whitfield's white-pillared porch.

"What?" Ben set his empty glass down and leaned back in his chair.

"Joe Chamberlain. Hannah and I hired him this Septembuh to help with the landscapin' and the maintenance. He dropped out of Georgia Tech to make enough money to go back, and we took him on. He's a Greene. His grandmother was a Nightingale."

Ben looked blank.

And Amelia laughed. "Family history's nothin' you take lightly around here, and I wouldn't presume to speak with real authority, but if I've got the generations clear, Joe's grandmothuh's grandmothuh was Nathanael and Caty Greene's daughtuh."

"I see." Ben gazed at the index finger that didn't bend and rubbed the scar on the palm. "Any chance Adam Clark doesn't know who Chamberlain is?"

"Nope. Not in a town the size of St. Mary's, or here on Cumberland eithuh. We know each othuh's business bettuh than we know our own. It's a blessin' *and* a curse. We watch out for each othuh, and each othuh's kids, but the watchin' can get to eatin' into you."

"Did Hannah ever ask to see Adam? Right before, or after, you hired Joe?"

"She did. She asked me to ask Adam to have lunch with her one day. He ate and she talked, is pro'bly the way it was. She couldn't hardly swallow much of anything by the end of the summer."

"But she never mentioned their conversation?"

"Not to me. And I'm pretty sure it would've been me instead of anyone else, since I'm the one he works for. There *was* somethin' else that happened. Nothing big or impordunt, but…" Amelia was staring at the live oaks, chewing at her bottom lip.

"Yes?"

"You won't make too much of it? I don't think it means a thing."

"I'll try not to, that's for sure."

"Well, earliuh that week when Hannah took sick with pneumonia—you were here then, it was right before you left for Charleston—there was some sort of trouble between Adam Clark and Joe Chamberlain. It was my day off. I didn't get involved and I don't know the details, but when I came up to Whitfield right before dinnuh I heard Adam talkin' outside Hannah's door. He was leavin', standin' in the doorway as I was coming down the hall, and I heard him say somethin' like, 'You bettuh watch yourself, Miz Hannah. You don't want to go pushin' me too far.' I couldn't see his face, and I don't know what he meant. Hannah told me latuh that night there'd been a misunderstandin' and she'd talked to both of 'em about it."

"Well. It's something to keep in mind."

"One thing Hannah did do that surprised me a good bit, that she never saw fit to explain. She asked me to put a cash box of hers in the safe. Let me think when that was." Amelia smoothed her navy blue skirt and pulled the belt down under a role of flesh. "It was the week aftuh Garrett Aiken died. Not that that has anything to do with it, but I remembuh I was askin' Miz Land to patch Johanna through to the opera in Atlanta, and Carrie came down and said Miz Hannah wanted to see me when I had a minute. Johanna came up here aftuh Garrett died, you see. Monday, I think, for the funeral in St. Mary's on Tuesday. Then she stayed anothuh day or two. She was livin' in New York then, but she'd been hired by Atlanta and was fixin' up the arrangements for what she'd be singin' and where she'd be livin' when she got there."

"What was in the box?"

"Don't have any idea. It was locked when I took it out of the dressuh. Hannah must've had the key somewhere in her things. Probably somewhere in her jewelry box. She'd had one of the girls lock it for her. Like she'd have different ones tack up the cards. I'm sorry, suguh, but I have to get back. Is there anything else you want to ask me?"

"Yes, but it'll take a while. Maybe we could talk tonight."

"Come find me aftuh dinnuh."

"Could I look at what's in Hannah's box?"

"I first ought to give it to Johanna, but I'm sure she'll let you see it. Aftuh the two of you talk."

"That'll be fine. I tried to see her last night, but she'd already gone up."

"What will you do now?"

"I think I might borrow a bicycle and go down and see

Kirkconnell. When will Johanna be done practicing?"

"S'afternoon sometime. Don't know when. She's been havin' some trouble concentratin'. As anyone could imagine."

CHAPTER TEN

BEN BIKED TWO MILES SOUTH TO KIRKCONNELL on the sand and shell road, listening to the birds and the scratching of the palmetto fronds and the scurryings of unseen animals. Unseen except for two deer in the distance who bolted into the brush because of Ben.

He passed the path to the Hill cemetery, and the track to the old Kirkconnell dock, and the first two sets of square pillars inside the Kirkconnell grounds.

He studied the jagged uneasy ruins that looked even wider than he remembered, as he pedaled the quarter mile of tall palm allée toward the last pair of stone pillars. He leaned his bike against one of them and walked up the center stone stairs, twenty feet wide and crumbling, cut by weeds and fallen rubble.

He stared up at the charred ruin, at the empty hulk without floors anywhere, at shreds of staircases and stranded stone, at the backs of fireplaces and tall brick chimneys standing sentinel over wide empty windows and many-sided bays, over twisted iron and glittering glass scattered on the basement floor.

He walked down and around, toward the west end of

Kirkconnell, toward an open-arched stone window with a medieval looking wrought-iron grill. He could see the west end of the basement from there—the brick rubble and ruined tabby that covered the ragged floor, the half-wall of wide brick arches, the large metal safe behind them, paint blistered and rusted raw, surrounded by broken stone.

It would've been an interesting shot, and Ben told himself he should've brought a camera, before he turned and walked toward Caty Greene's first house, a hundred feet past that end of Kirkconnell.

She'd lived there while her mansion was being built, and it was small and simple and newly whitewashed. And Ben could picture himself living there through cold northern winters, as he walked across the back lawn behind Kirkconnell.

He passed collapsing terraces and crumbling walls in wide wings and elaborate bays that looked largely overdone to him, with what he'd seen in Europe, with the old estates in England and Scotland he'd stayed in since the war.

It must've been a construction feat though, building Kirkconnell on an island. The revenge of the nouveau riche. Maybe. In cluttered Victorian excess.

*It's better as a ruin. **I** think. From the pictures up at Whitfield. The bones exposed without the powder and paint.*

Course, I could look at that marsh a long time.

He was walking toward the rusting iron railing where stairs went down toward the broad flat ground, edged by encroaching jungle, where the Greenes and the Hills had grown the big gardens that had made them self-sufficient.

The south marsh was straight ahead of him, framed by the garden's overhanging oaks and palms, golden marsh grass, as far as the far-distant dunes, rippling in an east wind.

But Ben was thinking about Hannah by then. And why he should've brought the camera. *Then I could've photographed the carved stone at the same time I make the tracing. Though that might've been too much to ask, to actually plan ahead.*

He took a deep breath and let it out slowly, telling himself not to dwell on it yet, to wait till he got to the Greene family cemetery and death stood and stared him in the face.

Once he was walking east toward the cemetery, he started picking at it anyway, thinking about who to talk to and what he ought to ask.

There was someone in the road ahead of him, someone who'd walked out of a driveway on the right. A woman wearing khaki shorts and a yellow blouse, who had short hair, and plump legs, and a squishy looking middle.

"Leah?"

She turned toward Ben and started to smile, before she said, "I'm sorry, I didn't see you. I've been looking at my cousin's old house. Seeing if Eddie Montgomery's keeping it locked and in some kind of decent repair. It's called the Grange." She was pointing to a large stuccoed house behind a line of trees. "It was the first Kirkconnell overseer's house, owned by my aunt for years. Are you going back to the inn?"

"In a minute. I'm being a tourist. I'm on my way to the Greene cemetery. I've been seeing Kirkconnell, and I thought I'd look at the old outbuildings. What's over here on the right?" Ben was shielding his eyes from the sun, looking at the wreckage of a large wooden building smothered by vines between the big house and the Grange.

"That's the recreation building. The Hills played squash there and accommodated bachelor guests. It ought to be torn down before it falls and kills someone. The stables and the carriage house are straight ahead, up at the curve in the road."

"What's behind the magnolias on the left?"

"That's the old laundry. Kirkconnell employed three hundred people in its heyday. There, and at Whitfield and Four Chimneys. But now the outbuildings are going to wrack and ruin, and somebody better repair them quick, or tear them all down. I understand Johanna's asked you to help her evaluate the situation with the park."

"Yes, though how much help I can be I don't know. I've been going through Hannah's things, trying to track down all the paperwork."

"Have you come across Hannah's photographs? She took too many nature shots for my taste, but she did have talent. She used to take a great many more, of course, before she became bedridden. Horrible, the last years of her life."

"I like some of her recent stuff too. The one with the deer, with the horses behind them in the mist."

"I don't think I've seen that one. No, I would've remembered. Did you find the picture of me putting the root table in the Jeep?" Leah laughed and wiped at her forehead as though she were after a bug.

"Yes, I did."

"Apparently, I had everyone at the inn worried stiff." They were walking toward Charlotte's old khaki-colored Jeep, parked on the east side of the overseer's drive.

"How'd you do that?"

"I came over on the Fourth of July to pick up some furniture from my house here, to use at my place in Beaufort, and I ran down to Whitfield to get my mother's Chinese table. Hannah had told me I could have what I wanted, and that was one piece I'd decided I did want. I was in a rush. The gentleman who ferried me had to get home to St. Mary's, and I didn't have time to write a note."

"I see. So then you—"

"I assumed Hannah would be down at the picnic. She'd always gone in the past. So I took the table and didn't give it a thought. Wasn't till a week or so later that I remembered to call her and tell her I'd taken it. She laughed and told me she saw me do it and had gotten a picture of me taking it red-handed. She thought it was pretty funny. Said she'd keep that photo of me forever and use it to blackmail me if I got uppity. She had a wonderful sense of humor, *I* thought, even when she was terribly sick."

"She was quite an amazing lady."

"She was. A good example for all of us." Leah smiled at Ben as she opened the door to the Jeep. "No matter what she was going through, Hannah could find something to smile about. Did you know my mother used to steal furniture from Whitfield?"

"How could she steal it when she owned it?"

"Taxes. She'd take a valuable piece of antique furniture from somewhere in the inn, hide it up at her house, or sell it in a city somewhere. Then say it was stolen and take the tax write-off."

"Really?"

"Charlotte was a law unto herself." Leah laughed and pulled her keys out of her pocket.

"Interesting the way the turkey vultures like to sit on the chimney pots." Ben was staring at Kirkconnell pointing to eight or ten huge black birds—five or six on the chimney pots, several circling, one flying straight at them, diving down between the trees.

"Get away! NO! KEEP HIM AWAY FROM ME!" Leah had jumped into the Jeep, and thrown both arms over her head as the turkey vulture swept above her, forty feet in the air.

"It's okay. He's gone. He never got close."

"They're horrible. With their bloody looking red heads. I was chased by them the whole time I was growing up. You think they aren't paying attention to you, and then they turn on you and attack."

"I didn't know they'd do that."

"Oh yes, any chance they get." Leah shivered then, as she turned the key in the ignition. "Can I give you a lift?"

"No thanks. I've got a bike up by the front drive. Did Hannah know about Charlotte?"

"She must've. She wouldn't have approved, however. Hannah wanted everyone to straighten up and fly right. I've got to go. I'm getting picked up at three. Come see me in Charleston if you need anything. I'll be there the rest of the week."

"I'll only be there a day or two. Then I go up to Tryon, North Carolina."

"Tryon?" Leah turned and looked at Ben as she shoved the gearshift into first. "Why Tryon? It's only a bump in the road."

"To talk to a man who's offered to donate paintings to my university. I may be back in Charleston after that. Arranging for insurance and crating."

"Well, get in touch if I can help." Leah turned around in the sandy drive and waved over her head as she pulled away.

"So you knew about Charlotte taking the chair?"

Amelia said yes, and handed Ben back the photograph he'd

given her of Charlotte carrying a Queen Anne chair toward her battered Jeep. "Hannah got her to stop after she moved here, but it happened three or four times before that. Charlotte hadn't listened to me. Just told me to mind my own business."

"What about this?" It was a copy of a charge slip—a three-by-five inch piece of lined beige paper with carbon paper attached to the back. "Stubbs Hardware" was printed on the top and it listed items purchased—two cartons of cigarettes, one fifteen-foot length of hemp rope, four gallons of kerosene—charged on a store charge to Red Johnson, Coleraine Road, dated June 16, 1951, with Red's scrawled signature across the middle.

In different handwriting, at the bottom, was written, "Found caught in a bush by front drive at Kirkconnell, Cumberland, four in the morning June 17th 1951." It was signed by both Hannah and David Hill.

"Are those their signatures?"

"It's Hannah's signature, and her writin', *that* I can swear to for sure." Amelia didn't say anything else for a minute. She leaned back against the sofa in her living room and pushed a pin in her French roll. "Poor Red."

"You didn't know about this before?"

"No, I didn't. Red works here. Hannah hired him aftuh Charlotte died. He works on the land, and doin' odd jobs of carpentry, and he's worked out just fine."

"Hannah didn't run from making decisions, did she?"

"No, she surely didn't. There were some folks who said Red was the poachuh who got shot at Kirkconnell. Before it burned. But I nevuh took it too seriously. There were lots of poachuhs from the mainland who'd come ovuh here during the Depression, and Charlotte's husband, Rafe, he let it go.

He talked Charlotte into overlookin' it and bein' sympathetic. Her mothuh had moved out of Kirkconnell in the twenties, then died in '33, and what difference did it make to anyone else if they poached down south there, or north of Four Chimneys, eithuh one? That was Rafe's opinion. But aftuh Rafe died, Charlotte took the poachin' up again and made an issue. But Red burnin' the place down? That's what this amounts to. The fire was set before midnight the night of the sixteenth."

"What if Hannah knew Charlotte shot him? Maybe Hannah saw burning down Kirkconnell as tit for tat. Would that make sense?"

"Hannah had her own views of mercy and justice. She didn't always see it the same way the law does. Course I nevuh heard that Charlotte shot the poachuh. Rumor was it was a watchman. Though now that you say it, she would've been responsible eithuh way. The person who was shot could see it that way."

"How would I find Red?"

"You've seen him. The little wiry guy with the real red hair. Had a terrible childhood. His dad beat every one of 'em something fierce. So I heard, anyway, after his daddy left St. Mary's. He up and ran off when Red was ten or eleven. Red went to work right then to help his mothuh and sistuh. Workin' on the turpentine stills where his daddy had worked before him. His mama cooked for the turpentine camps and did whatevuh else she could. His sister went off and got married real young. And Red got married not too much latuh. Nice girl. Had two little daughtuhs before he went to war."

"Sounds like a good guy."

"He enlisted right aftuh Pearl Harbor. And when he got

back he'd changed. Drank somethin' terrible, just like his daddy. And his wife left him and took the girls. He got worse aftuh that. Couldn't keep a job. Lived off in the woods a lot of the time. But he's been different the last four or five years. Sobuh. Workin' hard. Doin' a good job here."

"What changed him, do you know?"

"Don't know for sure. Just know how it looks from the outside." Amelia straightened a magazine on the coffee table and took a sip of iced tea.

"How *does* it look? I know I'm prying, but what else can I do?"

"Nothin'. I feel like I am too. Course, I have thought about it a good bit, 'cause I like him. And I figure it's connected to a car accident. He'd been drinkin', and he hit a little girl who ran right out in front of him. Broke her leg pretty badly, though it could've been a whole lot worse. Then Red was jailed for driving unduh the influence. And when he got out, he went to visit her, and he got a job and paid her medical expenses, and as far as I know, he's been real dependable ever since. He's been fine since he's been here."

Ben nodded and sipped his coffee and wrote a note in his notebook, before slipping it back in his pocket. "Okay, so what about this?" Ben handed Amelia a folded newspaper clipping and watched her read it.

Amelia dropped her hands in her lap and stared at Ben for several seconds. "I don't know what to think. I know Hannah read a lot about mercy killin'. I know she thought it was wrong. That we don't have the right to make that decision about us or anyone else. But I didn't know she kept clippin's about it. The girls who helped her out did her filing."

"Hannah's got a big file of articles on euthanasia. But this one was hidden behind a card in the armoire."

"Why, I wonduh?" Amelia stirred her coffee and crossed her legs and smoothed the skirt of her red wool dress.

"Look at the picture."

"What about it?"

"Not the nurse who was arrested, the one in the background leaning over the desk."

"The one the caption says is Harriet Betts?" Amelia looked and shook her head.

"Doesn't she look a little like a younger version of what's her name? The cook?"

"Estelle Baxter?" Amelia studied the picture again and dropped her hands with the clipping in her lap. "It does, doesn't it? I wouldn't have thought of it, with the hair bein' so straight and all in the photo, but now that you mention it, yes. A little. I mean you couldn't swear to it."

"No. But if it *is* Estelle Baxter, if she *did* talk a nurse into killing two patients in a hospital, it gives you something to think about. She'd know about pneumonia, presumably. About how to culture it, and make a solution out of it. She'd at least know how to find out. And if she's a real euthanasia enthusiast, here's Hannah, who's suffering slowly toward a painful death sometime in the not too distant future, lying there with information that threatens Estelle's life."

"Mercy."

"We don't know that she knew that. Though I suspect Hannah would've told her. Anyway, I think I'll call a friend of mine in Ohio. He's the chief of police in Hillsdale, and maybe he can do some tracking without taking too much trouble. That's not to say I'm convinced Estelle had anything to do with Hannah's death—"

"But it does seem more likely than anythin' else."

"Maybe. That we know of now."

"Oh, I forgot to tell you. You got a call while you were eatin' dinnuh from a woman named Kate Lindsay. She told the girl not to disturb you, but to give you this numbuh in Chicago." Amelia took a slip of paper out of the pocket of her dress.

"Kate? You're sure she said Chicago? She lives on a loch in Scotland."

"It's a Chicago number. And she said not to call her tonight. She'd be out until latuh, but maybe you could talk tomorruh."

"I'll call her first thing in the morning. Do you know anybody who works at the hospitals, or medical labs, in St. Mary's or Fernandina?"

"There aren't any medical labs in St. Mary's. The hospital's real small. Fifteen beds. But I do know a nurse there. And I have a friend who's the edituh of the papuh in Fernandina. I can find out about what's there pretty easily."

"Then could you do me another favor? Could you find out if anybody's been asking about pneumonia bacteria, or buying any, or anything else related to that? I don't know exactly how to formulate the question. It would depend on who you talk to, but you can see what I'm getting at."

"We might could see about hospitals in Jacksonville too. I've got friends there I might could get to look into it."

"Good. I appreciate it. Are there any military surplus places in St. Mary's? Or in Fernandina?"

"Not that I know of. S'pect they'd be in Jacksonville, with all the military people there. What are you lookin' into there?"

Ben was staring out Amelia's screen door looking across toward Whitfield. "This is going to get complicated."

"Course, nothing worth doin'—"

"Is ever easy. How many times did I hear that when I was growing up?"

CHAPTER ELEVEN

JOHANNA ELLIOTT STEPPED OUT OF THE big bedroom under the eaves, her dark brown hair twisted up untidily on top of her head, her dark blue eyes red-rimmed and distracted looking, and walked across the old attic storage room at Whitfield, where she and Leah and Mary had played when they were little.

She blew her nose on a Kleenex, while she gazed absently at the trunk room, which had been turned into the slant-roofed entry of the newly made suite. They'd left the bead-board walls, three old leather trunks, a stack of alligator suitcases, a shooting jacket, a pair of riding boots, and a big Victorian brass camera to help keep the feeling of the original room.

Which was comforting to Johanna, as she ran a hand along a big domed trunk and walked toward the tall front gable.

She blew her nose for the umpteenth time, and wiped her eyes with another Kleenex, then sat on the floor in front of the window the same way she had since she was six.

It wouldn't hurt you to do something physical. You haven't since she died, and it might help. Run down to Kirkconnell and back. Or go borrow a bike.

It's anxiety that's doing it. That's making this sick feeling in my stomach. Same as when I lie down in bed and can't even make myself breathe right.

I should've come to see her. And I don't know how to live with myself having taken the selfish way out.

She took you in. She loved you. She raised you when she didn't have to. And she died without seeing you and hearing one more time that you loved her more than you'd ever loved anyone else on this earth.

Look at it, Jo-honey. Call it by name. Don't lie to yourself and say it's something else. It was standard old regular everyday ambition. You wanted to work. To play a role you were ready for, and write it right there on your resume.

If I'd known how sick she was, I would've come home.

That's nothing. Everybody's worst enemy would've done that for someone they liked.

And if I'd come home when I should've, I wouldn't be crying all the time, and pacing the floor at night.

You're making yourself crazy doing this. You know you are. How many more days can you go without sleeping?

I still won't take sleeping pills. Regardless of what Dr. Tom says. I've seen what they do to people in the business. Pills to go to sleep, pills to wake up, pills to make you happy. I've got to learn to manage this like a grown-up. And face the world like Hannah did.

Are you a grown-up?

Or are you just a spoiled brat?

Lord, please. I can't keep going over this.

No? Can't you?

Then go get you a coat and get out of here.

rrr

"Hi." Ben was sitting on the big wooden swing at the south end of Whitfield's front porch when Johanna slipped quietly out the front door and started across toward the steps.

"Hey."

"Feel like company?"

"I guess so. Sure. That'd be fine." She didn't look like she meant it.

But Ben needed to talk to her soon. And she looked so sad, and drawn, and strained, he thought talking might actually be good for her. "You want to sit here, or—"

"I kind of thought I might walk to the beach. Of course, if you'd rather—"

"No, I'd like that. Anyway, there're a couple things I need to talk to you about."

"I'm not ready to think about Cumberland right now."

"That's okay. That's not what I wanted to ask you."

They walked down the wide gray steps and turned right down the oak allée without saying a word as they walked toward the north-south road. The moon was high, and brighter than it had been, and the Spanish moss shivered silvery above them, trailing in a soft breeze.

"How do you know the old man at the cemetery? Randall? Was that his name? It looked like you really like him."

"Randall's a wonderful man. He saved my life when I was little."

"How?"

"It's kind of a long story."

"That's okay with me. If *you* don't mind." Ben looked sideways at Johanna.

And she looked away. "I must've been six or so I guess. I'd

been living with Hannah in St. Mary's for a few months, and I wandered along the backyards from our yard into the neighbors', till I got five or six houses down to where there was this old broken stone fireplace made like an outdoor barbecue. It's kind of hard to describe. But it had two walled triangular sections to it, three or four feet high, on either side of the fireplace part, that were full of rotting leaves. Their inside walls were the side walls of the fireplace, but there were stones missing, and neither side had its top anymore."

"I don't think I've ever seen anything like that."

"It's the only one I've ever seen. Anyway, I was sitting in the fireplace part, pretending it was a castle, when Randall's shadow started moving toward me across the lawn. I'd seen him hoeing in the garden, and we'd said 'hey' to each other, but I didn't know him, and I could feel him creeping up on me, and it scared me. He was moving really slowly and quietly and it gave me a funny feeling. I couldn't look at him. I was afraid to. I just stared at the floor of the fireplace in front of me and quivered. I remember it as clearly as anything from my childhood, just like it happened today.

"And then, without saying anything to me, he raised the hoe up above my head, which scared me nearly to death, and smashed it down right behind me. He said, 'Sit still, Missy, don't be scared.' And he leaned over me, right up against me, I could smell the sweat and the fear, and he scraped up half a coral snake. It had crawled out of the leaves in the side of the fireplace, and he'd seen it coming right at me."

"It's amazing he saw it. They're not that big, are they?"

"No, but they're bright. Red and black stripes. Maybe there's some white, I can't remember. Randall took both halves of that snake and threw them into a jungly spot on the other side of the lawn. And then he came back and told me not to play in places like that where there were sticks and old leaves. He said coral snakes were poisonous, and I had to be careful. And then he thanked God for helping him get to me in time."

"Were you terrified of snakes after that?"

"Not really. I never had any other trouble. But it made me trust Randall. There was goodness on his face when he talked to me. You know what I mean? Shining there, right on his face. You don't see it all the time, and you recognize it when you're little. And then he lost his job."

"Why?"

"Well, that's kind of a long story too. One part of it was that Leah told the two old spinster ladies who owned that house that she'd seen Randall steal a statue from their garden. He'd put it in a wheelbarrow while he was trimming around it, and then covered it over with clippings and forgot about it. And the next day it was gone, so somebody took it, and Leah'd seen him put it in the wheelbarrow and push it away. It was only a part-time job for him. He worked for other people too. But the two old sisters let him go."

"Was this after he helped you?"

"A month or so, I think. Hannah tracked him down, though, and she talked to him. I hadn't told her right away. I was a coward. I thought I'd get in trouble for being in their yard. But she hired him part-time at the hotel then, workin' in the garden there. She never had a yardman herself. She couldn't afford one. Not with her husband the way he was."

"So you don't think he stole the statue?"

"No. Leah didn't like him, and I think she jumped to the conclusion he'd taken it when she heard the sisters say it was missing. She was selling Girl Scout cookies, was how she got to talking to them. Course, Leah's a much nicer person now than she was then. A lot more careful what she says about people."

"Why didn't she like Randall?"

Johanna didn't answer right away. She pointed to a tree on the right. "Doesn't that look like the torso and legs of a giant woman diving into the ground? I've seen it that way since I was little."

"Yes…but what were you going to say about Leah and Randall?"

"I don't think she liked Randall because he didn't kowtow to her as much as the people who worked for her family on Cumberland did. I don't know that. It's just the impression I got then. Having a job on Cumberland during the Depression was a big thing around here, and people catered to Leah and her parents. She knew Randall 'cause she visited the old ladies a time or two after school. After she sold them the cookies. And I think maybe Randall didn't treat her like she was as special as she was used to. It's hard on people who get fussed over. You get so you think everybody ought to."

"Yeah, you see it all the time."

"I don't know whether Hannah made too much out of thanking Randall when he helped me, or whether Leah didn't like the fact that he had. Leah wasn't too fond of me when I was a kid. She didn't like Mary either. Or anyone else that took attention away from her. Course, Mary was even more disgusted with me. And I guess I understand that."

"What was Leah's family like?"

"Eccentric, I guess you'd say. Charlotte didn't pay much attention to her. She traveled a lot when Leah was young, and she was busy with other things. The animals she raised. Wild ones who'd get hurt on the island. Partridges. She tried raising them for a while. Fawns too, she raised a couple after their mamas got killed. She had dogs and cats and tropical birds and her own horses. But Leah didn't like the animals and the dirt and the wildness of Cumberland. She was afraid of some of the birds, and she made a big deal about the wild boar, and she was afraid of boats and crossing water. And I think her parents were kind of disgusted by that.

"She wasn't afraid of heights, though. That was one physical thing she was good at. Climbing trees or walking over planks laid across the marsh ditches. I remember her daddy used to compliment her on that.

"Anyway, Leah came to Hannah's house in the afternoons after school to wait for the boat to Cumberland, and I think Hannah meant a lot to her then. Hannah *and* Mrs. Rutter. She worked for Hannah. She'd watch me and Mary and Leah before Hannah got home two or three days a week, and she cleaned and ironed and sometimes she'd bake cookies."

"Where was Leah's father?"

"He was gone a lot, like Charlotte was. Charlotte spent a lot of time in Africa. He sailed a boat all over the world. He started a polo club north of St. Mary's, and a country club too, and he was involved in local politics, and he didn't have much time for Leah. He'd spent more time with Charlie, her older brother, but not all that much even then."

"There's something I have to tell you, Johanna. It'll take a while, but you need to know."

"The wind's too strong for talking on the beach, but we could go sit in the gazebo. It's up here on the right. It's kind of protected by the dunes, but if it's too cold, we can go back."

They'd come out of the woods and climbed the high dunes and were looking down on moonlit beach and water, and she led him around earthworks of high dune to a small roofed shelter on short stilts with benches built between the posts.

Ben told her what he'd found in Hannah's room—the photos and the clippings and the receipt from the hardware store. And he told her what Hannah had seen—the figure with the gas mask and the spray bottle.

Johanna was quiet when he'd finished. And he looked away from the sea and saw tears running down her face.

He handed her his handkerchief and tried to think what to say.

A doe and two fawns stepped out of the woods thirty yards in front of them, and stood frozen on the ridge of a high dune. The doe's ears swiveled carefully in every direction. And then she dropped her head and nibbled a plant in the sand.

Her fawns lurched and leaped and then stood quivering. They leapt again, toward each other and then away, before they stopped and cropped the plants close behind their mother.

Johanna handed Ben his handkerchief. And the deer bolted into the woods.

"I wish I'd come back before Hannah died."

"How could you know she was going to die?"

"I still should've come back."

"Why? You can't read minds. None of us can see the future. You did what made sense, what Hannah and the doctor told you to do."

"But if—"

"You were coming here to spend all the time off you've got, from Thanksgiving till you go to New York, and then back for Christmas. *You* couldn't know she'd die. If *I'm* right, no one did, except the murderer. And you couldn't have predicted that."

"How could the murderer know she'd die from the pneumonia, even if he sprayed it in the room? She lived through pneumonia two other times this year."

"I s'ppose the concentration of the bacteria could've been higher than it would be naturally. But that's a very good question. One I've been giving some serious thought."

"Why would any of those people have wanted Hannah dead? Except as some kind of mercy killing. I guess I can imagine that. I don't mean that *I* think people should do that. I don't. And Hannah and I talked about it a lot."

"Fear of exposure, or retribution? She knew things about several people that could've been used for blackmail, by a different kind of person. What if one of those people she had information about was unstable, or felt threatened in a way we don't understand?"

"Hannah wouldn't have blackmailed anyone."

"I don't think she did, in the usual sense."

"And I still think I should've come back."

"Don't we do enough things deliberately in life that we know are wrong, that it doesn't do much good to blame ourselves for what we didn't know, and couldn't help?" Ben waited and watched Johanna's chin tremble. And then said, "I probably shouldn't say anything. It's not my business and I shouldn't stick my nose in."

"Feelings aren't very logical."

"No."

"And it feels like I caused her death."

"Why? I don't understand."

"I know it doesn't make sense, but…" Her voice trailed away in the wind, low and supple and fluid.

"Just because you didn't get here to say good-bye?"

"This isn't the first time." Johanna didn't say anything else.

And Ben waited a minute before he asked what she meant.

"It's not the first time I've caused someone's death."

"You didn't cause Hannah's death." Ben watched the clouds blow above the beach, and then he looked straight ahead at where the deer had disappeared. "Killing is something I know about, and it won't do you any good to blame yourself for nothing."

"How do you know about killing?"

"I was a scout in World War II."

Johanna looked at Ben like she had no idea what that meant.

And he looked past her at the moon—pale cream, with a strip of cloud slicing it in two, reflected on a jagged sea. "I'd go out at night, behind the German lines, and I'd find a German command post and kill whoever was in it. I'd do it quietly, without any warning. With another guy, usually, though sometimes there'd be four of us. We'd photograph every document we could find. The troop deployment and equipment lists, the codes and communication stuff, whatever passes the underground would need. And then we'd come back through the lines again, and take what we'd found to army intelligence. These weren't fair fights. They didn't see us coming, if we did it right. And that was on top of everything we had to do to make it there and back."

"You were a soldier. That was your job. You didn't have any choice."

"Wasn't that the argument the Germans used at Nuremberg? 'We were only following orders. Like you, when you bombed Dresden.'"

"I bet you helped save American lives."

"I think that's true. But there was an American journalist I talked to, the only time I got sent back for R and R, who didn't think that mattered. You'd know his name if I said it. And this one night, he came in drunk and called me an assassin. Said I wasn't a soldier or an 'honorable combatant,' like he thought I ought to be ashamed." Ben didn't say anything else. He rubbed the index finger that didn't bend without looking as though he'd noticed.

"What you did must've shortened the war. And Hitler had to be fought."

"*I* thought so. That's why I could do it. But killing your Aunt Hannah, if she *was* killed, there's no excuse for that. And what you did, by believing the doctor and honoring your contract, is not the same thing as killing her. One thing I don't understand, though, is what you said about other people's deaths."

"I'm beginning to get cold. Would you mind if we walked back?"

"No, of course not."

They were in the woods, in the damp and dark, listening to a horse stamp a foot in the forest, somewhere off on their left—before Johanna answered Ben in a quiet tired voice. "Mrs. Rutter, the housekeeper Hannah had? I was the one who caused her death."

"How?"

"I don't know that I want to go into it. Hannah's the only other person I ever talked to about it."

"I can understand that. The people I've really talked to about being a scout can be counted on one finger. But whatever I can learn about Hannah's background will help me examine her death."

Johanna walked in silence, breathing shallowly, pulling off the rubber band that held her hair back, before she sighed and said, "I was playing outside one afternoon. This was when St. Mary's was a good bit smaller than it is now, and it didn't take long to get past the neighbors' houses. I was older. Eight maybe. Pretending I was an Indian princess. And it got dark earlier than I thought it would. It was this time of year. Right around Thanksgiving. I didn't have a watch, and when I realized how dark it was, I'd gone so far it took me a while to get home.

"Mrs. Rutter had been worried about me when I didn't come in when I should've, but Hannah told her not to, and sent her home at five. Mrs. Rutter called back about five-thirty to check on me, and I came in ten minutes later. But she never knew that. When Hannah called to tell her, there was no answer at her house, so Hannah went over to check on her and found her on the floor. She'd had a terrible stroke and she died two days later."

"That doesn't mean you caused it."

Johanna turned toward Ben, and even though he couldn't see her well in the dark of the woods, he knew she didn't believe him.

"Other people thought so."

"Who?"

"And now there's Garrett."

"How can you be blamed for Garrett's death?"

"If I hadn't told him I was breaking the engagement, he would've studied that night like he normally did instead of driving into Louisville and getting killed."

"He might've gone out with the guys out of boredom that same night. You didn't know what he'd do. You weren't driving the car. We aren't held responsible for what we do in the dark. For not being clairvoyant when we can't be."

"There're several Greek tragedies and a number of operas that take a different view." Johanna sighed softly. And then stumbled on a tree root half a second later.

"You don't believe in the gods of the Greeks. How can you be held to that kind of worldview?"

"The saddest thing, from my perspective, was that Garrett died before he'd learned as much about himself as I think he would have. He could be very rigid and sanctimonious and I don't think he recognized that for what it was. He had wonderful traits too, but he'd been coddled by his mother and made to think he was pretty much perfect, while he got ignored and belittled by his father. That can be tough. He was arrogant and very insecure at the same time. And none of us holds up very well with that."

"No. But then all of us have stuff in our past we have to learn to get over. Who thought so? I'm sorry, who thought you caused Mrs. Rutter's death?"

"David Hill, Hannah's husband. Mary, their daughter. Mary threw more than one scene. Leah too, I'd be willing to bet. Mrs. Rutter meant a lot to her. Leah behaved better around her, and was able to show more affection."

"What was Mrs. Rutter like?"

"Kind. Humble. Gentle. Fun to be with too. She and her husband had moved to St. Mary's from up north somewhere after he'd had a heart attack. They thought he'd do better in a warm climate, and they'd just gotten settled here, when he died. She needed a job then, and Hannah knew her from church, and she gave her one. Most people had Negro maids, and they thought it was very odd to hire a white woman, but

Hannah wanted to help Mrs. Rutter."

"She would've had the stroke sometime, regardless of whether you were late."

"We don't know that."

"Did you mean to hurt Mrs. Rutter?"

"No."

"And you didn't want to hurt Garrett?"

"No, but—"

"Could you have foreseen what would happen?"

Johanna didn't say anything for a second. Then she sighed and said, "No."

"Does God think you meant to hurt either of them?"

"God knows what I thought at the time. But—"

"Then maybe you shouldn't blame yourself either."

"I'm not safe to be around. That's what's so terrible. I hurt people without intending to, and I can't control it."

"That's exactly right. You *can't* control it and it's not your fault."

"I'm not sleeping. I can't sing. I feel sick. And I think I may be starting to lose my mind."

"Why do you say that?"

Johanna shrugged and said, "Don't ask. It's too stupid to talk about."

Ben watched her in the moonlight, out the edges of his eyes, while they crossed the north-south road. "Do you have a good friend?"

"Hannah."

"Ah."

"I can talk to Amelia some. The trouble is I travel too much. That's what's hard about being an opera singer. Two months here, three months there. *If* you're lucky enough to be given roles, especially when you're young and you're a mezzo. I had to spend two years in Germany working with the small houses there. Anyway, it's difficult to make real friends. And the friends I had here when I was growing up, we don't have a lot in common now."

"If it hadn't been for my work, and a *very* good friend—who's dead now too, who badgered me after my wife died—it would've been a lot longer than it was before I could walk around in the world again and act like a human being."

"How long ago did she die?"

"Four years." Ben pulled at a string of Spanish moss and rolled it in a ball in his hands.

"That's not that long ago."

"It is and it isn't. Sometimes it feels like a lifetime. What can you tell me about Mary?"

"Funny you should ask. I saw Eddie Montgomery's mother on the street when I was waiting for the boat to Cumberland, and she told me, in 'strictest confidence,' that he and Mary are engaged."

"Are they? That's interesting."

"Mary wasn't pleased when she found out Hannah had given me Cumberland, I do know that. Though Leah didn't care. And she would've had much more reason to be upset."

"How did Mary react?"

"Yelled at the lawyer. Said she was going to get her own and fight the will. Course she hadn't seen her mother in six years, but it didn't seem to her that that should've made a difference. Even though a letter from Hannah was read with the will explaining that it was because she wanted me to fight developers and the park service, that it wasn't anything personal toward Mary, that Hannah loved her the way she always had. But Mary was pretty upset."

"Did that surprise you?"

"No, I guess not. Cumberland's worth a lot of money. *If you're interested in selling it.*"

"Why wouldn't Mary talk to her mother?"

"I don't know. She preferred her father. I think she thought her daddy'd married beneath him. Married a boring stick-in-the-mud working-class drudge who lowered him in the eyes of the prominent people who mattered. Her daddy would take her with him sometimes to Jekyll Island and Sea Island, to the polo matches and the card games, and Mary liked the excitement. Hannah had to worry about practical things, like paying the bills, because David didn't. And Mary got really put out by that. She hated the penny-pinching and the nagging."

"What does she do for a living?"

"She's a decorator in Savannah, and I'm sure she's very good at it."

"Why would it have hurt her to talk to Hannah?"

"One thing I do know is that once Hannah got sick, Mary thought it was understandable that her daddy'd have an affair, and she couldn't see why her mother made such a fuss about it. She was angry with Hannah too because David was living alone when he died. After the girlfriend left."

"Mary didn't take him in?"

"No." Johanna sat on the top porch step and gazed up at the live oak canopy woven almost solidly above her head. She set her elbows on her knees and her chin in her palms, and said, "She doesn't like ugliness. Or suffering. She'd run away when someone got hurt when we were young. She never liked St. Mary's or Fernandina. She sees herself in elegant clothes walking up curving staircases in gorgeous houses in beautiful places like Charleston and Savannah.

"Though that could just be me, being catty. She wasn't pleased when Hannah took me in. And that's understandable. What little child wants someone else taking part of her parents' time? Though, I think when she saw that David didn't much want me there either, that may've helped turn her toward him."

"Did she make your childhood a misery?"

"No, Hannah was so good to me it didn't matter. Mary was okay. I knew where we stood. We ignored each other generally. And we lived in the same house all those years without once having a serious talk."

"Funny how that is. And how lots of people don't even know what you mean by a serious talk."

"I'm sorry, but I'm getting pretty tired. I think I ought to go on up."

"Thanks for talking to me. Get some sleep."

"I'll try."

"Tomorrow morning, Amelia's going to give you a locked box from the inn safe that belonged to Hannah. Would you let me see it after you get it? Depending on what's in it?"

"Of course I'll let you see it. Thank you for taking the trouble with all this."

"Please. Would Hannah have helped me?"

CHAPTER TWELVE

SATURDAY, NOVEMBER 25ᵀᴴ

KATE LINDSAY LEANED AGAINST A STACK of pillows on the side wall of a window seat with her knees pulled up and her arms crossed across her middle, as she stared out diamond-shaped glass at a snow-covered side yard busy with birds on feeders.

She pushed her dark brown hair back behind both ears, locked her fingers together on the top of her head, then sighed and said, "Work!" Before she picked up her pencil and a stack of loose papers.

The phone rang, and she leapt at the desk across the room and grabbed the old black receiver before the phone rang twice.

"Hello?…Ben! I was afraid it was the hospital. Thanks for calling. I appreciate it…No, it's my dad. He's had a heart attack. Two, actually. He seems to be doing fairly well, but we still don't know what'll happen…Not really. I think Mom's doing okay…No, I don't. Not at this point, but I'll be here several weeks. What are you doing on Cumberland? I called you in Ohio and got your housekeeper, and she told me where you were…Really? That's strange. That you'd be involved in another murder. What are the odds of that happening?…I know. It does. But what else can you do, except investigate what you're confronted with?…

"Is that the new president of Alderton?…Ooooh, that doesn't sound good…You're right, though. You can't let that go… So when will you go back?"

Kate sat in her father's chair, twirling a letter opener in a circle on the blotter, while Ben told her about the paintings he had to examine in Tryon. She said, "I enjoyed your letter about the wildlife illustrators. I never thought about the kind of guts it would've taken to do what they did back then…

"No, I finished that book the end of September…Now I'm working on one that's set on Loch Leven…Right, the lake with the island right by Kinnesswood…It's about Mary Queen of Scots being sent as a prisoner to the family who owned the loch. The father kept her jailed in the castle on the island. Until she talked his son into helping her escape…

"I know. What must Christmas dinner have been like for them? Especially for the wife and mother…No, it was when Mary's second husband was murdered. Probably at the hands of her third…I'm not sure an American like me can do it, though. Can write well enough about Scotland then to even take it on…

"So this Hannah woman with the MS, she thought it was a dream?…Funny you should mention dreams. The night before I called you, I was dreaming about the first hospital in Wales where I was stationed, when you and Graham and I first met. And I dreamt that you were one of the wounded sent back after the invasion. Everything about that dream was unnerving, and I woke up and called you without really understanding why. I mean, I know you asked me to whenever I got to the States, but…

"Soon. We told them we'd get there by ten. They bathe him and all that in the morning…Why are you getting a safety deposit box?…Really? How many photographs had Hannah hidden?…

"No, but I'm still thinking about Georgina's murder. I want to write about that sometime too…Okay. Good. Pray for my dad if you think of it…Thanks. I'll let you know."

Kate set the receiver down and walked back to the window feeling ruffled and slightly bruised. As though she'd exposed some tender place she could hardly talk about, and no one wanted to hear about it—or she'd called out, "It's Kate," in a friend's house, and heard the back door slam.

She kept looking at it anyway. Asking herself what Ben did to make her feel off balance—as though she'd sounded interested when he wasn't, or tried to turn friendship into something he didn't want.

She couldn't put her finger on a single thing he'd said, or even a tone of voice he'd used. And yet her face was hot, and her stomach had twisted with the sickly, embarrassed, awkward feeling she'd hated all her life.

Maybe it was him hurrying to take the box to the bank?

That was probably it.

Though it could've been me telling him about the dream. It almost sounded as though he was afraid I was ascribing some really serious significance to that. When I wasn't. I just think dreams are fascinating. Strange unexplainable throw-offs from the subconscious that give me ideas I can use when I write.

What shouldn't I have done? He asked me to call when I got back to the States. I know he wants to talk to me. I heard it in his voice. And yet I end up feeling like I've crossed some invisible line.

Is it him? Or me?

Or all the years I've spent alone since Graham was killed?

I feel like an awkward kid again. Some of the time, when I talk to Ben. And I don't like that at all.

Then sit down and work on the plot, and don't ever call him again.

Ben was standing in the wooden phone booth in the lobby of the St. Mary's Hotel waiting to be connected to Chester Hansen, the chief of police in Hillsdale, Ohio.

"Chester? It's Ben…No, believe it or not, I'm embroiled in another questionable death, and I wondered if you'd…I know. It's nuts. It doesn't make any sense at all, but…" Ben smiled as Chester talked, because he could almost see him at his desk in his perfectly pressed uniform, one thumb hooked inside his belt, his soft gray hair floating around his head like baby bird feathers. "True. And if you've forgiven me for what I did in the Cook case, I thought…No, this time I'll owe you more than that."

Ben explained what he wanted—as much information as Chester could get on a case in Orlando, Florida, in 1950 in which a nurse name Annabelle Reed killed two terminal patients with large doses of morphine in a six- or seven-month period, at Seventh Day Adventist Hospital, and then committed suicide after the murders were detected.

"She left a note saying she'd been talked into it by another nurse named Harriet Betts, and she's the one I'm trying to trace. It doesn't sound to me like the police had much on her, but she ran after Reed was found…R-E-E-D. Am I talking loudly

enough?…Right. Could you run a check on someone named
Estelle Baxter too, from Augusta, Georgia? She's supposed to
have cooked in restaurants and hotels there, but…No, I can get
in touch with the paper in Orlando myself. I appreciate it,
Chester…I promise to do something spectacular to pay you
back…It'll take you three or four days at least, right?…

"Why would I want to become a private investigator?…
Yeah, but it's not as though I go looking for cases, it's…What
are you working on now?…Another Peeping Tom? You think
it's the same guy?…I don't understand it, that's for
sure…True…And I need to give you the phone number…"

Ed Montgomery stood in the sun with his well-groomed hands
cupped around his tortoiseshell sunglasses squinting at an
empty clapboard house that hadn't been painted for so many
years it had turned the lichen-leached greenish silver of a dead
tree stripped of its bark.

He gazed at the sewing machine on the other side of a half-
open lace curtain, at the thread threaded through to the needle,
at the bobbin sitting by the presser foot—all of it covered by
thick dust, as though the person who'd been sewing had died
in the chair or walked out and never come back.

He looked at the Georgian moldings on the outside of the
window that framed the inside still life and wondered if he
could market the house as an architectural treasure worthy of
restoration.

He considered the ruined rear rose garden, the crepe myrtle
and the gardenias, the bougainvillea and the camellia bushes,
overgrown and beaten looking—suffocating under weeds and
palmetto as the coastal jungle crept in—wondering how fast a

bulldozer could get it all cleaned out.

Nobody wants gardens today. All that work and expense. People like Charlotte MacKinnon, they're long gone and won't come back. Comin' in the hardware like she used to do, durin' the worst of the Depression, orderin' up all those plants for Cumberland. The summuh Papa got fired from the store, she was lucky she didn't get shot by some crackuh watchin' her gloat.

Ed Montgomery looked to make sure no one could see him, before he spat next to a camellia bush—then fought his way to the front through the tangled side garden, bound by honeysuckle and wild grape, stepping out, finally, onto the battered brick walk where he brushed off his khaki slacks and smoothed his shiny blond hair. He appraised the curling boards across the front facade, the advancing rot on the pediment above the door, the cracked sidelights between the side columns, the symmetrical windows in crumbling frames, the broken-toothed shutters hanging at desperate angles.

He stabbed the point of his pocketknife into the cedar siding and considered the softness of the hole, trying to decide which made the most sense. Tear it down and develop the half block into small cheap bungalows or smaller duplexes? Which he could rent to local military personnel, and then convert later to high-rent vacation units, once tourists were pouring in. Or would it be better to invest next to nothing, and sell the Dean house to a restoration nut as an eighteenth-century gem?

Latitia Dean won't be needin' it again. That's as plain as the wart on her nose. And why she nevuh had that removed is still a mystery to me. She's a hundred-and-two, for cryin' out loud, and been with her niece two years. Her kin won't turn down an offuh now, no mattuh how low it might be.

There're folks who'd spend their last penny fixin' it up the way it

*was. If St. Mary's were Charleston or Savannah, you could make
yourself a tidy sum on a veruh modest investment. 'Specially if you
did the work usin' your own construction company. And I should be
ready to do that within the next two months.*

But here in St. Mary's, the way the market is today?

*It wouldn't bring in as much as a half block of cheap housin'.
Ten years on, yeah. When we've had Cumberland a good while, and
we've got a tourist industry bringin' folks in on their way up and
down the coast, then I'll be makin' some real money.*

Edward Montgomery pushed his way toward the street
through the Spanish moss that had almost strangled an old
magnolia and closed the iron gate behind him, thinking about
other old houses in town that would justify the effort of reno-
vating, and the circumstances of those who owned them. He
took off his sunglasses and stared at the house again with blue
green eyes that cut and calculated and wrote off what they saw.

He smoothed his tie and started down the empty street
toward the only car parked on his side, brushing off the sleeves
of his navy blue jacket. *Course, **some** small progress is bein'
made. First step was gettin' Hannah gone, even if it didn't go just the
way I wanted it to. Johanna's an obstacle to climb ovuh, and I reckon
now it'll take longuh. But the park'll get Whitfield in the end.*

*Gotta do somethin 'bout Mothuh's house next. Get her outta
there and into a home. I'm not gonna put up with it anymore. The
whinin' about everythin'. The nosiness that nevuh will end. Her
wantin' to be dependent on me and not lift a finguh herself.*

*Once she signs that power of attorney, turnin' her affairs ovuh
to me, and Bill's puttin' it to her just the right way, I'll move her
outta there and sell the house. Gettin' the paintin' done was the first
step. That'll speed it up when the time comes.*

Women. The two of them togethuh would make me certifiable.

*Just havin' Mothuh in the house while they paint hers is drivin' me
to drink.*

*I hope Gladys got off her sizable derriere long enough to make
me lunch 'fore she left. I gotta be back by one-thirty, and I don't have
time to make my own.*

Ben checked house numbers walking up Osborne Street, his
back to the St. Mary's docks, and decided it was probably the
cream-colored two-story clapboard behind the picket fence on
the right.

There was someone sitting on the porch—a middle-aged,
dark-haired woman staring across the street toward a high
white house with Corinthian pillars surrounded by scaffolding
and a scattering of painters resting under trees eating lunch.

Ben opened the gate and started up the brick walk, saying
"Hello," loud enough to carry. Realizing as he got closer that
the heavy dark hair was a very artificial-looking black bouffant
wig, and the woman under it must've been close to eighty.

She didn't look at him, and didn't answer. And when he
got almost to the porch steps, he shouted, "Hello. I'm Ben
Reese. I was hoping to see Mr. Montgomery. I called his office
and was told he was on his way home for lunch."

"Mr. Montgomery will be here in only a few moments. If
you'd care to wait on the veranda with me I'm sure he'll be
pleased to see you. I am his muthuh, Mrs. Lucille Montgomery.
I'm stayin' here with Edward while my house is bein' painted."

"I'm Ben Reese. It's nice to meet you." Ben saw then, much
to his amazement, as he sat down in the chair beside hers, that
the wig was held in place by a gray elastic band pulled tight
underneath her jaw, half tucking up the folds of flesh dangling

under her chin. "Is that your house across the street?"

"No, sir, it's not. No, that's Orange Hall, our historical society museum. Though my family did have more than one home every bit as large as that in times past. My great-grandfathuh was General Nathanael Greene, hero of the Revolution and close personal friend of President George Washington." She looked at Ben coquettishly from under thick false eyelashes and badly painted black brows, her faded eyes half-hidden in layers of loose skin. The wrinkles crosshatching her whole face lay caked with powder and rouge, and one almost skeletally thin hand was clawing at the shawl around her shoulders. "Nathanael's daughtuh, Marthuh Washington Greene, known as Patty to her family and closest friends, married John Nightingale, my grandfathuh."

"Nathanael Greene was an honorable and admirable man."

"He was, sir, he truly was." Mrs. Montgomery looked grieved as she gazed at her hands in her black crepe lap, almost as though his passing were a matter of recent memory.

"His wife was an interesting woman too," Ben said. "I understand she gave Eli Whitney at least one idea for his cotton gin."

"Caty Greene was a brilliant woman, as well as a woman of spirit and elegance, and she suffuhed for it her whole life long."

"I'm staying at the inn on Cumberland, so I've seen Caty's house by Kirkconnell. Am I right in thinking that Kirkconnell is built on the ruins of Caty's big house?"

"You are, sir. Dungeness. The Hills nevuh have had the taste of an alley cat, and they couldn't do else but copy Caty."

"Have you seen Whitfield? I think it's—"

"I could nevuh bring myself to set eyes upon it. They stole Cumberland from my family. Yes sir, they did, they truly did.

My family lost its land there inch by inch to the son of an over-seuh of ours, in the early eighteen hundreds, when they were plagued by sickness and tragedy none could've prevented."

"That couldn't have been—"

"Aftuh the War between the States, aftuh my fathuh had scrimped and saved and was ready to buy the land there at Dungeness, from the disreputable descendants of his opportunistic formuh overseuh, these upstart Hills sashayed down from Minnesota—the drunken brothuh, you understand, not the Hill who'd built the railroads. No, the ne'er-do-well brothuh, Robert, who was no-account in every way, who'd been cast off by his brothuh. He snatched up the whole island! Payin' more money than any southernuh at that time could have paid for the earth." Mrs. Montgomery's face looked flushed suddenly, even underneath the powder and paint, and her mouth clamped shut in a thin-lipped line.

"That must've been hard to cope with. And I guess a lot of that happened after the war. Course, I do remember hearing that in one of the old spa towns in Georgia, where northerners came to vacation about that time, they used to say, 'A northerner's worth two bales of good cotton and is twice as easy to pick.' So maybe the Hills got taken advantage of too."

"Mothuh?" The door to the house opened and a shortish man about Ben's age, somewhere in his middle thirties, trim, carefully dressed, blond hair smoothed to one side, stepped onto the porch.

"Perhaps you could explain why is it you're helpin' Johanna Elliott decide what to do with Cumberland. I don't intend to be rude, Mr. Reese, but are you a lawyuh, or a real estate appraisuh? Do you have some sort of qualifications that make you the appropriate person?" Ed Montgomery had led Ben out onto his back terrace to a white wrought-iron table in a large yard largely shaded by thick overhanging trees. He watched Ben carefully as he asked the question, then bit into half of his chicken salad sandwich.

"No particular qualifications that apply to this. Hannah had been talking to me about it, and I'd discussed it with a lawyer I know on her behalf, so Johanna asked me to pick up where I'd left off. She's young. She hasn't had a lot of experience with business transactions of any kind."

"I see." Ed Montgomery swallowed another bite of sandwich and then sipped his iced tea.

"Have you lived here long? This isn't the house that was next door to Hannah's old house?"

"I sold that last spring. What can I do for you, Mr. Reese?"

"I wondered if Hannah had showed you this?" Ben handed Montgomery the black-and-white photo of the developer, the park official, the congressman and him—and watched his face blanch.

"I'll tell you exactly what I told Miz Hannah when she got herself carted ovuh here from Cumberland last spring. So what? So you got you a picture of me talkin' to some folks. It won't make any sort of difference to the future of Cumberland." Ed Montgomery looked Ben in the eye, ripped the photograph from top to bottom, and then ripped the two halves again. "Cumberland is the last large unspoiled island on the east coast of the United States. The American public will have a chance to enjoy that island and see its wildlife, whethuh you *or* Miss Johanna want them to or not. No one family, in the last half of the twentieth century, has the right to own that land to the exclusion of every othuh American."

Ben sat and watched him for a second, before he smiled. "So you think private property rights don't matter? You think the federal government has a right to decide what you should own, and what you shouldn't, and take whatever of yours they want when they want it? Or is that only okay when it's someone else?"

"There is such a thing as the greatuh good. Government has the right to provide for the interests of the majority."

"With force? By seizing it? The way Stalin, and Hitler, and Mao Tse-tung have?"

"It's not at all the same thing. We do it to build highways. Why shouldn't we do it to make parks?"

"We did do it to make parks in the past, but there weren't people living there who owned the land and got thrown off. It was unclaimed land when the big parks were established in the 1800s. Aside from Yosemite, where there were squatters who lost the fight. Have you read anything about land conservation in Britain in the last two hundred years? The land owned in private estates has been much better managed—the animal and the plant populations—than that owned by the government."

"That can't be true. I don't believe that for a second. They used to shoot ridiculous numbers of animals on estates, wipin' out whole populations."

"It *is* true. And I can send you the studies if you want to see them. Some did shoot ridiculous numbers of animals, but they didn't wipe out populations. They managed them and bred them and added to the populations in the vast number of cases."

Ed Montgomery didn't say anything else. He finished the last of his tea.

"Hannah had several copies printed the same day. And I've got the negative to the photograph too."

"Good for Miz Hannah. I'm shiverin' in my boots." Ed Montgomery leaned back in his chair and wiped the corners of his mouth.

"Exposing what you did wouldn't do much for your reputation, though, would it? If there were press conferences about Cumberland. If there were articles in Atlanta and Savannah and all over the South, and in Washington and New York too talking about the park service and the political side of the issue. About the pressure being brought to bear by a congressman and a governmental agency. If it were revealed that the real estate developer who'd bought land on Cumberland, and arranged to sell it to the park service, had brought in a developer to scare the owners into selling to the park people, and to drive the price up too. Someone who made money by selling his own parcel. And was also engaged to Mary Hill, Hannah's presumed heir to the island. It might spur a little more attention. It might even look like collusion."

Ed Montgomery carefully folded his pink paper napkin and laid it by his plate before he looked at Ben. "And where did you hear we're engaged?"

"It's a small town. Somebody told Johanna."

"Mothuh. I wouldn't pay much attention if I were you, sir. She believes what she wants to believe and closes her eyes to the rest of the world. Your logic's flawed too, as I expect you know. Mary *wasn't* the heir to Cumberland, was she? And who would care if she were? You're graspin' at straws, Mr. Reese. Seein' what rock you can turn ovuh, hopin' somethin' useful'll jump out at you and kiss you on the lips."

"You thought till the will was read that Mary was the heir.

She was surprised and put out that she wasn't. Several people saw her reaction, and now she's fighting Hannah's will. Cumberland Island's not an inconsiderable inheritance. I suppose it could even be a motive for murder."

"What murduh? Whose murduh? I don't know what you're talkin' 'bout."

"Why have you kept the engagement a secret?"

"Good day, Mr. Reese. If you're evuh lookin' for land on the Georgia coast, be sure to keep me in mind." Ed Montgomery was standing, buttoning his navy blue jacket.

Ben stood up and smiled down at him. "Thanks for talking to me anyway. I hope I didn't ruin your lunch."

CHAPTER THIRTEEN

BEN WAS WALKING TOWARD WHITFIELD from the dock, thinking about what he'd done, and what he had left to do, and how to finish his own work and still investigate Hannah's death.

He'd gotten her metal box into a safety deposit box at the bank, with its extra copies of the newspaper articles, the original of the hardware store receipt, and the negatives for all the photographs, along with copies of several.

The nurse who'd been with Hannah the night she died had had nothing new to say. But Amelia might've had more luck, talking to the people in the hospital labs. Though why anyone wanting to murder someone on Cumberland would risk getting pneumonia bacteria from a fifteen-bed hospital in St. Mary's, or even somewhere as close as Fernandina Beach, wasn't intuitively obvious.

Ben told himself to stop thinking about it. To walk and regroup and consider his own work, and let his unconscious grind on on its own.

The sun was warm and the breeze was gentle as he stepped out of the live oak path into Whitfield's side yard. And when he saw the sheltered stretch of open grass behind the house, edged with trees but cut with views of the marsh and the river, he walked toward the lawn, watching sunlight dance on the water that slipped sideways beyond it.

He didn't see any reason to resist an urge as old as he was, and he lay down on the warm grass, cupped his hands under his head, and watched the clouds roll by just like he had as a kid.

They were high and white and unpredictable, slipping into shapes of surf and sand and snow, and he followed them as they thinned across the soft blue sky, or rounded into watery whirls billowing across the sun.

One large swirl started as a mountain range and unrolled as a river, darkening the sun for an instant as it streaked off on his right.

And as it shrank, he saw Johanna running through a tall narrow pyramid of hot poured light in a thin white dress, her hair long and tangled in the wind, her blue eyes liquid and too bright to look at, rushing in a circle from someone who scared her, sobbing and whispering, "Don't hurt me! Please! Not when I'm all alone!"

Ben felt himself falling then, down an elevator shaft, blinding white and narrow, down toward the top of the elevator— till he jerked himself together and caught himself awake.

He was cold in the sun. Shivering. Wondering why it bothered him as much as it did that Johanna had been left alone.

He got up and brushed himself off, thinking about chiggers and ticks in the grass and whether they'd be dormant by November, before he walked in the back door to the big white-and-wood kitchen and asked the young girl scrubbing carrots if he could have some water.

"We've got lemonade made, and iced tea too." Tallie Helms

looked shyly at Ben, her smooth plump face freckled and pale, her hazel eyes shy, as she wiped her hands on her apron.

"I'll just have water, but thanks anyhow. You don't have to bother. I can get it."

"I can fix you a glass right quick." She was already reaching for a green glass tumbler on a shelf beside the refrigerator.

Ben said, "Thank you," walking along a long glass wall of china cupboards while he waited. "Did the crystal glasses in the cabinet belong to the Hills? I work in a library, and I had to look up the pattern when somebody gave the school a punch bowl just like this."

"They belonged to Miz Charlotte's mothuh, and when Miz Charlotte was here for suppuh, she drank from 'em. No one else used 'em, 'less she was havin' a fam'ly dinnuh. Miz Hannah used 'em too once after Miz Charlotte died, when the Hills come ovuh for somethin' special. It might coulda been the funeral dinnuh. Miz Charlotte was drinkin' iced tea out of one of 'em the veruh moment she died."

"Was she?"

"With a whole lotta sugar. She didn't, as a rule. Said she was feelin' real washed out."

"Didn't Charlotte's glass disappear the night she died? Seems like somebody told me that. Amelia probably."

Tallie handed Ben his water and nodded her head, but her teased, sprayed, home-dyed hair didn't look as if it had moved.

"So what could've happened to the glass that disappeared?"

Tallie didn't say anything. She stood at the sink scrubbing the carrots with a stiff brush, till Ben heard her swallow a soft sob.

"I'm sorry. Did I say something wrong?"

"*I* broke that glass. The night Miz Charlotte died. I picked it up and brought it in the kitchen, and I was puttin' it in the sink and it up and slipped outta my hand. I felt real bad about it, and I took it up to where I live and buried it there in the woods."

"Up by staff housing?"

"Yes sir, south of Miz Charlotte's."

"Why'd you decide to bury it?"

"I got real upset. Somebody was talkin' 'bout Miz Charlotte bein' murdered, maybe bein' poisoned or somethin'. That was that night, before they figured out she died of somethin' else. They were thinkin' 'bout all the fightin' ovuh Cumberland. And when I broke the glass, and I knew how much store everybody set by 'em, I got scared. I like it here. I didn't want trouble. And I couldn't tell Miz Hannah *or* Miz Amelia, they were so busy 'bout Miz Charlotte's death. So I took it away and buried it, and didn't know how to go back. I was gonna tell Miz Hannah latuh. I was. I felt real bad about it. Hidin' what I'd done the way I had. But I kept puttin' it off. And now she's dead. And I nevuh told her the truth." Tallie Helms was sniffling by the sink.

And Ben walked over and touched her elbow. "You couldn't help breaking it. Hannah wouldn't have cared. Just tell Miz Amelia now. She'll understand. And she won't hold it against you."

"I heard one of the maids say yesterday that maybe Miz Hannah was murdered. That can't be true, can it?"

"Miz Hannah? Why would anyone say that?"

"Don't know. Don't see how she could've been killed, but…"

Estelle Baxter had stopped in the doorway that led to the galley kitchen by the dining room, standing tall and narrow, staring at Ben and Tallie, holding a tray of pies, her face frozen and her eyes startled.

Ben said, "That's just the kind of rumor that gets spread when people die, when they've got some money, or they own something like Cumberland. I can't see why there'd be any truth in it."

"You can't?" Tallie was still snuffling, wiping her eyes on her apron.

Estelle set the pies on the counter, glanced sideways at Ben but not at Tallie, then walked out of the room.

Ben waited beside the road, a half mile north of Whitfield, sitting on a live oak branch photographing a fern. It was a resurrection fern, a foot away on the limb, that had just opened up and turned green again, after a quick afternoon shower.

It was just past four, and he wanted to catch the five o'clock boat from Cumberland back to the mainland, and he hoped Red Johnson would come along soon so he could talk to Amelia afterwards and still make the boat.

Then he saw him, walking around the curve, reading a letter with his head down.

He was wearing old jeans with a rip in one knee and a lot of mud on the other leg, with the sleeves of his green flannel shirt rolled up above thick muscular arms. His hot red hair was curling around his face and down past his collar on the back of his neck, and he was smiling to himself and reading his letter as though whoever had written it meant something to him.

A cigarette hung from the right side of his mouth, and his lips moved as he read—not as though he needed them to, to get around the words, but as though it added to his pleasure. His face was lined and leathery, partly from wind and weather, and tanned the sort of red-clay tan redheads often are.

When he looked up and saw Ben, the smile died, the green eyes shuttered themselves behind almost closed lids, the mouth tightened on the cigarette.

"Mr. Johnson?"

"Yes sir?" He'd folded the letter carefully and was pushing it into a shirt pocket.

"I'm Ben Reese. Amelia's nephew. I'm helping Johanna try to decide what to do with Cumberland."

"'Spect y'all got your work cut out."

"Yeah, I think you're right." Ben didn't say anything else for a second. He watched Red Johnson watch him—short and strongly built, wiry, and looking wary, sizing Ben up in silence. "Could I talk to you for a minute?"

"Reckon you are already."

Ben laughed, and said, "True. I'll walk on with you if you want."

"No, sir. Standing here suits me fine." He stepped on his cigarette, then pulled a pack out of his left breast pocket. And held it out to Ben.

Camels. Ben hesitated for a split second, and then shook his head. "Thanks anyhow. I pretty much stopped four or five years ago. Anyway, I bet you'd like me to come to the point."

"If you've got a mind to. Don't mean to rush you none. But gettin' cleaned up's gonna feel mighty good."

"I've been helping Johanna go through Hannah's papers, and I found a receipt from a—"

"Hardware store. Charged to me with my signature on it." Red Johnson squatted in the sand, picked up the butt he'd crushed, and squeezed the tobacco onto the ground. "Is Miss Johanna worryin' 'bout me?"

"She's not worrying exactly. But she asked me to look into it."

"She afraid to talk to me herself?"

"She's having a hard time with Hannah's death, and all the stuff that has to be done, and she needs some help. Still, Kirkconnell being burned to the ground would make any-one—"

"Yep. I reckon it would. Course it was a good long time ago. And a good bit's changed since then."

"Whatever you're willing to tell me will make it easier. I assume you'd like to stay here, and I'm trying to see that that happens. Hannah trusted you, or you wouldn't be here now, and Johanna wants to look at it from her perspective."

Red Johnson stood up, then sat on the branch where Ben had been sitting, his hands dangling between his knees, his eyes on the sand and shell road. "Does this stay between us? Us and Miss Johanna?"

"Yeah. Unless she says otherwise after she talks to you her-self."

Red considered for a minute before he said, "I reckon I don't have too many choices. Seein' it from her side. Not if I want to work on Cumberland."

"Maybe. I don't know."

"Well, the truth of it was that I was a drunk. My wife had left and took the girls. I had no use for Charlotte MacKinnon, and I used to come ovuh here and poach her game whenevuh the spirit moved. Lots of folks did durin' the Depression, and old Rafe MacKinnon, he kept her off our backs. Aftuh the war, aftuh he died, she got real testy, and we had words in town one day, and the next time I come ovuh I near got my leg blown off. Whethuh it was her or the overseuh she had then, didn't mattuh. It was her behind it, I knew that, and I was mean enough and mad enough not to let it pass. Once I was up on my feet again, I come back ovuh and burned Kirkconnell down.

"There's no way I wouldda done it today. Wouldn't even a thought of it. But I done it then." Red Johnson inhaled deeply, then exhaled slowly before he looked at Ben.

"And Hannah found the receipt."

"I was drunk when I done it. Musta pulled it outta my pocket when I was fishin' for the matches. I was nuts then. Doin' all kinds of stuff I shouldn't've. And then Miz Hannah stopped me on the street in St. Mary's. She was walkin' with a cane then, and still workin' at the hotel, and she asked me to come see her at home. I did. And she told me she had the receipt, and that if she heard of me gettin' into any othuh trouble, she'd know who to show it to. I was real mad. *Real* mad. Till I begun to see she weren't takin' Charlotte's side. Even when Charlotte's brothuh was her own husband. Said she didn't like the shootin' that'd gone on. And that the feudin' was gonna stop on both sides. Looked to me like she meant it. And I backed off."

"How'd you happen to come to work here?" Ben was looking north up the road with his hands in his back pockets.

"Somethin' happened, and I had reason to quit drinkin.' Got me a job at Gilman Paper, and I worked real steady. I'd get there and get it done. And it was a bettuh life than before for me, workin' on the stills before the war. Hated seein' all them trees come down, though. And then Miz Charlotte died. One day I just come ovuh here to Miz Hannah and asked for a job on Cumberland takin' care of the land. Doin' some carpentry, when she needed it. Maybe huntin' for her when the herds needed thinnin'. Maybe workin' as a huntin' guide sometimes too. On the mainland. If she'd put in a word with folks she knew ovuh to the huntin' club Rafe MacKinnon started. She listened real polite like. Told me she'd think about it. Two days latuh she called on the ship-to-shore, and I come to work the next week."

"Everybody says you've done a really good job."

Red Johnson shrugged and lit another cigarette.

"You don't much care what anybody says though, do you?"

Red smiled a crooked smile that exposed a missing tooth.

Ben laughed and said, "I don't either. Never did too much."

"Come home from the war carin' a lot less."

"Me too. I know exactly what you mean."

"Was you in Europe?"

"France. Belgium. Germany."

"Made me nevuh wantta see anothuh snowflake as long as I live. Nevuh thought my feet would thaw out evuh again." Red was standing with his broad hands on his narrow hips looking Ben in the eye. "What'll you tell Miss Johanna?"

"That it looks to me like Hannah knew what she was doing."

Red nodded, staring at the oyster shells and the sand he was standing on. And then he said, "Thanks," in a low quiet voice.

"How are the deer doing?"

"Need to be culled. Wild pig could stand some thinnin' too. Specially on the north end. Told Miz Amelia last week, but with Hannah's death and all and everything, nothin's gettin' done about it."

"I'll mention it to her too when I get a chance. Thanks for telling me."

"You're right welcome." Red Johnson nodded and turned north toward the staff quarters, pulling the letter out of his pocket as he walked.

The sky was striped salmon pink and purple on a scrap of cloud gathered around a sun that was burning down like a disk of backlit Merthiolate. Lights on docks and houses flared like fiery pinpricks in land and water, growing darker by the second as Ben watched.

It was chilly on the *Charlotte MacKinnon*, running toward St. Mary's, with the sun dropping and the wind up, slapping the waves, getting splashed by spray, with the engine whining, filling the night, making it hard to talk.

Adam Clark had finished speaking to the harbormaster in Fernandina and had hung up the microphone on the ship-to-shore, and he was holding the wheel easy in his hand, standing steady and relaxed and staring through the windscreen, steering between the red and green buoys, cutting the engine to keep from swamping a sloop that lay anchored off Cumberland's southwest shore.

He was broad backed with huge hands, a large head, and a heavy square jaw. And there were tattoos on his forearms—a clipper ship and an anchor—half-visible under well-pressed rolled-up blue work-shirt sleeves. He was younger than Ben, thirty, or a little older. He was quiet. He answered when spoken to. But he looked at Ben out the edges of his eyes when he thought Ben wasn't watching.

There was one other passenger, asleep on a bench in the stern, a kid who was there to help with the luggage when they met the incoming guests.

"How long will it take me to drive to Savannah?" Ben had to almost shout across the cabin against the rumble of the engine. And it took Adam Clark so long to answer Ben began to think he hadn't heard.

"Hunnurd and ten or twenty miles, give or take. Take you close to three hours though, road the way it is."

"I'm doing some work there for Miss Johanna. She's asked me to help her sort through Hannah's things." Ben waited. And Adam looked at him, but didn't say anything in response. "See if I can help her figure out what to do about Cumberland."

Adam glanced at him for a second, then answered the call on the ship-to-shore from the Whitfield office in St. Mary's.

Ben sighed quietly to himself and waited for Adam to finish. "One thing we found, that Johanna didn't know anything about, was a clipping from a Jacksonville paper about a bar fight ten or twelve years ago."

Adam didn't react at all. He just gazed past his running lights at the dark water ahead.

"Because of that, I think Johanna's a little concerned. Joe Chamberlain's a Greene descendent. She saw from the article that at *that* time at least, you felt some real hostility toward the Greenes in general. And then there was a disagreement a couple weeks ago between you and Joe Chamberlain. And she wants to make sure there won't be more trouble on Cumberland."

"There won't be. There was a misunderstandin' about when a chain saw was s'pposed to be delivered to the dock in St. Mary's. Chamberlain thought it would be there by noon. I had to come on back with passenguhs before one, and the delivery-man was late. I picked it up on the next trip. Didn't look to me like any big problem. And we got it straightened out."

."I guess Chamberlain acted kind of irritated."

"I don't know nothin' more about it."

"There was no conflict later between the two of you?"

Adam studied Ben silently. And then turned back toward the water. "Miss Johanna's got nothin' to worry about. You got my word. I was a kid when I punched that Greene boy. I'm not a kid anymore. You got a temper? You know what it's like?"

"Takin' out your own hate on somebody else? I do, yeah. And it wasn't easy learning not to."

"I reckon I had to learn that lesson too."

"I could still get pushed off the edge. I can imagine a circumstance where it'd be hard for me not to be."

"I s'ppose there's that for everybody. I don't feel that strong 'bout the Greenes today. That's one thing I know for sure."

Ben nodded. Then didn't say anything for quite a while. He smelled the water smells he loved, and hummed nothing in particular under his breath to the throb of the inboard engine.

When he looked at the clock and saw they were only a few minutes out, he cleared his throat and said, "One other thing I wanted to ask. The day you had that misunderstanding about the chain saw, you talked to Hannah that night?"

"Yeah."

"Something you said was overheard and—"

"By Miz Amelia."

"Yes, and she—"

"I thought maybe I shouldda explained to her. Aftuh the thing with the chain saw. But when I thought about it latuh, it didn't seem that impordunt. I reckon she heard me say somethin' like, 'Watch yourself, Miz Hannah, don't you push me too far.' Somethin' like that. Maybe not that exactly, but close."

"Yes. What was that about?"

"We'd been plannin' the next week. That was a Saturday we were talkin', right before she died, and she asked me to make a special trip into St. Mary's the following Saturday and bring back Reverend Michaels and his family. She wanted him to preach her a sermon, and give her communion, and she thought he might like to bring his wife and kids, or his grandkids, whoever was around, and let 'em have a picnic on her porch and spend the day on the island. She was talkin' 'bout gettin' strapped in her chair and goin' out on the porch with 'em."

"So how does that—"

"I know 'em. I been goin' to their church since I saw a reason to go to any. And she was sayin' she wanted me to sing 'Amazing Grace' out loud for 'em, in front of everybody, and I was sayin' I wouldn't. Over my dead body. She heard me one time on the boat. She was in the back, and I didn't think she could hear with the engine goin'. I never could sing in front of nobody else and she was teasin' me." Adam was cutting the engine, turning in between the channel buoys, into the St. Mary's River, and it almost looked to Ben in the light from the hanging lantern that Adam's face was turning pink. "So I was teasin' her back. Sayin', 'Don't you push me, woman. I'm not gonna be singin' for nobody.'"

"I see."

"I got a lotta reason to be grateful to her. And I kinda wish I'd thought to thank her more than I did."

"I think a lot of people owe her something. How many appreciate it, I don't know."

"She did push herself some into othuh people's lives. Some don't mind, when they can see why. Lots of othuh folks do. It makes some folks real mad."

"I know that's true for sure."

CHAPTER FOURTEEN

MARY HILL LOOKED AT HERSELF in the long gilt mirror leaning against the wall in the bedroom part of her studio apartment, wondering if shantung pants were all right, or she ought to wear something more casual. She did *not* want to give the impression that she'd dressed for a friend of Johanna's.

The next second she told herself there was no reason on earth she should care what this Mr. Reese thought. His mind had already been poisoned against her by Hannah and Johanna too, and she should wear whatever she wanted to wear.

She walked up closer to the tall French mirror and added more eyeliner and mascara. Then looked at her cheekbones and the sharp line of her jaw and told herself she shouldn't have eaten the half piece of toast for breakfast.

She wouldn't tomorrow. She'd skip breakfast and lunch for a day or two and make sure she lost another five pounds in plenty of time for the wedding.

She wondered why this Reese person wanted to see her, and how she ought to approach him, and wished she'd been able to get Edward on the phone after the man had called. *Funny that Edward didn't call me back. I expect something important must've come up and he couldn't get away.*

Mary opened the armoire next to the four-poster bed and took out the floor-length wedding dress that had come the week before. She unzipped the plastic bag, pulled it out carefully, and held it against her, smoothing it in around her tiny waist, sweeping yards of gathered skirt out to one side as she swirled toward the mirror.

It really is the most beautiful silk-satin I've ever seen. It's exactly the cream of a gardenia, and it complements my complexion perfectly. I may not be as good-looking as Johanna, but I do have perfect skin.

I wish my hair were longer for the wedding.

Do I? Why would I think that all of a sudden? I haven't wanted long hair since I was in high school. Since Johanna put hers in a ponytail right after I got mine cut.

It would be nice to fasten it back and tuck gardenias around it. Though I s'ppose I could pin one in front of one ear, even as short as it is now, if I decide not to wear a veil. If we do get married at the inn in Charleston, a veil might be too formal anyway.

How long would my hair be by Valentine's Day? I need to remember to ask Teresa when I get my nails done next week.

It's the most exquisite gown I've ever seen. Even in New York, when cousin Sarah got married. Course I never should've spent this kind of money. That's the curse of having elegant taste, you never are satisfied with less than what you know looks right. I used to feel so miserable when Daddy and I went to the Cape. The cousins' clothes were just gorgeous, and it was all I could do to scrounge something suitable to wear to Sea Island for dinner.

Daddy would've taken me shopping. Driven up to Savannah to look for something fine. He would've written a check, and found the money later. But Mother never would let him. Saving for my educa-

tion, that was the main excuse. And Johanna's schooling too, I don't doubt, even with her scholarship. If Johanna hadn't been there, we would've had money to spare.

Mother still made Daddy feel guilty. Making it look like overseeing his land at St. Mary's wasn't good enough for her. When he hadn't been raised to get some ordinary job, and making him worry wasn't right.

If I hadn't bought the cashmere sweater and both the silk slacks, buying the dress wouldn't have been so bad. But I'll use them for years, and they're part of the trousseau. I wish Edward would tell me where we're going on our honeymoon. It'd make it so much easier to buy the right clothes.

It was a ground-floor garden apartment in a narrow white-stuccoed house in a neighborhood going from bad to better, one block west of a boardinghouse where Ben had been surprised to see diners still lined up for dinner.

He parked on the street, once he'd found a spot. Then walked under the stairs to the main floor, and knocked on the ground-floor door.

"Who is it?"

"Ben Reese. I called you from St. Mary's."

The glossy black door opened as far as the safety chain would let it, and Mary Hill looked at him carefully before she unlatched the door.

It was a painstakingly decorated apartment—a small packed pink-and-green space, stiff with tassels and brocades and ruffles—grand style on a cramped scale.

And Ben searched for something safe to say, seeing how much it was expected by Mary, who was watching his face for a

211

reaction. He settled on, "Anyone could see you're a decorator," and told himself to smile.

"I wait and buy good pieces. The mantelpiece is carved Italian marble salvaged from a planter's townhouse. So is the marble I used in the bathroom. There're great sources here in Savannah. All you have to do is know what you want and be willing to wait to find it. Could I offer you a glass of iced tea?"

"No, thank you. It's late, and I feel bad bothering you. I have to get to Charleston tonight to do work there tomorrow, or I would've arranged a better time. I'm trying to help Johanna decide what to do with Cumberland. She feels uncomfortable the way things are, and she asked me to ask you what it is you'd like to see done with it. She knows what Hannah wanted, but she thinks it's only right to ask you."

"Sweet li'l old Johanna." Mary's fingers pulled at the bottom of her black cashmere sweater, then settled on the edges of her hip bones. Her long thin face was turned to the side, the brown eyes unreadable, the thin lips pressed against themselves.

"You think she should sell it to the park?"

"What *I* think is it shouldn't be Johanna's to decide." Mary motioned Ben to a green wing-back chair and sat on a camel-back sofa. "I'm not about to let my family inheritance go without a murmur, and that's why I've gotten my lawyers involved. My father was a Hill. *I'm* a Hill. Johanna Elliott never will be. My father never adopted her, and it's no business of hers what happens to Cumberland."

"I see." Ben was pondering the importance of Mary's makeup. The time she'd spent on it, that had made her good at it, that made an unattractive face almost striking. Though the expression in the eyes and mouth interested him more—the self-protection and the core of anger. "Then you think Charlotte should have left it to Leah instead of your mother?"

"No, I didn't say that, I—"

"It never would've come to you if she'd given it to Leah, to her own daughter, the way everyone expected then. Leah would've sold it and kept the money herself."

"Charlotte did what she thought best, and I was led to believe it would come to me as Charlotte's niece. As her brother's daughter. And that's what I intend will happen."

"Who led you to believe that? Not Hannah or Charlotte."

"No, but you'd expect that—"

"The deciding factor in both decisions, Charlotte's *and* your mother's, was trying to keep Cumberland a private island with very few visitors for the good of the land and the animals, as well as for the family, for the future."

"That's a very narrow view." Mary hadn't looked at Ben for some time, but she did then quickly, before glancing away.

"If Johanna found a way to give you the island, by refusing the inheritance, some way that kept her from having to pay inheritance taxes when she passed it on—and we don't know yet if that can be done—what would you do with it?"

"What would I do? Why, with the land the park already has, I'd find a way of making an agreement with them that would keep Whitfield as a private inn, and limit the visitors on the rest of the island."

"You'd keep the inn yourself, and sell the rest to them? You think they'd negotiate in good faith and be trustworthy once they got it?"

"I do. I'm sure they would. Despite what Charlotte and Hannah have said, I know for a fact they're very reasonable. I'm sure I could keep the inn for myself, and be able to control the numbers they bring on the island, in exchange for making an agreement."

"Have you studied the history of Indian reservations, or eminent domain, either one? There're a lot of consequences nobody sees ahead of time once the government takes over. I know Ed Montgomery thinks all of Cumberland should belong to the park service."

"Yes, but—"

"He didn't indicate anything like this to me, naturally, but having met his mother, I almost wonder if with him it isn't partly the Greene hostility to the Hills that's made it so important to get the land away from them. That, and the desire to profit himself. Course, he is marrying a Hill, so he may not be as prejudiced—"

"I beg your pardon?"

"You are marrying him, aren't you? I assume you must've both thought Hannah would die soon, and that that would enable you to sell Cumberland, or at least some part of it. You'd make a lot of money either way, and do what Charlotte and Hannah hated the thought of. Do you think that appealed to Ed? Edward Greene Montgomery. The final revenge of the Greenes?"

"I don't know where you get your information, but—"

"Must've been quite a shock for both of you. Not inheriting. You and Ed."

"Well, I—"

"You must not have felt a whole lot of sympathy for Hannah's wishes. Since you hadn't seen her in six years. Assuming I've got that right?" He'd been watching her face closely as he pushed her, and he saw just what he'd thought he might.

"I'd like you to leave right now. If Johanna wishes to converse with me, she may do so through my lawyers."

The phone rang as Ben was closing the door behind him, and Mary turned away from him to answer it. Ben stood outside with the door cracked, trying to listen without being seen.

"Hey, honey. I called you four or five times earlier, but...Why? Why does that matter?...Ed, honey, please, I don't want to postpone the wedding. We agreed to keep it quiet until after she...Why? What difference does it make about Cumberland, we still...No!...Suspicious in what way?...*I* see...Is that right!...Well, that kind of makes me wonder if you ever loved *me* at all, or if you were simply...No...No, honey, I trust you, but I don't understand the..."

Ben closed the door as quietly as he could, then started toward his car telling himself to ask Chester Hansen to use police channels fast and see if he could find a medical lab in Savannah or Charleston that had sold streptococcus pneumoniae to anyone, man or woman, any time in the last twelve months.

It was midnight when he got to Charleston, and it was raining hard. He found a parking spot on Church Street a block south of the house, and by the time he ran up the bricks of the side drive toward Robert and Sarah Sykes' front door, his raincoat was soaked through and water was running down his neck. He shot onto the veranda under the upstairs porch, hung his raincoat around a chair, shook the wet off his hair and slid the key in the lock.

The lights had been left on for him, and he turned them off in the hall before he quietly climbed the curving white stairs to the guest room he'd always been given.

He hung his jacket in the bathtub to let it drip.

And then stood at the foot of the bed and stared at the rain past the porch.

He knew he needed to get some sleep, but he was too restless to lie down right then. He didn't feel like reading. And he'd already planned the research he had to do the next day, on Twachtman and de La Tour and the rest, as he drove up from Savannah.

He felt cold and irritated and alone. He was tired of looking at the underside of human nature. At Alderton. To say nothing of Cumberland. And he opened his suitcase, put on a sweater, and took out a small plastic bag.

He stepped out onto the porch and lay down in the white woven hammock. He pulled out a Camel and took out the matches. And then dropped them both in the bag on his stomach, while he listened to rain rattle on the metal roof.

He thought about Hannah. And he saw Johanna's face again, pale and drawn as they'd walked in the moonlight, and the sadness that covered her every time they'd talked.

He thought about Cumberland. The behind-the-scenes manipulation. The jealousy and the ill will. The rush to justify anything to get what it is you want.

He remembered the image George Milton had used to describe Hannah. The well-meaning spider in the center of a web tying herself to the lives around her. And told himself to look at it later when he had the patience to think about details.

He thought about Alderton's new president. The look he'd had on his face when he asked Ben if anyone else knew about the will.

Which made Ben want to push it away. To get the taste of it out of his mouth. To think about something encouraging. Like what he wanted to do most—pick up the phone and ask.

He told himself not to do it. It was late.

It would give the wrong impression.

It could set things in motion that shouldn't be started.

So he lay there instead, wishing he were blowing smoke rings. Feeling his blood slapping at the hollow between his collar bones. The old squirreliness in his stomach, that came this time from knowing what he wanted and thinking it might not be wise.

He told himself not to do anything rash. For at least the fifteenth time. That being alone forever would always be better than getting somebody else involved, and deciding it wouldn't work. *Better than finding you don't want to come home to her. After leading her on out of ignorance.*

So safety first, is that it? Don't take risks. Because you know better. Protect yourself, no matter what.

What kind of life is that?

It wouldn't have gotten you halfway to Malmedy, and it wouldn't have brought you back.

Rational thought. Calculated risk. Taking charge of myself. I do that without much trouble.

Responsibility for someone else, that's what I don't do if I can avoid it. And why I wouldn't become an officer and send other people out to die.

So? Where does that get you now?

Stop worrying about what you don't know.

Listen to your gut as well as your head and do what you want to do.

Is that what this is?

Is it?

No. Not really. Not entirely.

Jessie deserves better. And always will.

I'll never have another marriage that's like the one I had with her.

True.

But you could have one that was different but good.

What would she want for you? That's worth asking.

Nothing for the rest of your life?

No one to talk to. No one to touch. No one to wake up with till you're too old to care. No one to tell you when you're wrong, or being pompous, or when you're terminally dull and boring and need to take on something new.

Jessie touched you everywhere. She took everything you could give her and gave you back more. There wasn't a cranny inside you she didn't fill. You know that. She made you whole. As much as you can be in this world.

Would she want you alone forever?

She wouldn't have wanted a man who played it safe. Not for all the wrong reasons. That I know for sure.

You haven't seen a single woman but Kate who's interested you at all since the day Jessie died.

So pick up the phone before she goes back to Scotland and say what you have to say.

He was standing in Rob's study, waiting for the operator to come on, clearing his throat, and walking back and forth as far as he could with the cord.

"Yes, operator, I'd like to place a call to a number in

Evanston, Illinois, and charge it to my home phone in Ohio." Ben gave her the numbers and waited, feeling silly, and young, while he stood there thinking about hanging up.

He heard Kate answer, and said, "Hi. It's Ben. I'm sorry to call so late. I hope I didn't wake you up...Working, huh? Why should I be surprised? How's your dad...That's good. So he may actually come home in the next few days?...Great...

"Oh, I'm trying to figure out Hannah's death. That's partly why I called. I need to talk to someone about it and there's nobody here who's not involved...You're sure? Okay, well, first of all..."

Ben tried to describe the personalities involved. The handful of facts. The situation surrounding Cumberland and the family conflicts that affected that. "But it doesn't seem to me like it's as simple as simple greed. There's something personal about it. Something twisted. Something emotional or psychological. Something I can feel under the surface, but can't see yet. Assuming that that makes any sense...Right. Some hidden intent or hatred. It's depressing to have to dwell on, but... exactly...Yes. So what about you? How are you doing with your mom and dad and all the tension there?"

Ben listened. He asked a question from time to time. And he heard the edge of coolness and hesitation she'd had when she'd answered the phone gradually melt away.

They talked again about Wales in '44. His helping her husband, Graham, train British commandos for the invasion. And the difficulty they'd had getting Graham's Scottish military papers, and her American ones too, in time for a wedding before the invasion was launched.

They talked about losing your husband in battle and never knowing what it was like for him. As opposed to losing your wife and son in childbirth, when you know entirely too much.

Then Kate said she probably ought to get to bed.

And Ben told himself to say it and pray that it would happen the way it should. "One other thing I wanted to ask you. How long do you think you'll be here? Before you go back to Scotland?...That makes sense. You might as well stay for Christmas, as long as you can work while you're here. Do you have to see your publisher in New York too?...Right. Well. I don't know if you'd want to do this—I mean, I'd certainly understand if you wouldn't—and I can't stay too long either, because I've got to get back to Alderton before term ends before Christmas. But I drove through Beaufort, South Carolina, last week, and it's a really nice small town on the coast, and I thought maybe, when I was done here, if it were convenient and you wanted to, I could book us two rooms in an inn I saw, and we could spend a weekend walking around and seeing the countryside and talking."

Ben waited. Listening to the silence on the other end. "Of course, you may not feel like you can leave your parents. I'd certainly understand that, with him as sick as he's been. And you may not be interested in spending that much time with me. That wouldn't surprise me either. I haven't talked to anyone much since Jessie died. And I'm probably not very good at it any more. But with Graham gone, and Jessie gone too, I thought maybe both of us could use somebody to talk to."

Ben nodded. And then smiled. And said, "Okay. I'll let you know how all this goes, and we'll see if the timing works. It may not, for you *or* for me. I'm going up to Tryon tomorrow, or the day after. And the murder investigation is still up in the air...Would you? Good. I'll let you know. I'll have to call you, since I'll be moving around a lot."

Ben hung up the phone and looked out at the rain and smiled to himself in the dark.

Then he shook his head, and swallowed, and asked himself what he'd done.

CHAPTER FIFTEEN

SUNDAY, NOVEMBER 26TH

BEN HAD THE TOP OF THE DESK in Robert Sykes's study covered with books about painters whose works were owned by Daniel Henderson, the donor in Tryon he was about to meet.

Claire Price, the woman who'd invited Ben to Charleston to speak to the Preservation Society of Charleston on early botanical illustrators, was a friend he'd made when he was studying conservation at the Brooklyn Museum in the fifties, who was now working in Charleston as a curator at the Gibbes Museum of Art.

She'd loaned him books of hers, and helped him track down what she didn't have at the Charleston Library, so that together they'd come up with books on the Peale family, on Chardin and Ingres, on de La Tour and John Singer Sargent, on Piero della Francesca and John Henry Twachtman, among others.

Ben had also brought magazine articles and photocopies with him on other painters in Henderson's collection. And he'd been working since six, reading and making notes, and he'd just told himself he needed to stand up and move—when the phone rang.

He yelled, "It's probably for me," and picked it up. Then thanked the operator for patching him through to Cumberland. "Morning, Amelia...Yeah, some progress. My police chief friend in Ohio will help check the hospitals and labs in Savannah and Charleston and Jacksonville. Over...Why's Johanna's voice teacher from New York coming down to Charleston?...Ah....So Johanna will take a lesson here today, and stay with her teacher and her family tonight, then go back to Cumberland tomorrow? I couldn't quite hear what you said. Over...So she'll give me a call when she gets in? Over...

"I've got copies of all the photographs with me, so that'll help. Including one of Estelle. I took it when she wasn't looking day before yesterday and got it developed in St. Mary's. I left a copy in the desk in my room for you. Could you get Estelle's personnel file and tell me who her references were, and give me their phone numbers too? Over...No, that's okay, I can wait."

Ben stood up and stretched his neck, until he said, "What d'you mean the file's gone?...Nuts. When did you see it last? Over...She never cooks breakfast, does she? Somebody else does that?...Her room's next to the office, though?...Then can you see if she's there? And check if her clothes are gone? Over...Thanks. Sure." Ben read the titles on the biography shelf in Robbie Sykes's library, while rubbing the back of his neck.

"*Everything's* gone! So she took the early boat? Over...Then what do you think about talking to the local police? Show them the clippings, take them the new photo, maybe tell them about the rumor Estelle heard Tallie telling me about Hannah's death. Keep them from thinking the rumor's true, though. Getting them involved now could slow things down a lot. Over...Right. But could you go to St. Mary's instead of doing it on the ship-to-shore? Over...Exactly. And speed is of the essence with what you and I are both doing. I'll call you later tonight. Thanks, Amelia. Over."

All I evuh wanted was to keep folks from sufferin' like Mama did. Dyin' in agony. Swellin' up and screamin'. I'll nevuh forget that. I'll still be picturin' it the day I die.

Daddy too, sittin' on the sofa drinkin' whiskey. Head in his hands sayin' "Why?" and cussin' like he was tellin' some real person somewhere what he could do with himself real quick.

No one should suffuh like Miz Hannah did eithuh. Not when you can set a person free. She deserved to be released, and it shouldda happened a good deal soonuh.

But I cain't hardly stand to be runnin' again. 'Leven years of runnin'. 'Leven years of gettin' old. And gettin' weary livin'. 'Fraid to even talk to folks, case I let somethin' slip.

Gotta get work first. And that's not gonna be real easy, startin' over with a new name. Course, with all the...What is that man doin' ovuh there?

Estelle was squinting across the bus station at the Negro side, watching a man with his hands twitching in his lap and a deranged look on a worn and dissipated face as he followed one woman and then another with hot irrational eyes.

Don't look, honey. It won't do you any good. Bus stations can be real weird. 'Specially in big cities like Jacksonville. Folks walkin' in off the streets who don't have no place to go.

What was I thinkin' 'bout before? Gettin' me a new name.

Gonna be hard to change aftuh bein' Estelle for seven years. Harduh, the older I get. All the lyin' you have to do. Nevuh gettin' close to nobody. Guardin' yourself 'gainst your own heart. 'Long with all the work problems. Like gettin' me a Social Security card.

Least Mama can't see what's happened. I wouldda hated that. She was such a fine person. Kind and sweet-tempered. I started out good 'cause of her. But then she went and left me. And kidney trouble like hers, it's one of the worst ways to go.

Course, I managed all on my own, when lots of folks would-n't've. Took that insurance money aftuh Daddy died, and got me through nurse's trainin'. Bein' a nurse was everythin' to me, 'cause of her. And now I'll nevuh nurse anyone again.

Least I did what I thought was right. Lots of folks cain't say that. And that's some satisfaction.

Still see Blackie with lumps all ovuh him. Daddy takin' him off to the vet's. Shootin' him in the yard, so he wouldn't feel pain again. Mama cryin' all that day with her own pain. Me askin' Daddy why he didn't help. Made him feel awful, but I didn't know. I wasn't but eight years old.

Nevuh did ask him latuh. Nevuh could say, "How could you up and leave me the day aftuh Mama's funeral?" Nary a word from him in four weeks' time. Me eatin' canned fruit and stale cookies and not knowin' what to do. Gettin' myself to school like nothin' happened. Nevuh tellin' nobody he'd gone off and left.

Don't know why I'm thinkin' about it so much today. But I gotta make myself stop.

*There were folks bettuh off at that hospital 'cause of me, no mat-tuh what anybody evuh says. Wasn't me put the needle in their veins, anyway. Just talked to Annabelle and told her how **I'd** do for people in pain if I was on the wards instead of surgery.*

*It **was** pretty clevuh. Seein' how you could draw morphine out* of a supply bottle just like usual, whatevuh dose was prescribed for whatevuh patient, then inject some of everybody's portion in anothuh dose bottle you'd hide away till you got you enough to ease somebody's pain for good. Course Annabelle **couldda** thought of that herself. It wasn't **my** fault she did what she did. But I'm glad she did it. Specially aftuh what she'd been through the way her husband died.

My mistake was writin' Paul aftuh he finished his residency. Wantin' him to see how special I was 'cause I could do what he just talked about. I felt so bad aftuh he went. Him stayin' with his wife the way he did.

Course, I nevuh did say right out that I was the one that'd done the mercy killin'. Just hinted at it round about when I sent the two obituaries. Nevuh thought in my wildest dreams he'd call the hospital pathologist and tell him to look again.

If his wife hadn't been rich, it would've been different. Puttin' him through medical school like she did. If **I'd** been rich, he wouldda stayed with me. He loved me. I know he did. Lot more than he evuh did her.

It's tough standin' up for what you believe. But I know the time will come when we'll be able to ease our loved ones' dyin' for their own good. I reckon there might be one or two who'd do it for some othuh reason. To inherit somethin'. Or get their relatives outta their hair. But I cain't believe there're too many folks who'd kill their relations for selfish reasons.

Like Daddy said, if there **was** a good God you could count on, you wouldn't have to take mattuhs into your own hands. But there isn't. Anyone lookin' could see that. Even him, the son of a preachuh.

How Miz Hannah could see it so different I nevuh will understand. Layin' there the way she did. Year after year.

What I gotta decide now is what am I gonna do once I get to

Nashville? Find me some sleazy short-orduh place? Where they don't care 'bout references and government cards, and start all ovuh again?

I want to go back to Orlando. I want to move into the old house on Marks Street. Get me a lab like Blackie. Get me a job in a nursin' home, maybe. Though aftuh you been a scrub nurse, cleanin' bed-pans wouldn't be much fun.

Sometimes I almost start to wonderin' if I oughtta go to the police. I didn't do nothin'. Just talked to Annabelle was all. Even if they call it bein' an "accessory" like they did, they couldn't keep me in for long. They can't prove I knew what she'd do. They can't prove anything.

You bettuh go ahead and eat your lunch early. Bus'll be in shortly. 'Membuh to buy you some hair dye in Nashville before you get a room at the Y.

"This your paper bag, ma'am?" He was wearing a shiny blue suit, and he had gray hair and a gray mustache and looked to be close to seventy. There were heavy gold rings on both his hands, and there was a dirty gray cowboy hat pushed to the back of his head above bloodshot eyes that had been watching Estelle stare off into space above the waiting room. He handed her the lunch she'd dropped on the floor and touched his hat when she thanked him. He moved a little closer too, across the slick plastic bench, as soon as he saw her smile.

"What are you doing in Charleston?" Johanna Elliott was gazing at Charleston Harbor, walking north with Ben up East Bay from the Battery past a row of large old planters' houses.

"Researching a lot of painters to get ready to meet a donor

in North Carolina. So tell me about Mary. What was she like as a kid?"

"Well. She was crazy about dolls. Ones that had outfits she could change. And she started buying wedding magazines when she was twelve or thirteen. She'd still cry then when she got dirt on her good clothes. And she spent a lot of time trying to make people admire her daddy. Telling everybody who'd listen when he got invited up to Jekyll. When she was in high school, she spent every waking minute she could at the country club, playing bridge and dancing, and not understanding why Hannah didn't."

"Ah."

"She wanted to be admired. More than most people do, I think. But what that comes from I don't know. Her daddy wasn't respected much by folks around town, and Hannah was. And I think Mary resented that."

"How's she deal with money?"

"She put everything you can think of on layaway in high school. And spent money that should've gone for college on clothes or furniture or jewelry."

"She puts an awful lot of energy into how she looks now, and you're a lot better looking, so that must've irritated her. You came into her house and took part of her mother's affection, more than she wanted to share, I'm sure, and made her look plain when you did it."

"There's not that big a difference in how we look, *I* don't think. She was born knowing what to do with herself, and I've had to learn by trial and error. She was heavier then, as a little girl, and as a teenager too. But never as heavy as Leah was. And not as unattractive. Leah had a harder time than she did. I don't mean in comparison to me, but in general. And I believe

Mary enjoyed that. It made her feel much better that the wealthy Hill-MacKinnons, the ones who hadn't squandered their money like her father had, who were catered to and looked up to, had a daughter who didn't get along with people and wasn't very attractive. Leah's much thinner now, and I know she's really worked at that."

"Could Mary be talked into doing something shady by Eddie Montgomery?"

"I s'ppose. If she loves him. She loves beautiful things, and she's never had the money to buy them the way she wants. I expect that matters to her more than it does to most of us. But I don't see her as being dishonest. And I can't imagine her killing Hannah. There's a big difference between not going to visit your mother and deciding to actually murder her."

"What can you tell me about Eddie?"

"Well, I'd say he bore the brunt of his mother's ways *and* his daddy's. His father was a handsome man, tall and distinguished looking, but he was from one of the mill-hand families, and I guess I'd have to say he wasn't particularly intelligent. They were good simple people, but they didn't have much in common with Eddie's mother and her Greene relations."

"And everybody knew that."

"Yes. People thought it was pretty funny, her marrying him. Getting swept up by the way he looked. That's what everybody figured. And then she hounded him, and corrected him, and belittled him for not being what she wanted till the day he died. He worked at the gas station mostly, pumping gas and filling tires, and it never was good enough for her."

"Not a great situation in which to raise a kid."

"No. Eddie got caught between them. Half-ashamed of his

dad, and irritated by his mother, and tired of being the butt of jokes around St. Mary's. He put on his own airs, in his own way. And seemed to grow up feeling hostile to whoever had money. He went out and stumped for every politician who said he'd take it from those who had it and give it to those who didn't. But he talked all the time too about wanting to make money himself, and how he was going to do it. Somehow I guess it seemed different to him if *he* was the one with money. I actually felt sorry for him, growing up. What I saw of him. He's ten or twelve years older. Older than Leah or Mary."

"Did Mary ever try to hurt you?"

"Depends on what you mean. They've fixed up most of the houses in this block since I was here last." Johanna was moving her purse from one shoulder to another, staring at a four-story beige stucco house with black shutters.

"Do I take it you're trying to avoid the question?" Ben was smiling at her, looking at her straight on, his gray eyes asking the question as much as his wide easy mouth.

"Children *are* mean. Anyone with eyes, or any kind of a memory at all, knows that very well."

They'd come to the corner of Tradd and East Bay, and they stood for a minute gazing across at Fort Sumter listening to drifts of conversation, to the laughter of a couple with their arms around each other, to someone singing in a high thin voice halfway down a side street.

Ben still managed to watch Johanna, and when he saw she was getting herself ready to say something, he stopped himself from interrupting.

"Mary locked me in a closet once, from early morning till it was dark that night, when Hannah had gone to help a neighbor lady who'd just come home from the hospital. I was five, probably. Or maybe six. It wasn't long after my parents were killed in a car accident and I'd come to live with Hannah."

"How old was Mary?"

"Nine, I think. Her daddy was supposed to stay home to watch us, or Hannah would've taken us with her, but he left right after she did. It was a hot day in the middle of the summer, and Mary locked me in a linen closet. She let me out before Hannah came home. She rinsed me off in the tub, and gave me a glass of water, and told me not to tell."

"Did you?"

"No. Mary said she'd kill me. Said she'd drown me in the St. Mary's River. I didn't tell Hannah till years later."

"Did you think she'd do it?"

"I don't think I did. But I knew she'd make my life miserable, and I didn't want to get locked in that closet again."

"Were you terrified of her after that?"

"Maybe not as much as you might expect. I saw what she did to me as a sign that something was wrong with her. That whatever it was that made her want to do that meant she was weak in a way I wasn't. I didn't *need* to be that mean. I wasn't that weird or that damaged. Does that make sense? That doesn't mean I wasn't afraid of her. I was. I knew she could make my life painful, but it wasn't as scary as it could've been."

"Did Hannah know what was going on between you and Mary?"

"She understood the general situation. She just didn't have all the details."

"Would you say Mary felt outshone by you?" The wind was blowing hard coming off the water, and Ben was buttoning his corduroy jacket.

"I don't think so. She was very artistic. Visual in a way I'm not."

"Did she care that you could sing?"

"Didn't seem to. Leah might've cared more about that. She tried out for some parts in musicals before she went north to boarding school and didn't like not getting them. Mary seemed more concerned about whether people she liked liked me…if I got invited somewhere she wanted to go, or someone said something complimentary."

"How was Leah about that?"

"Leah was a Hill. Charlotte Hill and Rafe MacKinnon's daughter. That meant something in St. Mary's in the 1930s when she was born, and the '40s when I came to live with Hannah. She got pulled in both directions, spoiled and resented too. She was unattractive and heavy, and she threw her weight around at school—"

"Pardon the pun."

"Yes, which didn't endear her to anyone. I think she did a lot better when she went up north to boarding school and could start over with people with backgrounds like hers. Does any of this make any sense? In terms of Hannah's death?"

"I have no idea, but it gives me a clearer picture of who everybody is. How did Leah treat you when she came back?"

"Fine. She ignored me pretty much when I was in junior high and high school. When I first moved here as a kid, she wasn't any too pleased with me, but that was pretty much my fault."

"Why?"

"We were over on Cumberland—we went there fairly often for a weekend, or when Hannah had a day off—and I was playing with Leah's dollhouse up in the old luggage room in the attic where I'm staying now. Leah's family lived in Whitfield then. They didn't move to Four Chimneys till Charlotte turned Whitfield into an inn. I guess I was five then, when Leah was ten, and she got bored with me. She went downstairs somewhere, and I did one of those really stupid things little kids do because they don't understand what'll happen." Johanna pulled her sweater together across her chest and held her hair back against the wind.

"Are you warm enough?"

"It would feel good to get out of the wind."

They turned their backs on the water then, and walked west down Tradd Street—till Ben asked Johanna again what it was she'd done in the attic.

"Well, it was winter, and I remember it was getting dark out, and I thought the dollhouse would look really beautiful if there were lights in it like a real house. There were candles up there in a box for when the electricity went out. There were always candles in every room 'cause the generator broke pretty often. And I lit two or three candles and put them in the dollhouse.

"They caught the house on fire, of course, and we had to pour water all over it to put it out. I had a glass with me, but we had to bring the rest from the second floor, and we were lucky I didn't burn Whitfield down. The dollhouse was ruined. And Leah was furious. Really angry. She loved that dollhouse, with all the fine furniture and the draperies and the dishes. Her Hill grandmother had given it to her, and she'd really loved that grandmother, who'd died when Leah was four or five. Shall we walk north on Church?"

"Sure. Did she do anything about it? Try to pay you back in any way?"

Johanna laughed like she meant it for the first time since Hannah's funeral. "You may not believe this, but she measured me the next day with a tape measure, head to toe, and then two or three hours later she asked me to walk to the beach with her. You know how there're tree roots that stick up across the path? She'd dug the dirt down in front of one of them and buried a rusty coffee can in the sand on the other side so the rim stuck up an inch or so above the ground right where my face would land when I fell."

"Geez. Did you get hurt?"

"No. I could see Leah was acting funny, getting me out there to go for a walk when she never wanted me to go with her anywhere, so I knew something was going on. Then I could see the path had been dug up, and I saw the coffee can, and I stepped right on over it and looked her in the eye."

"So she knew you knew?"

"She knew. And I don't remember her ever doing anything like that again."

They'd walked across Broad to Washington Park, and they sat on a green wooden bench without saying anything for a minute, watching the faces and the feet go past the obelisk dedicated to Confederate dead, listening to two elderly gentlemen on the bench beside them talk about the Depression and how they'd squeaked through.

"By junior high we got along fine. It didn't even bother Leah when Garrett Aiken started asking me out, after I'd graduated from high school. They'd gone out a few times before that, but I don't think it meant anything to her. They only went to some formal dinner or some dance up at Sea Island or somewhere when she was home from boarding school and had to dig up somebody to go with and wanted it to be someone good-looking, to irritate the other girls."

"Garrett filled the bill, did he?"

"Oh, yeah. Garrett was very good-looking. By the time he'd graduated from college and was working to pay for law school, they didn't go out at all. And I never had the feeling she cared about him. She dated someone up north where she went to college, and that was much more serious. Mary really liked Garrett, though. I think there was a time she wanted to marry him. And when she was in high school and part of college, she asked him to the same sort of society things Leah did, and I think he went more often."

"You had a lot to get over as a kid, didn't you? Your parents' deaths. Being resented by Mary and Leah. Sounds to me like you coped well."

"Whatever I did came from Hannah helping me. Explaining people's feelings. Giving me standards based on something solid that never changed, so I knew how I *ought* to behave even when I didn't want to. She made me feel loved in all kinds of ways. Because she *was* tough on me, that was part of it. Her expecting good behavior and caring enough to take the trouble."

"Hannah was a wise lady."

"It's odd, when you think about it. I did better when my parents died than I'm doing now. Garrett's death wasn't easy. But ever since Hannah died, I've felt like the one person I could count on for perspective and advice is gone, and I don't know if I can live the way I want to without her."

"Why wouldn't it be tough? She was your mother for most of your life, in all the ways that count every day. Your advisor *and* your mentor too. And maybe it's the combination. Her and Garrett and your parents. Grief is like that anyway. Like a large part of your body and brain have been amputated, and whatever's left doesn't function much, except to register pain."

"I can't concentrate. I'm doing stupid things. I'm more disoriented than I've ever been except—"

"What have you been doing that's so stupid?"

Johanna looked at Ben sideways, her finely drawn face, oval and well proportioned, her large blue eyes uneasy behind dark lashes, her soft red lips tucked sideways in indecision, as she pushed her black leather headband back through her shoulder-length hair.

"Oh, come on, what am I going to think that matters either way?" Ben said. "I've never done anything silly that I couldn't sympathize?"

"It's embarrassing. It makes me sound like a nitwit."

"So?"

"All right. I'll tell you if you promise not to laugh."

Johanna was watching a little boy in a dark blue coat with mittens dangling from his cuffs squatting on the bricks, trying to pick up a penny. "You ready to walk? There's a great grocery store not far from here, and I want to buy something special to take to my voice teacher's family."

"Sure. And I'll promise not to laugh if it makes you feel better."

"On Cumberland, the day of the funeral—or the day after, I don't remember which—I took a shower in the morning, and went back into my bedroom to make the bed and found sand between the sheets like I'd forgotten to wash my feet the night before. Which wasn't true. I'd cleaned my shoes downstairs, and rinsed my feet before I went to bed. I went downstairs to get clean sheets, and when I came back and started to pull off the old ones, there wasn't any sand on them anywhere."

"Really?" The bells in the old Episcopal church at Meeting Street and Broad rang the quarter hour. And then Ben asked Johanna what else had happened.

"At lunch that same day, I took a sandwich and a book of arias out to one of the tables in front under the oaks. I wanted to eat alone and go over the *Fledermaus* score, and I set the book on the table with the sandwich and went in to get some orange juice. When I came back, the book was gone. I knew I'd put it down there, but it wasn't anywhere to be found.

"I went all the way up to the attic where I'm staying, then down to the basement floor to the kitchen where I'd made my lunch, and asked everybody in there if they'd seen the music. Then I went out again to the table, and *there* was the music next to the sandwich right where I thought I'd left it."

"So that's all that happened?"

"Isn't that enough?"

"Well…"

"I wrote Amelia a note too thanking her for everything she did for Hannah, and everything she does at the inn, and telling her how hard I think it's going to be while we fight the park, and that I appreciate the support she's giving me in that, and I put it on her desk. When she didn't say anything about it, I asked her if she'd gotten it, and she said she'd never laid eyes on it. So I'm not sure whether I actually wrote it, or just planned it in my head and thought I had."

"When was it that all this happened? It's important. Was it the day of the funeral, or the day after, or the day after that?"

Ben and Johanna had crossed Broad at Savage Street, and had just stopped in front of Burbage's Grocery, when Johanna said, "It must've been the day after the funeral. Yes, because then you and I walked to the beach that night. I wrote the note when I got back, I *thought*, and took it down to her desk right before I went to bed."

"You're not losing your mind, Johanna. Somebody's decided to play games with it."

"You're sure?"

"Fairly sure."

"Why would someone do that?"

"I don't know. And whether it's more than that is definitely worth considering."

"You mean someone put sand in my bed? And then changed the sheets?"

"Are you saying you imagined the sand?"

"No. I mean I don't think I did, but—"

"Who would want to scare you? Or hurt you in some way?"

"I don't know. I really *don't* know. There're always singers who want parts they don't get, but I can't see how that would apply to this."

"Anyone in love with you?"

"No. No, not since Garrett."

"No spurned suitor making your life miserable?"

"No one."

"Who was at the funeral or was still on Cumberland the next day who's hostile enough to do something like that?"

"Nobody I can think of."

"What about Red Johnson or Adam Clark?"

"I get along fine with both of them."

"Estelle Baxter? You ever had trouble with her?"

"No."

"How were Mary and Leah at the funeral?"

"Fine. Leah was very nice. She's been a lot more pleasant

for years than she was when we were kids. Mary was awkward and kind of defensive because she'd been so estranged from Hannah. And I'm the one that had to tell her Hannah loved her right to the end. But Mary and I still had a perfectly reasonable conversation. We'll never be the best of friends, but it's not a hostile relationship."

"Even after she knew you inherited Cumberland?"

"That's true. She was upset about that, yes." Neither of them said anything for a minute. They both stood and stared at the food arranged in the windows. "Where are you going tomorrow? Where in North Carolina?"

"Tryon. I'll keep in touch, though. I'll call Cumberland every day. I'll be at the Pine Crest Inn. Amelia has the number, so call me if you need me. How long are you staying on Cumberland?"

"All this week. I think till Saturday. After Thanksgiving anyway. Charlotte's sister lives in Tryon, you know. Susanna Hill Smith. Her husband's a surgeon in Asheville. He spends a few days a week with her in Tryon, and the rest working in Asheville. She's the one whose children sold the land to Eddie. I guess I better get my shopping done. I have to get back before dinner."

"Thanks for taking the time to talk to me."

"Don't even think about saying that, when it's you who's helping us."

CHAPTER SIXTEEN

MONDAY, NOVEMBER 27TH

IT REMINDED BEN OF SCOTLAND, the land around Tryon—the narrow roads winding around soft green hills, the patches of woods cutting across them, the cool crisp moist fall air, the smell of wood smoke as you swept around a curve, the high mountains blue in the distance, the stone walls by small simple houses built in shapes born in Britain hundreds of years before.

Ben smiled to himself as he passed a horse dozing in the middle of a field, then looked for a drive on the left between the split-rail fences and crepe myrtles Henderson had described on the phone.

He slowed the car down a steep hill, till he came to the gravel lane, then climbed for half a mile, curving gently between rolling grassy hills, passing an old wooden barn, and parking a hundred yards farther on in front of a long log cabin sitting parallel to the drive on the right.

A second after Ben slammed his car door by a red Chevy pickup, a Dutch door opened in a smaller cabin, past and perpendicular to the house, and a black-and-white Border collie shot toward Ben, followed by a tall man in tan work pants and a green-and-black plaid shirt.

"Jeb won't bother you. He'll stay down."

"Hi, Jeb. How you doing? You're a good boy, aren't you?" Ben leaned over and patted Jeb's head, then scratched him under his black-and-white chin.

"I put on a pot of coffee. Figured you might could use you a cup after the drive from Asheville."

"Thank you, Mr. Henderson. I'd like that. This is a great piece of land."

"Call me Daniel. Mr. Henderson was my daddy." His blue eyes were smiling slyly at Ben, a blue so bright it was startling against his darkly tanned and freckled face.

"Thanks, I will." Ben was staring at the lean, low-looking shake-roofed house with four stone chimneys and a shed-roofed porch on either side of the front door. "Is it several cabins put together?"

"Three whole cabins, and parts of two others. All of 'em old. My wife designed it. She had a real good eye for business. Y'have to see the back to get the whole picture. She was a painter. Nobody you wouldda heard of, but *I* thought she was real good. Studied it at your university. That's why I'm givin' you folks some of the pictures Mr. Winthrop give me. Passin' 'em on to you in her memory. 'Gift of Hazel Remington Henderson.' That's what I want the plaques to say."

"We appreciate it very much. *I* certainly do, as the archivist."

"Quite a story, way I got them pictures. Nothin' nobody would've thought would happen. All the Winthrop paintings, Mr. Clarence's and Mr. Stephen's, comin' to me, the gardener.

Wonder what Mr. Clarence wouldda said if he knew. Mind if I ask you a question?"

"Of course not."

"I don't mean it to sound rude or nothin', but why've they sent you? Somebody who works in the library?"

Ben explained the parts of his training as an archivist that applied—his postdoc degree in painting conservation, his experience in dating and identifying works of art.

Daniel Henderson nodded and said, "Then that makes real good sense. So how you wantta go about this? Want me to take you in and let you see the ones I'm thinkin' you might could have? Let you look 'em over in Hazel's studio? It's over yonder by the workshop."

"That'd be great. I can hardly wait, actually. So you want me to look at the paintings you've put aside, and then decide—"

"Pick you the eight or ten you'd want from what's there. Whatever you think your school could best use. I've got other paintings I haven't decided what to do with. Old European pictures, most of 'em. Got to take my time decidin'."

"It's really good of you to do this."

"Nope. No sir. Nothin' to be said for my part in this. You'll see why later. I'll bring you a cuppa coffee over to where you'll be workin'."

Ben spent more than four hours examining the thirty-two paintings hanging or leaning against walls, or lying on work tables in the big open barnlike studio attached to Daniel Henderson's workshop.

Ben had moved from one to the next (notebook in one

hand, magnifying glass in the other), studying the size, the subject, the signature (if there was one), the paint surface, the pigments, the brush strokes, any evidence of restoration, the construction of the frame in front and back (the type of wood, the corner wedges used, how the fabric had been attached to the stretchers—iron tacks, steel tacks, staples, or something else), the canvas itself (or the paper, or the wood, or the paper attached to wood or canvas), counting threads when there were threads, identifying the content (European linen or some sort of cotton)—comparing what he saw with his own eyes to the detailed descriptions in the technical files that applied to each painting.

Ben would write his own observations on a painting in his notebook, add additional information from its technical file, pointing out any differences between the two, before he started on the provenance material on that particular painting.

Those files told him each painting's history—who painted it, what was known about the painter, when it was painted, when it was sold, who bought it and for how much, where and when it had gone from there, when and where it had been exhibited, how it had been shipped (if noted), estimated value (ancient and modern), references to it in books and articles, photographs and/or sketches of it made over the years, and what it was currently insured for. Ben would write that information in his own notebook—then go to the next painting.

It was an interesting group of paintings, this part of the Winthrop collection, which a liberal arts university like Alderton could use well. There were three idiosyncratic watery landscapes in oil by John Henry Twachtman, the nineteenth-century American impressionist—all of which Ben would've loved to hang on his own walls.

There was *Peacock in the Woods*, a beautiful example of the art of camouflage by Abbott Thayer, the father of camouflage, who helped the army in World War I (whose approach was used and expanded during World War II).

There were fine American landscapes, mostly painted in the '20s, by plein air schools in California, New York, and Pennsylvania.

And a wonderful collection of small oil landscape sketches from the eighteenth and nineteenth centuries that had been painted as notes for large formalized works by John Constable, Albert Bierstadt, Thomas Moran, and others.

Henderson had set out five really fine important portraits—Georges de La Tour's *The Magdalene at the Mirror*, Jean-Siméon Chardin's *The Washerwoman*, Rembrandt Peale's *Rubens Peale with a Geranium*, and two miniatures by Sir Henry Raeburn, which appeared to be his earliest known work.

The Peale, the de La Tour, and the Chardin were obviously worth a great deal of money. Any university would be glad to have them for that reason alone. But Ben saw interesting possibilities for student work as well with several of the other paintings.

The whole collection was staggering. And Ben sat on a stool in the center of the room and stared for the pleasure of it for half an hour.

"Let me know when you're ready for another cup."

They were sitting on a porch behind the dining room in the back of the house, watching the sun streak across the back slope, watching the field shake and shiver when the wind touched the woods below and to the left of them, shifting shadows across the grass and the wild flowers scattered through it—watching two ewes and a young lamb crop their way around the meadow.

"Thanks, but I haven't finished this cup." Ben sighed and sipped his coffee and sat quietly for a minute. "I'm glad you've got sheep. The land looks like parts of Scotland, and the sheep fit."

"Folks say that's one reason so many of the Scotch settled round here, that it reminded 'em of home. I wouldn't know. Never got over there, myself. Always kinda wanted to see the gardens in England and Scotland."

"*I* think they're worth the trip. Especially for someone who gardens like you do."

"Sheep've given Jeb a new lease on life." Jeb was lying beside Daniel Henderson's rocker, staring hard at the ewes and the lamb as though they were his responsibility even at such a distance, and nothing they did would escape his attention. "Give him somethin' worthwhile to do beside torment the 'possums and the 'coons. Had to fence two fields with pig wire inside the split rail, but it cut down on the mowin'. Gave me more time in my own gardens."

"I'd like to look at your gardens while I'm here."

Daniel nodded his large broad head, his face creased and worn looking, the copper hair faded, but without the first sign of gray, even though he was probably seventy. "Herbs are by the studio. Got perennial beds all over the place. Shade garden's on the edge of the woods."

"And you're still a gardener by profession?"

"Been workin' all my life at it. Worked for Clarence Winthrop and his son, Stephen, after him, for forty-five years or more. 'Spected to work for Mr. Roy too, Mr. Stephen's only boy, but never got the chance. He was killed in Korea in fifty-two. I 'member the telegram comin' like it come this mornin'."

"Too many telegrams since 1914."

"That's the truth. Course, some wars you gotta fight."

"Oh yeah, some wars you gotta fight."

Daniel Henderson pulled a pipe out of the breast pocket of his wool shirt and tamped fresh tobacco into the bowl. "Miz Sylvia Winthrop passed away right after that, right after her son died. Brain tumor. Lost her reason before the end. Wasted away right quick. Real hard on Mr. Stephen. He held on three more years, then went on yonder too."

"How'd the Winthrops make their money?"

"Up in New England with a foundry makin' farm tools to begin with, then motors and engines durin' the First War. Got into tractors in later years, till they took up the war effort in the '40s."

"Ah."

"Mr. Stephen sold the business in '49 to some big concern up north, and spent his last years givin' money away and buying art like his daddy had before him. He'd always been one to collect paintin's. Mr. Clarence got him started. But he gave it more attention once he sold the business. After Roy died, and Miz Sylvia, Mr. Stephen kinda give up hope somehow. You could see he wasn't gonna last long. Course he wasn't no spring chicken. Seventy-six when he passed away, but before Roy died, he looked to last forever. After that, Mr. Stephen gave a couple paintings to some museums. Big paintings. Famous ones. And then one day *he* was given a painting he wouldn't've traded for anything." Daniel Henderson lit his pipe, then sat and stared at the back field as though he'd forgotten Ben was there.

"What painting was that?"

Henderson glanced at Ben with a closed and quiet smile. "I was up at the house that day. Workin' in the front, clippin' boxwood with another fella, when this young boy drove up askin' to see Mr. Stephen. Mr. Stephen was readin' on the side terrace, and I took the boy round to him. He was usin' a cane and limpin' real bad, carrying this package all done up in brown paper.

"Mr. Stephen called to me after he'd opened it, told me to come see, 'cause it was a painting of young Mr. Roy. Face and shoulders. Wearing battle gear. Smeared with dirt and blood. It weren't the kind of paintin' Mr. Stephen collected. My wife didn't call it a good paintin', but you could see Roy's likeness, and the young man standing there had painted it and brought it yonder. Said that Roy had saved his life, had carried him out of the line of fire back to their own camp. Roy'd died bringin' him in. Shot in the back by somebody."

"Really?"

"The young man, Bobbie Tillotson his name was, he wanted Roy's daddy to have the picture, and his daddy was right glad to have it." Daniel sucked on his pipe five or six times blowing rich-smelling spicy apple smoke into the afternoon breeze.

"When was this?"

"1953. After Miz Sylvia had passed away. More coffee?"

"Thanks."

Henderson came back with a steaming mug and set it on the table by Ben. "You know what the old gentleman did? Mr. Stephen walked in the house and took down a paintin' in his livin' room up above the mantelpiece, and hung that paintin' of his boy. Took down somethin' by somebody famous. Don't recollect who. Somethin' French with fruit."

"So how'd you get the paintings?"

"Well sir, after Mr. Stephen died, the lawyer announced that accordin' to the will, all the artwork had to be auctioned off. You can just imagine all the museums and the collectors who come down here chompin' at the bit. The Winthrop Collection was famous, I guess, all over the world. And the day come, and they was all there in the livin' room at the house, and the lawyer was there with the auctioneer, and they started the biddin' with the picture of young Roy.

"I was there. I come to try to get me a memento of the family, and I wanted the picture of Roy. Figured too that in a few years time nobody'd remember Roy. Hardly any Winthrops left, none that really knew him. And Hazel and me, we wanted to remember him. Everybody kinda snickered when the painting of Roy was bein' held up, and it got my goat. Bid five dollars for that paintin', and nobody bid against me. The auctioneer, he called out, 'Sold to the gentleman in the seventh row.' And then he said, 'Thank you, ladies and gentleman, that concludes the auction.'"

"Why?"

"Well, nobody could b'lieve their ears. They got to grumblin', and then the lawyer got up to talk. He said, 'Stephen Winthrop's will provides that whoever buys the painting of his son will be made a gift of the rest of the estate—lands, buildings, works of art, and all other effects.'" Daniel Henderson shook his head like he still couldn't believe it, and stroked Jeb's muzzle.

"That's amazing."

"Yep."

"So you didn't know anything about it ahead of time?"

"No sir, I didn't. Mr. Stephen kept it secret. It was the last line of the will that explained it. 'Whoever seeks the Son will be given everything, pressed down and overflowing.' Comes from somewhere in the Bible. He was a real religious man, Mr. Stephen. If you can see your way to what I mean."

"Do you think he knew that you'd want to buy that painting?"

"Don't know. Don't reckon he could've. Maybe he wondered what I'd do. He knew I had a feelin' for Roy. Roy used to come over to our house a lot. Him and Hazel were real close. Hazel, she lost six babies altogether. Miscarriages or stillborn. Mightta been part of why we thought so much of Roy."

"So what've you done with your inheritance?"

"I sold the big house to some folks from Brevard. Kept five hundred acres between my place here and theirs, though. Added it to what I had to let it stay wild. Then give most of the house money to the charities Mr. Stephen cared about. That's what would've happened if nobody'd bid on Roy's picture. Everythin' wouldda been sold, and the money given to his charities around the world. That's what I did in his name."

"Good for you. Too bad more people don't."

"Quite a few folks do. More than you'd think, I guess. Hazel read where some real famous guy who plays the cello, a guy from Europe who's kinda old now, he said that what he liked about America, that everywhere you go, small towns everywhere, some rich family built a library or a concert hall or an art museum, but that hardly ever happened in Europe where he come from."

"Pablo Casals maybe?"

"Yep, exactly who it was. I used some of the money to care for Hazel. She got cancer. Got pretty bad 'fore we knew it, and

she passed away last year. Sold some of the paintings. Ones I
didn't much like. Gave some to some museums, and then
decided to give some to Alderton. Hazel had to work real hard
to get through school. Took her a long time. She was from
Ohio. Down by Marietta. She spoke real highly of the teachers
at your school, and the work she done there. Said she
would've wanted our children to go there. If they'd wanted to
too. If some of 'em had lived. And I bet I know what you're
thinkin'."

"Do you?"

"It's what everybody thinks, even if they're too polite to
come right out with it. Why would some real educated
woman, a painter who got to Europe and saw all that art there
in Italy and France, why would she marry some fella like me?
A farm boy who's spent his life hoein' in the dirt and never
been much of anywhere."

"That's not what I was thinking."

"No? That's what *I* thought near every day I lived with her."

"I guess I think I understand something about what she
saw."

Daniel Henderson looked sideways at Ben as he knocked
his pipe out in a clay saucer sitting on the cedar table.

"Look at the way you did the tree line over there. You're an
artist. You work with plants instead of paints. And you care
about what's important."

"I don't know 'bout that."

"Don't you?"

"So'd you decide what paintin's you want?"

"Not completely. I need to talk to the man who's head of
the fine art department at Alderton and discuss it with him. If
it were up to me, I wouldn't necessarily take the most valuable

paintings. I don't want to pick a painting that'll go in the president's office just so he can show off."

"That's good."

"I'd want to take the ones that can really help students see how great painters work. So I've got to consult with other people, and give it some more thought. Could I come back for a while tomorrow?"

"Sure. And you're welcome to stay to supper tonight."

"Thanks. I appreciate it, but I've already been invited to have dinner with relatives of someone I know from Cumberland. Susanna Smith and her husband. I think I may need directions."

"She asked me to work for her some this summer, but I don't have any extry time. She's got horses. Puts a lotta store by 'em. I'll have to draw you up a map. Lotta the roads aren't marked."

CHAPTER SEVENTEEN

"IT'S A NICE ARENA." BEN WAS WALKING DOWN a steep green hill from a large, expensive, not-very-interesting house toward a covered dressage ring and an elaborate barn surrounded by three large paddocks where two dark bays and a smaller gray were watching them walk down the path.

"It's hot here in the summer, and I'd lose too much riding time if the arena wasn't covered. My trainers come here, and I don't have to trailer the horses. It took a long time to get the footing right, but it was worth the time and money."

"I'll bet." Ben looked sideways at Susanna Smith, Charlotte Hill MacKinnon's sister, who was short and very thin, veins and tendons cutting through skin, making her look stringy and shriveled, the bones of her face so uncovered it made him think of mummified parchment stretched across a skull. Making him wonder how old she was too, and whether or not she was well. Seventy at least, Amelia had said. Always a perfectionist. And always driven.

"I just got a new jumping saddle, and it's making a big difference. I think the old one was restricting Dawn Dancer when he jumped. Pinching him across the withers."

"That wouldn't help, would it?"

"I'm hunting with the Tryon Hounds, and I belong to the Tryon Riding and Hunt Club, and I'm planning to start another hunt next year. Though how much I get out depends on how Spencer shapes up this next spring. Spencer's my hunter. The smaller bay. I have trouble keeping him sound, but when he's working, he'll tuck himself up and jump pretty much anything. Dawn Dancer's the one who's made to do dressage. I need a new dressage saddle for him too, *plus* a new trainer. I'd like to develop him as a three-day-eventor. He's a timid jumper, though, even though he's athletic, so I have to wait and see. Of course, if Spencer's sound, I may try to ride him in the Block House Steeplechase in April."

"Really?" Ben was wondering why someone her age would push herself that hard at riding that dangerous. Or whether it was because she *was* at least seventy. And time was running out.

"I judge at some of the local events as well, but that's a thankless task, believe me. Do you show?"

"I never really wanted to. I worked with a good dressage teacher, and did some cross-country too. But now I've got to find another horse."

"I know of a mare who's trained to Prix St. George. They're only asking four or five thousand. The owner's had a stroke and has to give up riding."

"I can't afford more than three or four hundred."

Susanna gazed at Ben quizzically for a second, as she opened the last stall door. "You can't just buy any old nag and expect to do much."

"I want to give some horse a good home and have some fun. One with good gaits, and a good brain, and a generous attitude to people. Of course, everybody wants that, so I'm not going to find one overnight."

"No."

Will Smith caught Ben's eye and smiled as though he'd read his mind, before he leaned down to Susanna's level and wrapped his arm around her shoulders. "Susanna had to wait until last year to move here and get her farm going the way she wants it, so I humor her. Horse people are like golfers. Obsessed with what they do." Will smiled at Susanna like he actually admired the single-mindedness and was only teasing.

But Susanna looked at him as though she were none too pleased as she started out toward the paddocks.

Ben said, "You want me to help?"

But she shook her head and turned toward the farthest paddock, a tiny figure in a pink knit shirt and Levi's, leaving Ben and Will leaning on the fence by the barn.

"I was serious you know, when we talked at dinner. Johanna really does want your opinions about Cumberland and what should be done about the park."

"You'd think she'd be disgusted with us. When it was our children who sold to Ed Montgomery."

"I think she wants as much family input as she can get. This is going to be a long painful fight."

"I hate to see Cumberland get taken over by the park, but I'm not a Hill, and I can't get involved. If the kids had asked me first, I would've said what I thought, but they didn't. Both of them are city lovers. They never cared much for Cumberland. Couldn't see beyond the heat in the summer. I'm from Scarsdale, and I'm not crazy about heat, but I hate to see that island change."

"Government takeover of private property seems like an issue to me too."

"Yes, and if you take one sort of property against an owner's wishes, it won't be long till you justify taking every other."

"I love parks, myself. I'm glad we've got the ones we've got. But in this case, national park people, backed by a congressman, are threatening to *condemn* a person's land for no reason except to take it themselves. They'll pay for the land, but—"

"Probably not what it's worth."

"Right."

"Oh, one thing I'd like you to pass on to Johanna for me. I called her at the time, but I'd like you to mention it too. I wanted to come to Hannah's funeral, but I had surgeries scheduled I couldn't postpone, and Susanna was hosting the hunt breakfast." Will Smith must've been six-three, very long-legged and lanky, and he shrugged his narrow shoulders and raised his thick gray eyebrows and smiled as though Ben would understand exactly what that meant.

"I'll tell her again, but I'm sure Johanna understood. So has Mary Hill ever seen your house here? I know she'd love the antiques."

"She was here this fall. Early October, I think. She was working on a house in Asheville, and we had her over to dinner. Don't know why she wouldn't talk to Hannah, but she and her Aunt Susanna have always gotten along."

"What'd you talk about?"

"Architecture. Art. Some politics. That sort of thing. We didn't always agree, of course, but I enjoyed it. At one point, we were talking about differences between life today and when I was young, and I said I thought people aren't as honest as they used to be. She didn't agree, but I may have given her something to think about before we were through."

Ben looked over at Will Smith and asked him what he meant.

"I told her about a lab technician we've got working in the hospital where I operate in Asheville, and I said no one *I* ever met in my generation, *or* my parents', would've behaved as he has. It's hard to believe anyone would. You see, I began to notice," Will Smith lowered his voice and leaned closer toward Ben, "that when this one technician did the routine blood work on my patients, there seemed to be a higher than average discrepancy between the results he got and what other lab techs would get on the same patients. More than was indicated by any perceptible change in patient condition.

"I've been compiling data on his results since the middle of October, going back earlier as well, and it appears to me, and to several of my colleagues, that he's simply filling in the forms to reflect a fairly normal blood workup without doing the analysis. He doesn't always do that, but enough to be noticeable."

"That's incredible."

"It is. He reads technical journals, he places an inordinate number of personal calls—many of them to racetracks, according to rumor—and he's thought to have a gambling problem that's led to financial trouble. That's not anyone's concern but his, though it could indicate the pressures he's under."

"Right."

"I learned this morning that the decision was made yesterday to terminate his employment the fourth of next month, so the right action's been taken. Is that next Monday? The Monday after Thanksgiving? Yes, it must be."

"How could you live with yourself, doing that to an unsuspecting patient? What kind of person would do that?"

"No one I'd want to take home for dinner."

"Not without counting your spoons. So you told Mary about him?"

"She pooh-poohed it. Can't seem to imagine someone doing what she wouldn't do herself. I told her I've got solid evidence. And that St. Joe's hospital deserves better. Any hospital anywhere does."

"Absolutely." Ben was watching a big glossy bay gelding canter toward Susanna at the gate to his paddock, wondering who he reminded him of. And deciding it was Malamaze, Alex Chisholm's big bay at Balnagard in Scotland.

"Johanna and I talked about the lab technician too. She came to visit before Mary was here. Sometime in September. She was driving from New York to Atlanta, and she spent a night with us. I'd only just begun to suspect Fred, and she and I had quite a conversation. I like Johanna. Always have. Have you heard her sing? Her voice is really remarkable. A beautiful deep, rich mezzo. I enjoyed talking with her about New York too. I did my residency in Manhattan."

"Where I bet you saw what there is to see about human nature anywhere. I read William Carlos Williams's autobiography and found his residency in a big city hospital really interesting, even if somewhat depressing."

"Someone else told me to read that."

"Has Leah MacKinnon ever come to visit? She'd want to buy your desk, if she had the chance."

"She came to dinner this fall too. Around the time Johanna was here. She was up on business, in Asheville and Tryon, and we had a good time together. She's a very intelligent person."

"Did you tell her about the lab tech?"

"I did. She reacted very much like Mary. Couldn't believe

anyone would do that. Johanna wasn't so surprised. And that surprised *me* in a way. You'd think Johanna would be the naive one of the bunch, and yet she doesn't seem to have any very optimistic opinion of what human beings will stoop to."

"Maybe she's like me. Maybe she thinks we're all born terminally selfish and capable of almost anything. I guess traveling like she does, working with artists, some of them fairly egotistical I suspect, competing for a very limited number of jobs, singing in big cities and in Europe the way she did, it can't be a very sheltered life."

"No, I suppose not."

Ben turned to watch Susanna lead the big bay down the aisleway into the farthest stall, before he said, "He did a great canter across the paddock."

"Oh, Dawn Dancer's gaits are spectacular. I've got to find him a new dressage teacher who's able to develop him the way he deserves. The one I was working with moved to Connecticut."

"Good dressage teachers don't grow on trees."

"Nobody around here will listen to me. They've all got their favorites, and can't seem to see they're being taught incorrectly. First you've got to have a horse with the talent *and* the temperament, and most people don't. And believe me, nobody wants you to say their horse doesn't have the potential. Dawn Dancer's wonderful. He's the best athlete I've ever had. Although sometimes he anticipates too much."

"My horse did that, and then worried too."

"If you want to ride while you're here, you're welcome to ride Bobby. He's the gray. He's not up to a lot of hard work, but we could take a trail ride. Where are you staying, Pine Crest?"

"Yes. I appreciate it, but I don't think I'm going to have time while I'm here."

CCC

Ben was standing in a phone booth across the street from the entrance to the Biltmore Estate, the receiver against one ear, a finger muffling the other, trying to hear Amelia over the noise of the traffic. "Is there any word on Estelle? Over...I guess I would've been surprised if there had been this soon...Right. How long is the guy with the boat who brings Leah over to Cumberland going to be out of town? Over...So he left to have the surgery done the beginning of November, and he's staying with his daughter till after Christmas? Over...What kind of boat does he have? Over...Could you? I'll wait."

Ben watched the cars climb the hill toward the center of Asheville, and then looked at his watch. "No, that's okay. A Dyer 29. *D-y-e-r?* What's that like? Twenty-nine feet long, obviously, but what kind of a boat? Over...Okay. That helps a lot. Over...Really? So what you're saying is the last week I was on Cumberland, the week Hannah saw the person with the spray bottle, Ed Montgomery's boat was seen just after sunset at the old Kirkconnell dock? And the person who saw it was a shrimper captain you know?...That's interesting, isn't it? And it was seen there again by the same guy the night after Hannah's funeral? Over...I agree. It is. Over...No, I don't know yet when I'll be back, but it may be sooner than I thought when I left. I've got to run, Amelia. Thank you."

He hung up, humming Vivaldi quietly to himself, then climbed in his rental car and drove north on Biltmore Avenue to St. Joseph's Hospital, where he turned right into the parking lot.

He got out and leaned against the fender of the shiny new navy blue Chevy and looked at his watch. It was after nine-thirty. And Ben was asking himself what he ought to do if Fred

Todd didn't show—when a medium-sized man in a trench coat, carrying a cardboard cup, came out of the emergency entrance. He stood for a second and studied the lot, and then walked toward Ben.

"Fred?"

Fred didn't answer. He climbed into the passenger seat and shut the door.

Ben looked at the grim watchful face gulping coffee beside him, while he pulled four photographs out of his breast pocket. "Have you ever seen any of these people?"

Fred looked at them, and looked back at Ben, and said, "You are making it worth my while, like you said on the phone?"

The swagger when he said it irritated Ben—the snide smile, the sly glance, the small mousy chin cocked toward him. But he told himself to wait, and bite back the first phrase that had popped into his mouth. Instead, he pulled out a fifty-dollar bill and laid it on the dashboard between them.

Fred nodded almost smugly and reached for it.

But Ben grabbed his wrist before his fingers touched it. "Tell me what you know first."

Fred studied Ben for a second. Then handed Ben one of the photographs. "This one came to see me. Five, six weeks ago. Said she was a mystery writer working on a book. Needed to see if a plot she was working on would hold up."

"What did she say she wanted it for, and what kind of questions did she ask?"

"Said she wanted to buy pneumonia bacteria. Wanted her murderer to spray it in a room and use it to kill somebody. Said she'd been talking to some doctor about how to do it, and she needed the pneumococcus to see what it would be like. Had to find out how to make the right kind of solution for spraying it. And see that a normal person could get it from a hospital lab and learn all the technical stuff that would go into using it right. Paid me five hundred bucks right then. So I gave her the bugs on a plate, and I—"

"On a petri dish?"

"Yeah, and I made up a bunch of isotonic salt solution. Gave it to her the next day and told her what to do. So why do you care? What's this all about."

"Murder."

"What murder?"

"The bacteria you gave her worked. I guess that might make you an accessory."

"Wait a minute!" The small face with the small chin turned gray while Ben watched, and the mouth fell open as Fred Todd straightened suddenly in his seat. The hustle almost disappeared and the swagger faded as he spilled the last of his coffee down the front of his trench coat. "*I* didn't know what she was gonna do! Never occurred to me she was doing anything but what she said—"

"Never? Not once?"

"Well, I mean, it wasn't illegal to give her what she wanted. Any med student, any resident would've done the same. You got any idea how little we get paid?"

Ben didn't say anything. He looked at Fred Todd consideringly, and then told him he believed him, and asked him to sign the back of the photograph. He also picked up the legal pad between them on the seat and asked Fred to write down what he'd said about giving her the pneumonia and the salt solution, and then sign it and date it.

Fred quibbled. They discussed alternatives for a minute or

two till Fred reconsidered. Then, while Fred wrote, Ben gazed out the window at Memorial Mission Hospital across the street from St. Joe's.

"Why'd she do it? What'd she get out of it?"

"Plenty. Exactly what she wanted."

Fred Todd studied Ben. But he didn't ask again.

When he'd finished writing and handed Ben the pad, Ben gave him his Ohio business card, having already written the radio phone and address on Cumberland on the back.

Ben said, "I don't know what your plans are, but I need to be able to get in touch with you. If you change addresses, or you change jobs, I'd like you to let me know. This is going to come to trial, with any luck at all. And you'll be needed as a witness."

"Wait a—"

"If you help, if your attitude is cooperative, I think things will go fine. But if you try to disappear, or you refuse to talk to the police, then it could get very nasty."

"Are you threatening me?" It was a face like a ferret's at that moment, the limp brown hair sleek against his skull, the glitter in the dark eyes, the lips pulled back against small yellow teeth.

"Not exactly. But this isn't the only trouble you're in at the moment—"

"Wait a minute! What'd you mean by that?"

"So if I were you, I'd make it as easy on yourself as you can."

Fred Todd didn't answer. He stuffed the card in his pants pocket and slammed the door behind him.

CHAPTER EIGHTEEN

TUESDAY, NOVEMBER 28TH

THE CAR COASTED TO THE END of the long sandy drive, head-lights off, easing to a stop inside a curve of pine woods bent and contorted by the coastal winds, that hid a small weathered wooden house on the tip of Point Peter from new houses half a mile north.

The driver's door opened and closed quietly, and a figure in a hooded raincoat climbed out, then stood by the car and listened, looking south toward the clapboard cottage.

The house was surrounded by marsh and water, on the edge of Point Peter Creek, yet it was hidden on all sides, blocked even from water traffic by a ring of dense pine.

There was a dog barking on the west, past North River toward St. Mary's, and another answering it from farther west, probably somewhere in town. But no sounds came from the peninsula, except for the sighing of water and wind. Which was why 2:00 A.M. had been chosen—that, and the safety of navigating at high tide.

The back car door was opened and a duffel bag was

taken out. Then the door was closed silently before the hooded shadow started toward the house forty feet away to the south.

The moon was out, half-hidden for half a minute by drifting clouds, a pale buttery three-quarter moon throwing shadows that shivered in the wind. But the house was dark, in the shade of the trees, as the raincoated figure hurried behind the back porch.

The boat dock stood straight ahead on the east, sixty feet from the house in the waters of Point Peter Creek, a quarter of a mile north of where it flowed into the St. Mary's River.

The marsh grass swayed in the moonlight, swirling in patches in wisps of breeze—as short legs hurried past it up onto the dock, tennis shoes slapping on hollow-sounding wood.

Short broad fingers grabbed an upright corner post at the upstream end of the dock, and the head hidden by the hood leaned out over the water and retched. The torso stayed bent for almost a minute, hands on knees by then, face flushed, breath audible, heart pounding, throat raspy and burning, nose fighting back vomit.

Then the back straightened slowly and the shoulders turned. And the body they belonged to boarded the boat.

It was a black-and-white New England style fishing boat, almost thirty feet long—a trunk-cabin hard-top made for recreational fishing with a large open watertight cockpit, its wheel on the starboard side, *Almyra* in gold on the stern.

The duffel bag was set temporarily on the foam seat that covered the engine in the cockpit, and a ring of keys with a cork bobber attached was pulled from a jacket pocket.

The companionway door was unlocked and opened, a

flashlight was aimed at the companionway steps, the lower tread was pulled up, and the battery switch inside was thrown.

A small silver key was turned in the ignition, on the instrument panel above the wheel, and the diesel engine caught, rhythmically vibrating the boat.

Where did I leave the strip chart? It should've been with the…You're not going to throw up again. You can stop yourself. You've got to calm down and search the boat.

The flashlight beam swept the cabin—the two-burner propane stove-top on the counter, the inside of the drawer below the sink, the drawer on the left of the refrigerator below the stove—before a harsh low voice whispered, "Swallow." *Relax your throat. It has to be here somewhere.*

Nautical Chart number 11489. St. Simon's Sound to Tolomato River. Why would I have put it behind the breadboard?

The figure climbed from the galley to the deck, stepped up onto the dock, and untied the bow and stern lines from their cleats, coiling the lines carefully while boarding the boat, and securing them fore and aft.

Short shaking fingers wiped both eyes with the sweatshirt cuff underneath the raincoat. And then gripped the metal wheel.

The left hand turned it tentatively to port, as the right pushed the clutch lever forward and eased the throttle after it, so that before both hands gripped the wheel again, the boat was sliding left toward the center of the creek.

The moon was hidden, half a mile later, by thick clouds blown in from the southeast, just after the *Almyra* had eased out into the St. Mary's, running toward Cumberland in a silent night, through the mouth of Point Peter Creek.

No! It's not fair! They said it was going to be clear tonight, but I can't see what's…There, that's a little better. Good. It better not cloud up again.

You have to turn on the lights, now that you're out of the creek. You may need the flashlight to find the right switch.

It was on the instrument panel on the console above and to the left of the wheel, and the compass light came on too when the switch was thrown, along with the white bow and stern lights, and the red and green running lights forward of the helm.

Watch what you're doing when you get to the Inland Waterway. It's shallow on the left, and you have to stay between the buoys.

One more time. That's all. There and back in the dark and you'll never have to touch a boat again.

It's got to be done by Thanksgiving.

And it will be. I should even have two days to spare. Then while the rest of them weep and wail and feel sorry for themselves, I'll celebrate in Savannah.

I'll drive up tomorrow night and treat myself to a suite in a really lovely inn. One with excellent food and old style elegance. And there I'll begin again. I'll start at that very moment to put a lifetime of pain behind me once and for all.

*I'll make it the first step in creating a life arranged on my own terms. On my **own** desires, and my **own** plans, for now and for the future.*

Santa Barbara would be nice. I don't want to live up north, not in the winter, certainly. A place on Cape Cod for the summer might be good. With a house in Santa Barbara too.

*I've always wanted to spend time in France. Live in Paris. Normandy. The Rhone valley. Learn about winemaking and visit the vineyards. I **was** given **some** token of an inheritance. Why shouldn't I finally do something fun and travel where I want to go? I've been* *thwarted my whole life. Prevented from having everything I really want. And that's going to stop now.*

*Of course, there **are** things to look forward to right at this very moment. Making her fear it before it happens. That'll be worth the wait.*

Making her feel what it'll be like to fall.

Making her stare at those stones, and those bricks, and imagine the edges breaking her bones and battering her head to bits.

I want to hear her whimper when I explain it. When she looks down on her own destruction. When I make her admit she killed them all. When I force her to see the justice of it and admit she deserves to die.

***She** caused Hannah's death.*

***She** killed Garrett.*

***She** murdered Mrs. Rutter.*

And if it hadn't been for Randall, the good-for-nothing yard man, none of the rest of it would've happened.

*Maybe I should make **him** pay too.*

That's worth serious consideration. Though why it's only occurred to me now I can't begin to explain.

This wouldn't be the time, of course. That's patently obvious. A year or two from now perhaps. When the rest of this is forgotten.

My own sweet Garrett. Gorgeous and young and full of life. Grinning and laughing and running toward me on the beach. Big and broad-shouldered and breathtakingly handsome. My very own Garrett.

Torn and bleeding. Dead on the side of a road.

I can smell his skin if I breathe carefully. Woodsy and warm and spicy. And I still remember every single word he ever spoke to me. If I close my eyes, I can see him that first August. When I stood and stared at him across from the hotel. When he was walking toward the docks in his football uniform, his jersey thrown over his shoulder pads, sweat on his tanned skin, the muscles on his stomach rippling in rows as he walked barefoot, carrying his cleats in his hand.

I can't bear it.

I can't.

How can I go on without him?

He loved me. He always had. He would've killed Brad for treating me the way he did. Leaving me stranded in that bar. After he'd lied and forced me into it and told everyone he knew. **He** deserves to be paid back too. That's as true as anything in this world.

I never did tell Garrett. I couldn't have. Not then. He was too clean and too shy. And I wouldn't have wanted him to know.

I can feel Garrett's arm around my waist. Sweeping me across the dance floor the way he did that Christmas. As though I were tiny and graceful, and as physical and fluid as he. My own dear Garrett. The man I should've married. Smiling at me the way he always had. Wanting to kiss me and holding himself back, because he loved me too much.

Because he did, till he saw **her** all grown up.

Beautiful strong Garrett. Drained and white.

Limp and cold. Soaking in a pool of blood.

Waxy and shrunken in a wooden box.

Dead because of her.

Nobody takes what belongs to me without paying me back with their own blood. Not now. Not never again.

Watch the buoys. You almost ran aground here before.

I've got to get the timing exactly right tomorrow night. Light enough for her to see. Dark enough to bring the boat back afterwards without being seen myself.

Sleep tight, sweetie pie. It's your last night before you lie rotting in your own juice.

This must be the Intracoastal. Get the boat over between the buoys. Green on the left. Red on the right. And don't miss the tip of Drum Point Island. Get west of it. You can't go east toward Whitfield.

It's not only because of Garrett. You know it's not just that. It's the sum of the parts. The preference. The perfection. The perfect classic face. The body she was born with. The way she runs and plays tennis and dances. The effortless popularity. The voice that can't be accounted for anywhere in her breeding. The full scholarship to college, forever discussed by Hannah. The never coming in last at anything, that can't be tolerated any longer.

*It's that, on **top** of the death and destruction she causes everyone who gets close to her. While everyone drools and does her bidding like the blundering fools they are.*

I hope these last ten days have been sheer unadulterated hell for her. With nobody to talk to. Or care about her the way Hannah did. I hope the sorrow of Hannah's death has made her want to lie right down on the ground and die.

Yes, and all you have to do is wait. My little chickadee. Dismemberment. Death. Nothingness. Coming around the next corner.

Ben caught a 7:00 A.M. flight to Charleston, got there before nine, and made the phone calls for Alderton he should've made earlier.

He'd gotten through to the head of Alderton's fine art department and got him thinking about the paintings. He'd called Daniel Henderson and postponed his next visit there. He'd called Claire Price at the Gibbes Museum and gotten her recommendation for a local fine art insurer. And he'd arranged for him to go up to Tryon the following week and give an esti-mate for insuring the paintings during their shipment to Alderton—once he himself had had enough time to make the final selection.

The curator hadn't known anyone in Asheville who had experience crating paintings for shipment. The man the Winthrops had used for years had died the previous year. So Ben called the Biltmore Estate in Asheville, the Vanderbilt home that was now a museum, to see if they could recommend someone.

He finally got through to the person on their staff who did their crating and shipping, and that gentleman agreed to make the crates and rent a truck and drive the paintings to Ohio, using his own vacation time.

That took Ben back to what *he* had to do—put off what he was paid to do for Alderton and do what had to be done right then.

I don't see what other choice I have. I've got to hunt her down, especially now. Because if I understand her at all, she's working on another murder.

He was driving his rental car toward Beaufort on autopilot, trying to make sense of it with most of his brain, thinking about jealousy and revenge and why they come more easily than most things in life.

Forgiveness isn't unrelated to that. It's just the last thing we want to get to.

We start our grudges in diapers. We won't give them up even when we're old enough to see we do the same things. Not always in the same degree maybe. But the same things, with varying degrees of excuse. Human nature. Needless to say. Being exactly what it is.

We compare ourselves to Hitler, and Stalin, and the gossip who lives down the street. Not David Livingstone. Or Eric Liddell. Or someone who copes the way Hannah did.

We don't like being measured against people who make us feel small and creepy. We'd much rather look at the worst people we can think of and pat ourselves on the back.

That's part of the significance of **us** being told to ask to be forgiven the same way we forgive.

And why is jealousy what it is?

Cancerous. Gangrenous. The worm that eats at the insides of families that won't even die when they do.

Look at Ed's mother. And Ed. And Mary. And Leah, obviously. Leah, as much as any.

Yes, and maybe you should look at why **you're** in such a rush to gloss over forgiveness and revenge.

You're so disinterested and so forgiving?

No.

No? What would you do if you saw Mitchell?

That's it, isn't it? What if I saw him walking toward me on the street? Could I keep my hands off his throat? Even after sixteen years?

Seriously.

Literally.

Maybe. But it wouldn't be easy.

And if I **did** control myself in public, could I keep myself from tracking him down and figuring out how to kill him later without getting caught myself?

He doesn't deserve to be living out his days anywhere in peace. Not after what he did. After the GIs I know he killed. The ones I know about but can't prove. Not to mention the ones I don't know about, directly, but know enough to be convinced existed.

So you're in a position to decide that?

No. Not strictly speaking.

Once you saw him, it'd all come back again and start waking you up at night. Everything he did in Belgium, and Germany, and more than likely France. And kept on doing after you got hit and got shipped back to the States.

So you're so much better than she is?

No. Except she doesn't have a reason. It's just jealousy and hatred and wanting what she wants with her. Mitchell did things he would've been executed for by a military tribunal, or a regular court, either one, if they could've proven what he'd done.

You better pray you don't see him, boy, because you're a long way still from wanting to learn to forgive him.

Which is not to say that bringing him to justice would be an ignoble thing.

No. But I don't see how to do that. Legally. Not after all these years. And unless he's dropped right in your lap, it's not up to you to worry about it.

It's not what I need to be thinking about, either.

Because I have to prove that Leah was on Cumberland the night that Hannah died.

Ben started in the old part of Beaufort in a public phone booth on Bay Street close to the marina. He called Leah's house and was told by the cleaning lady that Leah was in Charleston. He called the house and store in Charleston and was told both places that she'd gone to Savannah on a buying trip and wouldn't be back till after Thanksgiving.

Then he got the number of Garrett Aiken's family in St. Mary's and asked what they knew about any woman besides Johanna who'd kept in touch with Garrett over the years.

Garrett's mother told him everything she could, and gave him the number of Garrett's friend in Lexington, the one who'd lived through the crash.

Ben got him on the phone.

And got the answer he expected.

And stared out the glass booth toward Port Royal Sound, holding his breath, with his jaw off to the left, tapping his canine teeth together.

Then he wrote down the addresses of every hardware store and locksmith in town.

There weren't many, fortunately. Seven hardware stores and three locksmiths. And he started with the one closest, in the interests of thoroughness, without expecting it to be the one she used.

If she copied the keys in Beaufort. She could easily have done it in Charleston, where she'd be harder to recognize and track down. Except Charleston was farther from St. Mary's. And she probably would've wanted to get the keys back to the boat owner there before he'd noticed they were gone.

That's if I'm lucky.

And she didn't do it in Savannah. Or Atlanta. Or somewhere else where I don't have a prayer of pinning it down soon.

Ben kept looking at his watch as he drove from one store to the other. Telling himself not to panic at noon, when he was almost out of Beaufort on Route 21, heading away from the water toward the last hardware store on his list—"Scott's Hardware and Collectibles." Whatever that might mean.

It was raining and raw and Ben was getting damp and chilled from running in and out of the car, but there was wood smoke in the air when he opened his car door at Scott's—a long board-and-batten building behind a rusting gas pump from sometime in the thirties or forties, with old tools and garden implements displayed in the front window.

"Mornin'." He was tall and broad with long white hair, slicked back without a part, curling on his plaid flannel collar. He stood behind a handmade counter, crumpling a receipt he'd just pulled off the cash register, watching Ben with an experienced eye.

"Morning. I'm Ben Reese. I'm helping someone who thinks the keys to his boat might've been copied without his knowledge, and he—"

"From around here?"

"The boat's not from around here. We think the keys might've been copied here."

A woman came up to the counter carrying paint brushes and two quarts of paint, so Ben walked over and stood by the fire. It was an old broad brick fireplace putting out a whole lot of heat from a bed of white-hot coals under pine logs that smelled like woods and resin. And Ben warmed his hands, while he kept an eye on the counter.

When the woman left, he walked back to the cash register and handed the man the photographs of Mary Hill, Johanna Elliott, Ed Montgomery and Leah MacKinnon. "Do you remember any of these people? Did any of them come in and ask you to copy some boat keys?"

The old man took the photographs closer to the window and held them up to the light. "Yep. This one here. 'Membuh thinkin' for someone wantin' to copy keys to a boat, she didn't know nothin' about 'em. Five, six weeks ago I'd say. Sometime in Octobuh. Tried to be friendly with her, but she wasn't. She was real dressed up. Had a fancy car. Left a sour taste in my mouth. Being polite and hittin' a stone wall."

"How'd you know they were boat keys?"

The old man gazed silently at Ben as though he could see he was simpleminded, but would try to figure out how to explain without making it sound like he thought so. He spoke slower and more carefully, while he crossed his arms on his belt and said, "Big cork on the key chain. Keeps the keys from sinkin' in watuh. There was two reguluh keys, like usual. Ignition and companionway door. And a gas-fill key too, those're different. A barlike thing with two pointy deals on the side. Letcha unlock the cap on the tanks."

"That helps. I don't know much about boats. Rowboats. Small sailboats. Nothing else to speak of."

"Figured that." The old man smiled and pulled a Lucky from a pack on the counter.

"Would those keys be right for a twenty-nine-foot Dyer? Or should I say a Dyer 29?"

"Yessir, just what you'd figure. Could've been to some othuh boat too. Ordinary keys. Made by Cole Hersee. Used on all kinds of boats."

"Would you be willing to give me your name and address? And write your name on the back of the picture?"

"Why? You gettin' the police in on this?"

"Maybe. It's possible."

The old man flipped the lid of the Zippo back and spun the tiny wheel, closing the lid again with a sharp click as soon as the Lucky was lit. He inhaled and laid the cigarette in an iridescent purple metal ashtray half-filled with his and other people's cigarette butts, before he looked at Ben. "It's not like I know her. Not like I owe her nothin', is it?"

"Doesn't look like it to me, but that's for you to say. Stealing a boat's a nasty thing to do."

Ben handed him the photograph again. And Leonard Scott wrote his name on the back.

Then he took the legal pad Ben had ready and wrote what he remembered.

CHAPTER NINETEEN

IT TOOK BEN MORE THAN THREE HOURS to drive to St. Mary's, and he spent a lot of that time picking it apart, trying to tack down what he could prove and what he couldn't. He thought about Alderton too, and how to fight the president, to keep him from selling Harrison Hall without starting World War III in the middle of Hillsdale, Ohio.

He thought about the paintings he had to choose from. Considering possibilities and enjoying the diversion, until somewhere south of Savannah, where he found himself treading the same worn paths, tearing at the tangle between Leah and Johanna.

She's going back to Atlanta Thursday night or Friday sometime, no later than Saturday, and then up to New York from there. And Leah's not going to let her go without some sort of direct attack.

*Giving in to the hatred's gone on too long. It's gone too far too, to stop short of killing Johanna. Because **if** I'm right, Johanna must've been the real target when Leah murdered Hannah.*

*I doubt that Leah liked Hannah. Hannah was probably an irritation. But killing her, **I** would say, was Leah playing with Johanna. She blames Johanna for Garrett's death. So Leah's making Johanna* *suffer because* **she** *suffered when he died.*

I don't **know** *that that's true. The motivation stuff is speculation. But this is a woman who called Garrett every week or two for years, and made sure she saw him every couple of months, even when he didn't encourage her. At least according to his mother, and his room-mate from Lexington too.*

She holds grudges really well, we know that. And she works at getting even. Look what she did to Randall after the coral snake. And there was the tree root and the coffee can too.

There's the sand in the sheets. And the hidden music. And Johanna's letter to Amelia that mysteriously disappeared. All that tells you something about the kind of games Leah plays.

Which means I wish I'd been able to start back to Cumberland earlier than I did.

And you know there had to be jealousy going on. Out of her own vanity, probably. The all-consuming assumption that "I deserve what I want simply because I'm me. A superior and deserving person whose desires ought to take precedence over everyone else's around me."

That turns into "If someone else gets what I want, I have a right to take it back, or hurt the one who's got it," unless you make yourself stop.

Johanna could sing, when Leah wanted to. Johanna was athletic, when Leah's one claim to athletic fame seemed to be that she wasn't afraid of heights and sometimes climbed a tree. Johanna was good-looking too, when Leah wasn't. And people seemed to like Johanna, even though she was shy and didn't shove herself forward.

Johanna burned the dollhouse that had come from the grandmother Leah loved. And then she "killed" Mrs. Rutter. The only person back then, apparently, who was able to make Leah feel appreciated the way she wanted to be.

Of course, Leah learned, like most of us, to grow up and curry favor. She obviously knows how to be pleasant now, and she's made people think she's changed.

But then Johanna "killed" Garrett. Who "would've been hers," if it hadn't been for Johanna. And that tipped the scale. Unbalanced as it may be. Which means she's not going to let Johanna live. She'll go after her on Cumberland where she can come and go without anyone thinking she's capable of it. As long as the guy who owns the boat is safely down in Florida. Which adds another time limit, and makes it even more likely she'll make a move now.

I'll have to charter a boat to get to Cumberland. Because I'll probably get to St. Mary's long before five.

There was a smell of death in the dining room. Dead meat. Dead dreams. Dead plants. Dust. Damp. Decay. The death of love that means anything. And more than one kind of innocence.

It festered on the table, from the smeared food and dirty dishes. The cups and plates thrown on the floor and broken. The coffee and milk and wine spilled on the walnut top, left to eat through the finish.

On the other side of the dining room archway, across the hall in the living room, an arm hung off the couch, the fingers dangling above a blood-colored oriental carpet that matched the painted nails.

The hand on the stomach twitched. The eyelids flickered twice. The head turned toward the fireplace—before the eyes opened on the ruin around them.

Leah threw herself off the sofa into the squalor on the floor, looking at her watch while she kicked at the piles of clothes and papers tangled around her shoes. She leaned over and put her hands on her knees, and sucked air in loudly for a minute, once she'd made sure she hadn't overslept.

She picked up the open bottle of nail polish and threw it onto an upholstered chair. Then stood and thought for a minute, before crossing the hall into the dining room and turning right toward the kitchen.

You've crushed the pills already. So now you ought to make the coffee. Boil enough water to make tea for you too, or otherwise she'll think it's odd.

You washed the thermoses when you got here, so that's one less thing to do, and the cookies are still in the duffel bag.

You should've made homemade. What kind of a hostess are you? Hannah's little princess is accustomed to the very best.

Leah laughed and leaned on the cool metal counter, one broad hand on her low forehead, holding her bangs up above her face.

Watch for the grounds crews when you're driving south and don't let them see the Jeep. It shouldn't be much of a problem today, with them working on Old House Road. According to your most reliable source, the corruptible Roy Black. Books could be written about **him** *and his well-developed taste for spending money. Yes, and I'd hate to think what Amelia would say if she knew he takes bribes without blinking.*

I wonder how well she'll run the inn, now that Hannah's dead?

Or should I say I **would,** *if I cared whether or not it survives.*

Leah put the pan of water on the greasy electric stove, and thought about making something to eat. A peanut butter sandwich. Or toast and honey. But decided not to make either. To eat the extra chocolate-chip cookies, and enjoy a late dinner in Savannah.

She took the only egg out of a basket on the counter and threw it against the wall by the wing-back chair. Then smiled as she stirred instant coffee into the boiling water she'd added to the powdered pills. She poured the combination into a gray metal thermos and screwed the lid on tightly.

Make yourself tea in the pan. And remember to brush your teeth. Your mouth tastes terrible and you don't want to offend Little Miss Goody Two-shoes. Who's never become accustomed to any such thoughtless behavior.

The clothesline's in the bag.

The ladder's in the Jeep.

What else is there to remember?

Wipe your prints off the thermoses and everything else that goes with them. You probably ought to drive down the beach too, to keep from being seen near Whitfield.

Leah looked around the kitchen at the grease spills and the dried food, at the broken dishes and the buzzing flies. And wondered why it gave her so much pleasure to make a mess in Charlotte's house.

Mother was a pig. She wasn't neat and tidy like you are in your own houses. But you do so love to make a mess here.

Why wouldn't I? I'm ruining her things. The few paltry bits and pieces she actually chose to leave me.

She *never took care of anything. She's the one who threw silk brocade draperies from the master bedroom at Whitfield in the garage here, because they were "too good to leave for the tourists," and then let them rot right there on the floor.*

The only practical thing she ever did was bury the old phone lines between the houses. Course then she wouldn't repair them, so they crackle so much now nobody here will use them.

*My back's crippled from the sofa again, but how can I sleep in a bedroom with a leaking roof? And the thought of sleeping in **her** room absolutely turns my stomach. Seeing her rags in the closet and her comb on the table, looking at her fantasies hanging on the wall, her spears and her pictures of Africa. I should've thrown all of it out the second she finally croaked.*

Her office is even worse. With the eyedroppers, and the incubators, and the peculiarly intricate pet feeding instructions stuck under bones and rocks. She spent her life caring for the smallest least-sentient toad, but never gave a fig for another human being.

I wish she could've known what I did to the birds. I'd love to have seen her face. All my life I got pecked at and bitten, while I listened to her defend them. And watching those birds eat that poison almost began to make up for it. The flea-bitten dogs too, shedding and puking all over the house. Burying them was equally gratifying. The whole garbage load of them together.

Hannah was the only one all last year who didn't believe I'd given them to the naturalist near Macon. And she made sure I saw it too, and did it in a way that ticked me off. I wonder if she was thinking about that when I held the pillow on her face?

You have to stop this. You're getting too worked up. Take a deep breath, and force yourself to calm down. This is a time for thinking coolly and making logical decisions.

She walked to the fireplace and arranged six candles on the mantelpiece—three on either side of Garrett's silver-framed photograph with the lock of his hair curled inside the glass at the bottom.

She looked at her watch and said, "You've waited patiently all your life. And now the time has come."

It's on the turntable.

Go ahead and light the candles.

She lifted the lid of the old Motorola, listening to the hum of the tubes warming up as she lit the candles with a kitchen match.

She set the needle near the end of *Götterdämmerung,* at the immolation of Brünnhilde, where she rides off into the fire after Siegfried's death.

Leah stepped in front of the mantelpiece, staring at the face and the flames, as the crashing wailing frenzied world of pain and desire rose around her, swirling against her head.

She gazed at the wreck of the room, then back at Garrett and his candles burning on the mantle, and carefully took up the frame in both her hands. She kissed it and cradled it against her cheek, while weaving along with the music.

She set it back. And turned the phonograph off. Then stood in the middle of the mess staring at her hands, at the bloodred polished nails stretched out in front of her. "Now. For Garrett. And for Mrs. Rutter."

Leah MacKinnon walked into the hall and turned to the right toward the back, then right again by the back door into Charlotte's study. She didn't look at the dust and grime, at the cobwebs and mouse droppings and old dog hair, as she reached for the black trumpet-shaped receiver on the wooden phone cabinet on the wall by the hall.

She held the receiver against her ear and reminded herself to turn the metal crank three times slowly for Whitfield, and wait for someone to get over the shock and actually pick it up.

Someone did. Shy and hesitant. A woman with a soft southern accent.

Leah said she was a house guest of Ed Montgomery's at the

Grange and asked to speak to Johanna. Then she said, "Hey, Johanna, this is Leah. You'll never guess…No, I'm up at Mother's. I got someone to ferry me over. You'll never guess what I found, but you're going to like it…The combination to the safe at Kirkconnell. I found it in Mother's things. In *her* safe, as a matter of fact…I know, isn't it great? We can *finally* see what's in it after wondering all these years…Why don't we? I'm not on any schedule. I'm packing some of Mother's dishes to take back to town for Thanksgiving dinner. I could meet you now. Have you finished practicing? I know you usually work in the afternoon…Good. Why don't we meet at Kirkconnell? Say, four-fifteen?…That'd be good. I'll bring tea and coffee and cookies, and we'll have a picnic on the terrace the way we did when we were kids…Don't tell *anyone* what we're doing, though, okay? Even where you're going. Let's *really* surprise Amelia tonight with what we find in the safe. You know how much Miz Amelia has always loved surprises…Fine. Four-fifteen. Around back."

Ben rolled his window down to get the wind on his face, and then turned off the radio.

Why do I feel like I've been on Route 17 for most of my adult life?

A better question is why do you exaggerate whenever you get bored?

It's one way to avoid swearing?

Maybe. Having had to retrain yourself once you got out of the army.

I passed Woodbine. It can't be too far to Kingsland.

No, here it is. Route 40 East.

Ben told himself to think about something else besides how much time it was taking, and worrying about Leah when it wouldn't help, when he'd already gone over everything he knew to do.

Think about something interesting. How to start looking for a new horse, maybe. Or the work you want to do next.

Studying Constantine Rafinesque would be worth doing. "The odd fish," as he called himself. Which shows more insight than you'd expect from someone who spent half his life mocking everyone else. How did he manage to describe more than a hundred plants and animals before anybody else did?

The research would take a while. You'd have to spend some time on his other professions. Geologist. Historian. Poet. Philologist. Not to mention the ten or twelve others.

I'd also like to work on nautical engineering in Charleston. Because if I remember right, Charleston blockade runners during the Civil War were the fastest sailing ships ever built, except for the clipper ships in the China trade. With the Alderton connection to the whaling and trading families in New England who built the clippers, there might be interesting nautical stuff to learn and compare there. Especially with all the artifacts they gave us. The Harrisons foremost among them.

There's Gilman Paper.

Osborne Street.

Finally.

Main Street St. Mary's.

Ben parked the car where Osborne Street dead-ended at the docks, and went into the hotel to the public phone and called Chester in Ohio to ask him to call the police in St. Mary's to vouch for him whatever way he could, so that if Ben needed to call them in they wouldn't refuse to listen.

It was twenty-five of four when he came out. And he started toward the docks, toward the fishing boats and the shrimpers, looking for someone to take him to Cumberland.

"Hey, Johanna. My, that's a beautiful blouse. Isn't this the perfect day to have a picnic?" Leah had spread a tablecloth on the wide shallow stairs in the center of the terrace behind Kirkconnell, and was pulling a thermos out of a sweetgrass basket. "There won't be too many more eighty-five degree days with the sun out and no wind. Not the end of November."

"Thank you for doing this. I never would've thought of a picnic. And I still can't believe it. You finding the combination. I gave up hoping we'd ever open your granddaddy's safe a good long time ago."

"Could you get the other thermos? Thanks. That's your coffee. I've got my hands full with the cookies and the mugs."

"Remember all the stories we made up when we were kids? Remember Hannah's boys, and your brother, Charlie, scaring us to death with tales about ghosts, and what they'd hidden in the safe before they died?"

"We had a lot of fun at Kirkconnell then."

"Yes, we surely did." Johanna sat down on one of the solid stairs and took the mug Leah had wiped with a napkin and poured herself a cup of coffee. Then she sat, staring out across the back lawn toward the south marsh. She was wearing shorts and her elbows were on her tanned knees, both hands wrapped around the mug, her blue eyes smiling, and her mouth serious. "It was a healing place for me when I was a child. Cumberland. Kirkconnell. Magical almost. Larger than life. I could come here and play pretend, and watch the wild animals, and forget my parents had died. Thanks for the coffee."

"Sure. Here, have a cookie."

"One, maybe. I ate a late lunch. I can certainly use the coffee, though. I've been sleepy since I got up. Even this afternoon, the whole time I was practicing."

"There's plenty more in the thermos."

"Did you think Kirkconnell was a beautiful house before it burned?"

"Not very."

"I did. I s'ppose I didn't know enough not to. You've always had much better taste than I have. I thought it was astonishing. Like a castle in England or France."

"Grandmother gave it a certain style, but once she died, it was never the same."

"I wish I'd known your grandmother."

"I was only four when she died, and I didn't get over it for a long time. Everything I had that reminded me of her I still have now in Beaufort. Everything but the dollhouse."

"I really am sorry about that."

"I know you are. Don't worry about it. I've taken all the photographs that mean something to me, of her and whoever else, and I've put them in frames that belonged to her."

They talked about Hannah's twin sons, the ones killed in Korea. They talked about Leah's brother Charlie, killed in the Second World War. They touched upon the opera business. And making a living in antiques.

"The key is to develop a return clientele. Clients who trust your taste and your judgment and will come back time after time to ask you to find particular pieces for their homes, or their collections." Leah tugged at the waistband of her slacks, without taking her eyes off Johanna's face.

"I don't know anything about antiques. Most starving opera singers shop at the Salvation Army." Johanna yawned and stretched her arms over her head. "I'm sorry. I don't know what's wrong with me. I seem to be getting sleepier."

"It could be the letdown of the stress from Hannah's death. I remember that after Daddy died. Being so tired I could hardly think. You ready to open the safe?"

"Sure. How will we get down?"

"I've got it all taken care of, and I've got a surprise for you too. You have to close your eyes, though, and let me lead you."

Johanna glanced at Leah and laughed once. It sounded tentative by the time it ended. Maybe even slightly uneasy. But she yawned and stood up, looking down at the marsh. "It better be an exciting surprise. The coffee hasn't helped at all."

"You won't be bored, I promise. Close your eyes and let me hold you by the arm. That's right. I'm leading you around a big hole in the terrace so stay close to me. Don't worry at all, I can hold you up. Now, put your arms behind you. Don't ask me why, it's part of the surprise."

Leah led Johanna right to the open edge of the burned-out first floor—the edge above the exposed basement—up to the end of the stone terrace where French doors had once stood.

She'd pulled a length of cotton clothesline out of the pocket of her jacket, and she slipped the already-made loop around Johanna's wrists before Johanna knew what was happening or had time to pull away.

"What are you doing?"

"Open your eyes." Leah had tied Johanna's wrists hard and was holding both ends of the rope.

Johanna had opened her eyes as soon as she felt the cord,

and she'd started pulling against the clothesline even before she saw how close she was to the open edge. Looking down from where she was made her stomach roll over and her knees weak, and she said, "Leah, please—"

"We didn't talk about Mrs. Rutter when we were reminiscing. You do remember Mrs. Rutter? The first person you murdered?"

"I didn't murder her! I *loved* Mrs.—"

Leah shoved Johanna at the edge, and Johanna's upper body bent above it, fighting against the push, tensing her legs and her feet.

"You remember Garrett? The second person you killed? The most beautiful man I ever saw. Did you know his head was crushed?"

"No!"

"*Garrett's* head. I want you to imagine that. Garrett's brains smeared across concrete. Garrett Aiken, Johanna. The life battered out of him for no reason! *That's* what I'm going to do to you. Push you over onto all those sharp edges so your brains get sprayed across the basement. But first I'm going to hear you tell me how many people you've killed!"

"I didn't—"

"He loved me before he saw you! He would've married me. He would've! I would've gotten him back. If he'd lived. Once *you* threw him away. That's what you always do, take what you want and throw everyone away!"

"I never would've hurt Garrett—"

"You killed him! Don't even say his name!" She was hissing in Johanna's ear, shaking as she spit the words.

"Leah—"

"You killed Hannah too, you know. You made it absolutely

necessary for her to die. To make *you* feel grief for once. To pay part of the price of me paying you back."

"No!"

"How do you like looking death in the face?"

"Leah—"

"Speaking of faces, yours won't be so pretty when they pull you up, will it? Johanna's face will be crushed like Garrett's! Splattered across all those stones!"

CHAPTER TWENTY

"AMELIA, WHERE'S JOHANNA?" Ben was standing in the side hall, across the front hall from the sitting room and the stairs, watching Amelia in the small wood-paneled bar as she checked the glassware, and the lemons and the limes, and set out bottles of wine.

"Hey, sweetie, how'd you get ovuh here? Find you a fishin' boat to—"

"Yeah, I did. What about Johanna?"

"She hurried off a while ago, but I didn't hear where. She's bein' mysterious this aftuhnoon. I b'lieve she's feelin' bettuh since she came back from Charleston, though why I don't—"

"How do you mean mysterious?"

"She got a phone call earliuh. Don't know who it was, 'cause somebody else went to fetch her when the call came through. And then she took a notion to borrow the station wagon, and went off."

"She didn't say where?"

"No, she said, 'I'm gonna go solve an old mystery,' or some-thin' like that. And smiled like she meant it, for once." Amelia was smiling at Ben, her soft dimpled face looking younger then than she was.

"Who took the call for her?"

"Tallie, in the kitchen. Where're you goin', suguh?"

Ben was running down the U-shaped stairs toward the ground floor—the dining room-kitchen-office-level—rushing around the guests in the halls, not taking time to apologize.

"Tallie, who called Johanna this afternoon?"

"I don't know. I didn't recognize the voice. Said she was stayin' at the Grange." Tallie was holding a huge salad bowl she'd just taken down off a shelf, and was walking toward the cutting-block counter at the end of the big center table. "Whoever it was made Miss Johanna laugh. First time I heard her since the funeral."

"What did Johanna say?"

"Didn't hear nothin' to speak of." Tallie set the bowl down and moved out of the way of one of the waiters.

Ben looked across the big kitchen, at the rush of predinner activity. He hadn't expected it to be that busy, when most of the cooking was done in the galley kitchen, between this old one and the dining room. But maids were organizing supplies for the nightly turndown, waiters were setting up bread baskets and butter crocks, and two naturalists who took guests on drives around the island sat at the center table drinking iced tea and talking—which made Ben ask Tallie to step out to the back-yard.

"I don't listen in to folks in the office, Mr. Reese. It'd get me in trouble, and it wouldn't be right." Tallie was looking at the stack of mailboxes nailed to the side wall of the small back porch, checking hers as she walked past.

"You must've heard *something*, and this is important."

She stood stock-still in the sandy back drive and stared past the bathhouse to the marsh behind the oaks as though she were seeing something farther off. Then she stuffed her hands in her apron pockets and looked down at her feet. "I went outside when she was talkin'. Took garbage out to the big cans in back, but when I come back, I heard Miss Johanna say, 'Combination? Did you? That's great.' Something like that. I know she said 'combination.' And that's when she laughed. Then she said, 'I'll meet you there.' Or 'I'll get there as soon as I can.' Maybe not those very words, but somethin' close to that."

"When was this?"

"'Round four o'clock, I reckon."

"Thanks." Ben shot across to the back porch and grabbed the handle on the kitchen door.

"Mr. Reese!"

Ben turned and looked at her rosy freckled face.

"It wasn't the ship-to-shore. It was the old phone. The crank one on the office wall that goes from Whitfield to the Grange down by Kirkconnell, and up to Miz Charlotte's house, and the Suttons' too. The one that just works on the island. Hardly ever rings. Not since Miz Charlotte died."

"Thanks, Tallie." Ben ran through the kitchen and up the stairs and found Amelia in the paneled sitting room arranging white chrysanthemums on the grand piano in time for cocktails and hors d'oeuvres.

There were two guests looking at Hill family scrapbooks on the sofa, and Ben motioned to Amelia to follow him down to the library.

"Johanna said 'combination,' on the phone. What does that mean to you?"

"Nothin' whatevuh. Did I evuh tell you that Mary called me when Hannah was in the hospital to ask how she was—"

"Think in terms of Johanna and Leah. What combination? Combination of colors? Or flavors? Something like that? Something from their past?"

"Nothin' I know about 'em fits that."

"How 'bout a combination to a safe?"

"Well, I guess it could be that. There's the safe here. And Charlotte had a wall safe up at Four Chimneys. Is that what you mean? Though, now I come to think about it, Johanna did talk to Leah about paintin' her room in the apartment she shares in New York. Told her about the fabric on her furniture and asked her advice. So I reckon it could've been a combination of patterns or colors."

"Johanna laughed after she said 'combination.' Does that mean anything?"

"I don't know, suguh. Doesn't mean a thing to me. Hannah might could've told you right quick."

"There's a safe in the basement at Kirkconnell. The door's still shut. It's burned on the outside."

"That was Leah's grandfather's. There's a safe at the Grange too. Ed Montgomery's stayin' there, you know, startin' today. Came over for Thanksgivin'. Little rat that he is."

"Is there a car I can take?"

"Latuh, when the crew brings the truck back. Half an hour, pro'bly. They've been workin' on Old House Road."

"Too late. I can't wait."

Ben was down the front steps before she answered, sprinting toward the old stables where the yard equipment was stored and repaired, and the bikes used by guests were kept.

He saw two rows of black Schwinns when he ran through

the open door, praying that he'd know which one—the safe at Four Chimneys or the one at Kirkconnell. Thinking, as he grabbed the biggest of the old black bikes, that it'd be easier for Leah at Four Chimneys, inside her own house.

More dangerous too, though.

Easier to connect to her.

He pedaled east past Amelia's cottage along the sand drive out toward the north-south road, where he turned left toward Four Chimneys, saying, "Think!" while he pedaled.

He stamped on the foot brakes a hundred feet later, turned the bike around, and started south.

She laughed when she said, "Combination."

She was fifteen or sixteen when Kirkconnell burned. She played at Kirkconnell as a little kid. Kids would love an abandoned house like that. Making up stories about scary stuff. A safe like that would've been a big deal. Trying to open it. Imagining what was in it. That's why she would've laughed. Being able to open the safe now after all these years.

At least it makes more sense than anything I know about Charlotte's house. Which is next to nothing, and can't, therefore, be evaluated.

I'm gonna have to go on gut reaction.

And hope it's a whole lot more than that.

Ben pedaled south as fast as he could through stretches of deep sand and easier patches of packed shells, sweat sliding down his neck and along his sides, telling himself for the twentieth time that he should've warned Johanna as soon as he'd talked to the lab guy in Asheville.

I thought I'd be here fast enough. And I didn't want to use the ship-to-shore. Not with the operator listening in the way she does. Which means if Johanna dies I'll be partly to blame.

A deer jumped out ten feet in front of him, a quarter of a mile south of Whitfield, crashing through saw palmetto rattling like dried sticks—startling Ben in a stretch of unstable sand, so that he almost fell when he hit the brakes.

He avoided two armadillos. Who didn't seem to know he was there.

Right before a wild boar snorted somewhere in the woods on his right and charged away through the undergrowth.

Half a mile later—right after he'd congratulated himself on making really good time—the chain on his bike broke, and he was thrown forward and smashed his crotch on the metal frame and lost all sense of time and space.

When he could breathe again, when he could get off his hands and knees and stand up, he threw the bike in the palmettos on the right of the road and told himself to get moving.

All he could do was shuffle to begin with. But he was running twenty yards later, with a mile and a half to go, glad he'd worn his desert boots that morning instead of his hard-soled shoes.

His mind kept throwing pictures up in front of him while he ran, cutting from one to the other—imagined glimpses of Leah with Hannah, starting with the one that haunted him most and nearly made him froth at the mouth. Hannah lying helpless on her bed, not dying fast enough to suit Leah, looking up at a pillow held in Leah's hands.

He saw Leah at ten or eleven, short and chubby with a pudgy face, staring at a buried coffee can, measuring to make sure it'd hit Johanna's face, once she'd tripped on the root.

Ben said, "That's sick," as he ran past the entrance to the Hill graveyard. And wiped his forehead on his shirt sleeve.

He leaned down to pull up a sock that had started a blister, and as he straightened, he caught movement out the edge of his eye.

It was a young stallion trotting into the road from a side trail in the saw palmetto.

None of the wild horses had made any attempt to come near him, but this one was coming up behind him, trotting faster the closer he got, with what Ben hoped sincerely was a half-amused gleam in his eye.

Ben stood where he was and yelled, "No! Get outtta here!" while waving him away with one arm.

The stallion stopped and considered Ben. Who stood and stared the horse down for a few seconds, before turning back toward Kirkconnell.

He was walking quickly, looking over his shoulder at the mud-covered bay—when the stallion started after him again, in a trot that threatened to turn into a canter thirty feet away.

Ben wheeled toward him with his arms spread wide. "GET OUTTA HERE! GO ON! GET OUT!" Ben slapped his hands, and waved his arms, shouting at him and standing his ground.

Till the little bay stopped ten feet away and looked confused. Then stood and watched Ben watch him.

Ben pointed up the road and yelled, "GO ON. YOU HEARD ME. GET OUTTA HERE!"

But the young stallion didn't. He dropped his head to a soft strip of green grass growing at the edge of the road, and kept his eyes on Ben.

Ben watched him for half a minute, then turned and walked away. Looking over his shoulder every few seconds, waiting to run till he was farther away. Having learned from past experience that horses think it's *very* exciting and quite peculiar when a two-legged person runs.

He walked on, for what felt like way too long, looking at the stallion every few seconds, who had his head up now while he watched—till Ben couldn't stand it any longer and picked up the pace and ran.

The stallion studied him, chewing slowly, and stayed right where he was.

Thank God. That's a fight I couldn't finish.

You gotta remember to tell Amelia about him. She can't leave him loose with all the guests around.

You have to arrange an autopsy on Hannah too, to find out if she was suffocated. If there's an experienced pathologist here who'll recognize the difference between forced asphyxiation and normal respiratory failure.

Having a pathology book right on Rob's shelf made it easier. One with photographs of the signs of asphyxial stigmata. I can show the photocopies to the police here too. If they haven't had a case like this. Which most small towns haven't.

Fine. So how far can it be before the split in the road?

It wasn't much more than a quarter of a mile, and when Ben got there—where the track to Kirkconnell dock went off on the right and the drive to the house went straight ahead— he stopped for a second and listened.

He trotted through the woods to the first pair of stone pillars as fast as he could and watch carefully. Then ran up to the second, where he could see Kirkconnell.

The station wagon from the inn was there, next to Charlotte's old Jeep, in front of the broad center stairs.

And he mumbled, "That's a relief." *And a gift too.*

And scanned everything he could—the palms, the palmettos, the gray tabby and redbrick ruin of Kirkconnell standing up against the sky, turkey vultures perched on the chimney pots—without seeing Leah or Johanna.

He ran the last quarter mile to the pillars up by the house, hiding behind one long enough to listen and watch again. *There're too many places.*

In too many buildings.

So start where you know to start.

Ben ran, low to the ground, straight to the ruins in front of him and vaulted on one hand over the low stone retaining wall onto the raised grassy strip.

He edged to the right, toward the arched-stone iron-barred window, where he could look down on a narrow section of the basement, onto a floor covered with rubble and crushed stone.

The safe was there, in plain view on the far side, four feet square and blistered on the outside, the door still closed and presumably locked, from what he could see from there.

He could hear voices now, above him. In front of him. Drifting down from somewhere in back. From up near the back terrace.

Two voices. Thank God. Which is more than I've got a right to expect.

He dropped off the retaining wall onto the sandy drive (and took enough time to check and find there were no keys in either car), before he ran the width of the house, past the broad front stairs, past the library wing and around the east end of Kirkconnell—where he stopped, and started edging across the back toward the wide veranda.

He crouched and ran to the east end of the terrace, close up against the house. Then stepped silently up the rubble-covered narrow stone steps.

He crawled up the last five, and looked over the top step

toward the biggest of the two-story three-sided bays that stuck out into the veranda.

There was no one between him and that bay, and its walls and climbing vines hid him from anyone on the other side—but kept him from seeing Leah too, and what she was doing to Johanna.

He could hear Leah talking, as he crept toward the center bay, picking his way around sixty feet of rubble and collapsed floor. She was droning almost mechanically, the monotone cut by separated phrases that rose in pitch and intensity, then fell again, slower and quieter, without being any less menacing.

He edged sideways toward the glassless east window of the bay, where he was hoping he could look through to the west side window frame and see what Leah was doing.

He leaned over to the right, across a broad gap in the terrace, to take one quick look around the open edge—and saw Leah's short broad back off a little to the right between him and Johanna.

Johanna's arms were tied behind her, and Leah was talking nonstop—holding her hard, shoved up against the stone edge of a precipice, above the open ruin of the ground floor—her right hand gripping the rope, her left arm wrapped around Johanna's throat.

Ben pulled back away from the open window and eased to the left toward the short retaining wall around the corner of the bay, where he saw two mugs and a basket on a solid strip of shallow stairs.

He worked himself toward those stairs, toward Leah and Johanna on the other side, winding his way through weeds and rocks and holes in the veranda floor—listening to Leah hiss in Johanna's ear.

"You've killed everyone I've ever cared about, and now you're gonna admit it. Go on, say it! 'I killed Mrs. Rutter and I killed Garrett!'"

"Leah, please—"

"HUSH!"

"I never meant—"

"You didn't think about *them*. Ruining their lives. Taking them away from me. Taking Hannah away. I used to like Hannah. She used to like me before you came. You know what I heard my daddy say? 'Why can't Leah be like Johanna? *She* doesn't sit around eating cake in the kitchen, she's outside running with the dogs. Everybody likes Johanna. Why can't Leah be more like her?'"

"I *never* tried—"

"Mother couldn't stand to look at me. Once I drowned the kittens. I was only five, but she never even asked me why. She never cared what *I* thought. I didn't like birds in my hair, and cats climbing up my dress or dogs slobbering on my legs. I didn't like alligators or turtles, so there had to be something wrong with *me*. When everyone else in the world could see she was mad as a hatter."

"Your mother—"

"They never knew who I was, and they didn't care because of *you*. 'Johanna doesn't throw temper tantrums. She's taken her parents' death just like a little trooper. Johanna's so beautiful. She's so talented—'"

"People didn't think that." Johanna was slurring her words. Her head hanging, limp and loose, her whole body sagging. "I was miserable. I was shy. I never thought I'd live through my parents' death. You had everything—"

"SHUT UP! I had nothing I wanted!" Leah pushed Johanna's

feet halfway over the edge, shoving her upper body over the basement, over the house-sized hole littered with cut stone and sharp-edged concrete slabs, piles of brick, tangled metal, beams burned and bent in the fire, crumbling brick pillars connected by arches, twisted trees and tangled vines, the safe at a disconcerting angle twenty feet below Johanna.

"They'll know someone killed me. I'll still be tied up."

"You think I'm stupid after all these years! I brought a ladder, dimwit. The thermos has your prints on it, just like the mug. You've been depressed since Hannah's death. You're sedating yourself, and you jumped or fell."

"Ben won't let you get away with it…What'd you put in the coffee?…I think I'm gonna be sick."

"Stand up! Stop leaning back! Say it! NOW! Tell me you killed Garrett and Hannah and Mrs. Rutter!"

Ben was holding his breath, his back to the solid south wall of the big bay. He turned around, laid his chest against the warm stone wall, edged his way back to the open east window, and grabbed a clump of vine. He slid his face around the corner fast, checking Leah's position, then leaned out over the basement, through the open frame, studying that part of the stone floor between Leah and the bay's west window.

"NOW!"

"Leah, *please*—"

He'd have to edge around the window frame, along the inside lip, and he was wondering how solid the window frames were as he grabbed the south corner of the east window, leaning into the void above the basement, his eyes on Leah's back—and stepped out onto the rotting ledge.

He felt the narrow bottom edge of the south wall with the toe of his right boot, scanning the stone wall for a place to grab with his right hand. He told himself not to look at the ruins below him, to concentrate on crossing those walls without making a sound.

Leah was still talking, rocking Johanna forward-and-back and side-to-side as though she were a cloth puppet—while Johanna hung limply in Leah's hands. Leah whined with her lips up against Johanna's ear, repeating herself over and over—before she suddenly switched topics. "I could've sung as well as you if I'd had teachers who were good. I could've played tennis as well as you too if Daddy had wanted to help."

Ben's left foot slid off a sliver of ledge and he fell toward the ruin under him—till he grabbed at a tangle of woody vine and pulled himself back, throwing his chest flat against the south wall of crumbling stones—before he found a toehold for his right foot on a ridge of broken brick.

Leah stopped and listened.

And Ben hung above the basement and held his breath.

"No one ever encouraged me. Not like Hannah did you. All I had were servants who lied to me and parents who hated the sight of me."

"Charlotte didn't hate—"

"Garrett wouldn't have wanted you, not if he'd lived. He didn't live because you played with him. Pushing him away and pulling him back, making him go through hell."

"No—"

"Nobody's going to do that for *you*. Pull you back from the edge. Nobody's coming to save Johanna. So look way down there, Little Miss Goody Two-shoes. See all those sharp, sharp stones? Look at the safe right below you. I want you to think about how it's going to hurt, when your head cracks open like a melon." She stopped talking for a second and froze. As though she'd stopped to listen.

Just before Ben's right hand came at her from the right, fingers cupped and arm swinging fast, arcing toward the right side of Leah's head.

It hit her ear hard enough to break the eardrum, and she screamed and reached her right hand toward her head—just after Ben had grabbed Johanna's left arm.

Even so Johanna was falling forward, and Ben leaned back, holding her up by the upper arm, pulling her away from the ruins. Making her sit on the veranda floor, slumped against his legs.

Leah was moaning and whimpering, staggered by the agony in her ear, crumpled against a section of wall that had once been the side of a stair. Her eyes were shut tight against the pain. But when she opened them and saw Ben bent over Johanna, blocking her own escape in the one reachable piece of floor between ruins and bottomless bays, Leah straightened against the wall with fury on her blood-smeared face.

Awkwardly, painfully, she started climbing the broken stair, the few fragments of narrow stone treads hanging above the ruins—while Ben pulled Johanna, limp and shaking, farther from the ragged house toward the veranda stairs.

He left her in a solid spot of stone floor, safe between craters in the terrace.

And then turned to face Leah.

"Don't come after me! If you make a move I'll jump!" Leah had made it to the top of that single-story stair. And there she'd grabbed the twisted branches of the tall woody vine, and was standing now on the second-story frame of the center bay almost directly above Ben.

"I take it you killed Hannah to hurt Johanna."

Leah laughed, and then wiped at the blood trickling out her ear. "Hannah died of pneumonia!"

"Streptococcus pneumoniae you bought from a not very upstanding member of the St. Joe's staff in Asheville."

Leah looked taken aback for a second, but then she said, "I wasn't even here on Cumberland. Nobody ferried me over."

"You took Mr. Terry's boat at least three times, and you had the keys copied at Scott's Hardware in Beaufort. He's identified your photo and written what he remembers about you copying the Dyer's keys."

"You can't prove I had anything to do with her death!"

"I've got enough to get you to trial either way, even if you ended up suffocating her."

"You don't know—"

"She was getting better, and Johanna was coming home in two days, and you didn't want her to talk to Hannah. You wanted Hannah to die fast, and I'll bet you suffocated her. It wouldn't have been too hard, would it, with Hannah in her condition?"

"She had nurses with her all the time."

"All you had to do was wait for the nurse to take her break, and pick up a pillow from the bed. It'd be easy, with someone as helpless as Hannah. And there wouldn't be an autopsy. Not with a small-town doctor, not for someone who'd been sick as long as Hannah had. But there'll be an autopsy now, I can promise you that. Now that you've tried to kill Johanna."

Leah took her jacket off and threw it at Ben, and then started climbing again, sideways to begin with, along the second-story west window in the big bay, toward the south window frame above the first-floor wall.

Ben had seen one route that might work. But he said,

"There's no way down from there except the way you came. You don't want to die here. Not like that. You want to write your side of it. Explain what your parents did to you. Tell people how it felt. Tell them about Mrs. Rutter. Justify what you did. You're a Hill. People will want to read it."

Leah paused where she was, looking around for the next foothold.

Ben could see where she was headed—right to the path he would've taken. Because if she could cut sideways across a ten-foot section of brick wall to the only twisted I beam that crossed any part of the pit—*if* she could slide down the I beam, and climb from it to the one half-wall of brick attached to the front of the house—she'd make it to her Jeep before Ben could get Johanna's car keys and run around the house.

Leah was moving again, inching along the window frame toward the broken brick wall between her and the I beam—when she stopped to think about how to get across.

Three black turkey vultures, their heads red like raw meat, were watching from the chimney pots of the highest chimney, when Ben said, "Leah, wait, you can't get down that way. The bricks are loose and the I beam doesn't look steady. Come back toward me before you lose your balance."

Leah paused for a second, listening to Ben, holding her ear with her right hand, looking unsure and disoriented, not seeing a safe-looking place to set her left foot.

She was staring down at the veranda, at the gaping holes in the stone floor, at the broken slabs sticking up on end, twisted at strange angles—when the largest of the vultures swept down off the chimney and flew at Leah's head.

She shrieked and put her right hand up to protect her face and fell, screaming, onto the point of a broken stone slab.

CHAPTER TWENTY-ONE

WEDNESDAY, NOVEMBER 29TH

"ARE YOU SURE YOU CAN'T STAY AND RELAX for a day or two?" Johanna was sitting next to Ben on the big wooden swing at the south end of the Whitfield front porch, pouring coffee in Ben's mug.

"I can't, but thanks. I need to get back to Tryon and finish my work there."

"So you don't think there's much I can do about the park right now?"

"I wouldn't say *that* exactly. No, go see Robert Sykes, my friend the lawyer in Charleston. I've known him since we were both in graduate school, and I've talked to him about it in as much detail as I could. He thinks you need to make your case public. Maybe even hire a publicist to organize a publicity campaign, or at least a series of press conferences."

"What would we have to say?"

"Talk about Cumberland from the historical perspective. How worn the land was when the Hills bought it, from the cotton plantations and the lumbering, how the Hills cared for it and brought it back. How committed Charlotte was to preserving the animals and the land, while she limited the rattlesnakes and the alligators enough to make it usable for people. How she started an inn in the old family farmhouse so that a small number of outside people could come and appreciate the island without hurting it, and help her and her heirs continue to care for the island. You know the sort of thing I mean. All of which is true."

"Yes."

"Talk about how the developer was brought in, and how that scared a couple of the owners into selling to the park. That you've inherited most of the island from Hannah, telling them about the MS and how she was murdered, and trying to get feature articles in all kinds of magazines and newspapers. Which sounds really tacky, I know, on the one hand. But Rob thinks you need to make enough of a public splash that the park can't take you over without a public outcry."

"I can see why that would be true, but it's not something I'd look forward to."

"No, I understand that. But what can you do, except use the old 'David fighting Goliath' approach? A small landowner with not a whole lot of money trying to keep the federal government from condemning the land for no reason except to take it for themselves by force."

"The whole situation sounds pretty overwhelming."

"It's a long-term, large-scale fight, and you shouldn't start it if you don't have the energy to go through with it."

"No, I'll do it. I want to for Charlotte and Hannah. *And* for Cumberland too. But I don't feel very confident that I know what I'm doing."

"If it were me, right at the beginning, I'd get Rob Sykes to talk to Eddie Montgomery. Rob will tell him he's got the dated photograph of him with the developer, the politician, and the park guy, and that you'll be only too happy to make that public, that whole behind-the-scenes deal they pulled, if he doesn't stop trying to push the park to take over your land."

"Then if he won't back down, I do make it public?"

"Yes, you do. Once Rob's found out all the pertinent facts. If he still thinks you've got a case."

"Do you think Ed would've married Mary if she'd inherited Cumberland from Hannah? So he could sell it to the park and make more money himself?"

"Looks like it to me. Although I think they would've kept the inn if they could've. For a steady source of income, on top of all the money they would've made right away."

"He would also have been the Greene who got Cumberland back from the Hills."

"Right. Don't forget the rock he carved as a kid. The one I found in Caty Greene's tomb. The vow to get back what the Greenes had lost. Which must mean Cumberland as much as anything. I'm actually beginning to feel sorry for Mary." Ben smiled and finished the last of his coffee.

"A friend of Amelia's works for the same decorator in Savannah, and she says Mary's taken a leave of absence for a month, and she's beginning to talk to people about the wedding and how Eddie's called it off."

"Maybe this will be good for her. Unless she wallows in being a victim. She seems to like doing that now."

"I don't know what she'll do. I've never been able to predict with her. Did you talk to Amelia this morning about Estelle?"

"No."

"Amelia got a call from the police in St. Mary's, and they said Estelle walked into the police department in Nashville and gave herself up. Apparently she'd taken up with some man who was on the bus with her from Jacksonville, and he went off with her wallet and left her in a restaurant with an unpaid bill. She walked into the police station and said she was tired of running. That she'd had nothing to do with killing the two patients in the hospital. That all she'd done was talk to the other nurse about how she'd do it herself, if she ever got her nerve up. That the other nurse did it on her own."

"Wonder whether that's true."

"How could you do that to someone else? Why would you assume you've got the right?"

"I don't know. I guess maybe the more life-and-death decisions we can make because of modern medicine, the more we assume we've got a right to play God and decide who dies when."

"You'd think seeing Hannah might've given Estelle another way of looking at it. But you never know."

"I wonder how much evidence there is of Estelle's part in those deaths? I guess intent is something they'd try to assess."

"Speaking of intent, I want to pay you for all your time, and work, and the airfares and rental cars you've paid for yourself. You're having to fly up to Asheville now because you've lost so much time. Archivists don't make a lot of money, and I won't let you pay for any of that."

"I won't take a fee. Not for Hannah, and I don't—"

"I'm not going to have a huge amount after taxes. The inn's going to have to make a profit to keep Cumberland going, that's for sure. As long as the government lets it. But I've got enough to pay your expenses, and pay you a fee for what you've done, and I'm going to do it. I'm not going to let you wriggle out of this."

"I won't take a fee. I really won't. But if you want to pay for the airfare and the car rentals, I'll agree to that. That would help me a lot. I *would* like to ask a favor, though."

"Good. I'm glad to hear it." Johanna was smiling at Ben with her whole face, finally—her dark blue eyes and her soft wide mouth and her dark delicate eyebrows.

"The library here has some interesting books. Things by and about nature illustrators that could help me with my work. I talked to Hannah about some of them. I've found others since too. And I wonder if you'd let me photocopy them. If you'd let me copy them up at Alderton, and bring them back to you in the spring sometime."

"No, I don't think so. No, that'd be too much to ask." Johanna laughed.

And Ben smiled at her, thinking what a rich, deep, real laugh she had, and how good it was to finally hear it.

"What *I* want you to do is keep them. Nobody else here knows what they are, *or* cares, and you should have them. Write me a list and I'll get them shipped up."

"That's not right. Some of them are worth a lot of money. I don't know how much, but you could—"

"I want you to have the books. Please. Don't say anything else about it, all right? For you. Not for your university."

"You're sure? You ought to think about it more than that. You've even got the thirteen-volume autobiography of Chinese Wilson. He's the guy who first brought regal lilies to the West from the Himalayas, and almost died in the process."

"I want you to have all the books that interest you."

"Thank you, Johanna. I really appreciate it. But I think you're being way too kind."

"Not after what you've done for me. Really. Take whatever ones you want."

"If you're sure." Ben waited and watched Johanna nod. And then said, "If I could get them up north without shipping them it'd be better. There're several, and they're fragile, and a couple are really rare. I've got a student at Alderton who's from Jacksonville, and maybe I could have him pick them up here when he's driving back to Ohio after Christmas."

"That'd be fine with me."

"Alec Hill's name's on the flyleaf of a few of the books."

"Charlotte's brother. The one who died of TB."

Amelia had stepped out onto the porch carrying a large white mug of tea, and she said, "Four Chimneys was his house. Charlotte bought it from his widow," as she sat down in the rocker closest to the swing, facing the front lawn. "This has been an easy mornin'. No one leavin' today except you. You two talked about the lawyuh in Charleston and all?"

Johanna said, "Yes, I'll call him Friday and make an appointment."

Amelia paused and stirred her tea. "I reckon the park *is* bettuh than developuhs. I couldn't stand to see the island cut up."

"Yeah, but it's still a Hobbesian choice." Ben laid his cup down and stretched his arms over his head. "And I'd hate to see Cumberland get taken without a fight."

"I think I'm about to find out more about fighting than I probably want to know." Johanna set her book of arias on the table, then leaned forward with her elbows on her knees.

"Rob'll help because he believes in the fight, and he'll

charge you as little as he can. And if there's anything I can do, I will. Have you found a home for the stallion? The little guy you said was driven out of the herd?"

Amelia nodded and said, "I have. A friend of mine by Fernandina. He'll geld him and get him trained. He's coming for him next week."

"Good. He didn't seem mean, really, but you can't let that go on."

Johanna leaned over and touched Ben's arm. "I've got one other question for you. Did Charlotte die of natural causes, or did Leah do something to her?"

"The autopsy report said she died of an aortic aneurysm, and I don't see much reason to doubt that. We know what happened to the glass. Anyway, I guess I better bring my bags down."

"They're down. I had Roy Black take 'em to the boat already," Amelia said. "You tell your mother I want to see her down here real soon. She'd stay with me, so it wouldn't cost her anything." She patted Ben's knee, then finished the last of her tea.

"I'll tell her, but I think she's kind of tied down now. Dad's not well. And she still works some. And she does a lot of baby-sitting for the grandkids."

"It's about time you gave her some grandkids yourself." Amelia looked appalled as soon as she said it, and started back-tracking, saying she'd forgotten, and what was she thinking, that she'd never met Jessie, and not to pay any attention.

Ben said, "Don't worry about it. I know what you mean," before he turned toward Johanna. "Will you let me know when you're singing places I could get to? If you were at Lyric in Chicago, or with the Pittsburgh Opera, or even in New York, depending on the timing, I'd find a way to get there."

"*If* I get any roles. It's not that easy at my age, especially when you're a mezzo. In Germany they've got a whole network of small-town repertory companies, and there's a lot of work to go around. Here I take secretarial jobs. Part-time work as a Kelly Girl."

"You'll get roles. And when you do, let me know."

"If I do, I will. Thanks."

"Give your old aunt a hug." Amelia stood up and hugged Ben hard and then held him at arm's length and shook her head at him. "I hate to think of you bein' up in Tryon all alone workin' your fingers to the bone on Thanksgivin'."

Ben hugged Johanna, then said, "I'll be fine. Don't worry about me."

Both women said thank you for the fiftieth time, as he started down the stairs.

"Anyway, what makes you think I'll be alone?"

Amelia said, "What do you mean by that, sir? Ben!"

Ben laughed and waved to them and trotted down the sandy path under the two arching lines of live oaks that led toward the Whitfield dock.

THURSDAY, NOVEMBER 30TH, THANKSGIVING

"I kind of wish we could've met in Beaufort. It's a great town. We would've had fun there, walking around, looking at the houses on the water, poking into all the history. But I didn't get enough work done early enough."

"Tryon's fine with me." Kate Lindsay was tucking one side of her just-longer-than-chin-length brown hair back behind her left ear, looking out the window as Ben drove, as they curved through green hills cut across by thickets of trees losing their leaves now in a wet wind, gusting after a shower. "It's beautiful country, the sun's about to come out, and we're staying in a nice inn. Course *I* have the better room. I like being in a cottage instead of the main house, and so would you I'm sure, so thank you for giving it to me."

"It's the least I could do when you came all this way."

"I would like to drive up north of Asheville one day, if we have time, and see more of the mountains."

"I'd like to too. But it is amazing how far you can see from here, on a clear day. There're quite a few places you can see the Smokies."

"So what do you have to do today?"

"Look at the paintings one more time and make the final selection. It's a wonderful collection. Even just the ones I've seen, and I know there're a lot more. Then tomorrow I'll meet the insurers, and the man from Asheville who'll make the packing crates and drive the paintings up to Alderton. If you get bored this afternoon, feel free to do something else. Work yourself. Or go for a walk. Or whatever you want to do."

"I did bring my briefcase, but it wouldn't kill me to take a day off."

"No. Especially Thanksgiving."

"I've decided not to do the book about Mary Queen of Scots. Not now, anyway. Maybe I'll feel ready to do it later."

"Then what are you going to do now?"

"Write the book about Georgina's death last summer, and the way you did the investigation."

"Really?" Ben glanced at Kate as he stopped at a stop sign.

And the look on his face made her think she ought to ask him again what he thought about her doing that. "Is that okay with you? We talked about it in Scotland and I thought you were willing then."

"I am, as long as it's fictionalized. So nobody can connect it to me."

"That's what I intended to do. A fictionalized archivist. A fictionalized murder written like a classical mystery novel. But make it a serious novel too whatever way I can, with a lot of emphasis on character."

"Good. Then that's fine."

"I may have to bother you with questions from time to time. There're a lot of things I'm going to have to study. Microbiology. Falconry. Stone sculpting. And, of course, abandoning one book and taking up another means I'm already a couple months behind."

"Whatever you need, let me know."

"Oh, Ben." Kate was looking at a watery blue-green-and-gray river scene Twachtman had done in France, misty and impressionistic, but spare and clean and unexpectedly modern. "I could live with that a long time."

"I know. It's one of my favorite paintings. Compare that to *Fish Sheds and Schooner, Gloucester*. Not an appealing title perhaps, but there's water, there's landscape, there're ordinary unprepossessing buildings, and yet it's just as unexpected and as beautiful."

"It is. Twachtman was great, and I've never even heard of him. Don't let me interfere, by the way. You go ahead and work and I'll just watch."

Ben smiled and handed her a leather portfolio, and said, "I thought you might like to see those," then started moving paintings till he had the eight he thought he wanted hanging on one wall.

"These are incredible, especially for pencil drawings. So there're real bones that have been arranged with others from different animals, or from different locations on the same animal, put together to create new forms. Right? And some of the bones are enlarged? But they're drawn absolutely realistically. Kind of like Dürer, don't you think?"

"I do. Jensen's from Minnesota, and from what the paperwork says, he started the bone drawings thirty years ago. I'd never heard of him myself, but to find somebody who creates forms like that, and draws the way he does, I've never seen anything like it."

"Has Mr. Henderson offered you these for Alderton?"

"No, he's just letting us look at them."

Ben and Kate stood a foot apart, the light coming over their shoulders, and stared at the paintings Ben had arranged on the west wall.

Kate put her hands in the pockets of her brown tweed jacket, and leaned forward to study the brushwork of the big blue-and-green Twachtman, before she said, "What's the organizing principle, other than landscapes?"

"Paintings that will teach the students something specific, then lead them to other fields of study. Pardon the pun."

Kate laughed and said, "Very amusing."

"Twachtman was from Cincinnati, but he trained all over Europe in the late 1800s, so students can compare him to other European and American impressionists and see the differences in what he did. With the added interest of him being an Ohioan from no very distinguished background, like most of Alderton's students.

"Abbott Thayer was also an American, who was both a well-known painter and a naturalist. His book *Concealing-Coloration in the Animal Kingdom* was important for naturalists studying animals, *and* the military too trying to protect men and equipment. The allies and the Germans implemented Thayer's theories of camouflage in World War I, and everybody's worked from them since.

"The oil landscape studies are from Europe in the late 1700s and early 1800s when painters sketched small landscapes in oils to use as studies for huge, formal, public works done for competitions and museums. Students can look up the big pictures and see how the sketches were used, and think about how the quick broad-stroked momentary impressions might've affected the impressionists later. *If* they did. Which is something worthy of investigation.

"Thomas Moran was famous too for the grandeur of his landscapes, primarily of the American West, and yet, here we've got two quick wonderful watercolor sketches of Yellowstone that he probably used for his bigger works. You can compare his concept of sketching landscape to the Europeans', and study his big canvasses in comparison."

"Art majors will love all that, but I think regular students and people like me would find it interesting too."

"Good. That's what I was hoping. Now, Edgar Payne's *Sierra Divide* is an impressionist oil from 1921 that shows the California school's approach to plein air painting. Which can take you to the Bucks County school in Pennsylvania, and the Hudson River School in New York too. So all these different approaches to landscape, with heavy emphasis on Americans, can be studied and compared. Which leads me to the Peale—"

"Where I don't see an obvious connection."

Ben looked at Kate and smiled. "That's because there isn't

one. It's Rembrandt Peale painting his brother, Rubens, beside a potted geranium. They're earlier than most of the other painters I've chosen, and they're two very fine artists in the most important painting family in American history. If you start looking at one or two Peales, it takes you to a whole history of American portrait painters that can take a student off in lots of other directions."

"Interesting." Kate stood there and looked at the wall of paintings. Then walked up next to them and moved from one to the other.

"You folks mind if I come in?" Daniel Henderson was hesitating in the doorway carrying a large pot of coffee.

"You're giving us all these works of art, but no, you can't come see what we're doing! Please, come in. What do you think of the selection?" Ben cleared a space on the worktable and then turned back toward the wall.

Daniel Henderson put the coffeepot down, then studied the wall of paintings. "If that's what you want, it's fine with me."

"You don't think it's a good choice?"

"I wouldn't say that. I don't know much about art, but I kinda like the de La Tours, and I know they're worth a lotta money. The Chardin too, and the Raeburns. Kinda thought you mightta picked some of them."

"They *are* worth a lot of money, and that's probably what the board and the president would want me to take. But I wasn't thinking of it just in terms of cash value. I was trying to emphasize landscape painters who might be models for our students today. Show them the American and European traditions, and something about the different landscapes that exist in their own country. Then throw in the Peale portrait to get them to study portraiture."

"Makes sense. Sure. I'm used to these collectors and muse-ums houndin' me, talkin' 'bout money more than most else and wantin' the Europeans. You like *Magdalene at the Mirror?*"

"Oh yeah, very much. It's one of my favorite de La Tours."

"You can have it too if you want it. My wife really liked that one and it might as well go to Alderton."

"You're sure? You said eight or ten paintings and I've got eight. I was trying not to get grabby."

"That's okay. Why not? Take the Raeburns too. Help keep the president off your back." Henderson laughed, and then smiled at Kate. "I hate to think of you folks eatin' in a restau-rant on Thanksgivin'. You wantta come to my sister's with me? She'd be happy to have you. There'll be a whole pack of kids there, family from everywhere, lots of commotion and all-and-everything. Course," Daniel looked from Ben to Kate and back again, "maybe you'd rather be alone."

The phone rang then, in the hallway between the studio and the garage, and Daniel went to answer it.

He came back a minute later and said the call was for Kate.

They'd left Henderson's number with the inn in case there was an emergency with her father, and Ben could see Kate wor-rying as she started across toward the door.

When she came back she looked stunned. White. Drained. And Ben said, "Is it your dad?"

"No. No, he's all right. It's nothing serious. We'll talk about it later."

An hour later, when they were driving down the drive heading back toward Tryon, Ben pulled the car over right before they got to the road, right where the evergreen woods almost hid the entrance to the drive. "You want to talk about the call? Or you want me to leave you alone?"

Kate didn't look at him. She didn't say anything for a minute. She stared out her window toward the hills, toward the blue green mountains in the distance.

She sighed and looked back at him.

And he saw death and dying in her eyes.

"It was my mother. A man from the post office came to see me. He's retired now. He used to work for the dead letter office somewhere. Milwaukee, maybe, I don't remember. He's been trying to find me since 1944. Off and on, I guess. Sort of took it on as a personal mission. He's been walking all over Evanston the last three days." Kate didn't say anything else for a minute.

And Ben told himself not to ask and interrupt.

Finally she looked at him again, her dark blue eyes half hidden under eyebrows tucked against each other—and then she looked out the window. "He's got a package for me that was sent from Holland during the war. From Arnhem. After Graham was killed. The outside of the package was ripped. He could see only parts of my last name, and that was Lindsay, my married name, not a name that would make it easy to find me in Evanston. Only part of 'Illinois' was readable. Very little of 'Evanston' was decipherable. Only a letter or two of the street name too. No numbers. No return address except 'US Army–Europe.' Something like that. But on the outside layer of ripped paper it said, 'Personal Effects Of Army Personnel Killed In Action.' On the next layer of brown paper, under that, the section he could see beneath a ripped part, I guess, it said, 'Personal. Physical Specimen. Only To Be Opened By Widow.'"

"Geez."

They were both silent for quite a while. Breathing quietly.

Fogging up the windshield. Till Ben turned away from the window and looked at Kate out the edges of his eyes.

"Mom didn't want to open it."

"No, I can see that."

"The post office guy hadn't either. He said his son had been killed in the war too, and he promised himself he'd get this package to me no matter what. He'd kept the box all these years, working at the spellings of a bunch of cities, narrowing it down to several. And when he retired this month, he started looking for me like a full-time job. My parents have moved since the war. Another house in Evanston. He must've had to go door-to-door till he found someone who remembered us."

"Yes." Ben had slipped the car into gear and was turning right up the long green hill. "So you want to go home tomorrow instead of Sunday?"

"Maybe. Maybe I should."

"You have to do what you want to do."

"I don't know. I could call her and ask her to open it now. As soon as we get back to the inn." Kate looked at Ben, at the self-contained carefully neutral face, and said, "I hate to bother you with this."

"You're not bothering me. Are you kidding? Graham was my friend too. No, you have to do whatever will make it easier for you."

"I was looking forward to being here. Seeing what you do. Walking the mountains, if we had time."

"We can do it another time. If you decide to go back now."

"I live in Scotland. I won't be back for a year."

"Ah."

"What would you do if you were me?"

"I have no idea. Except once my curiosity's up-and-running

I have a hard time not going after whatever's got it going."

"That's the way I am too."

They were facing each other, standing by the car in front of the dark green white-trimmed inn, Ben's hands on his hips, Kate's arms crossed across her stomach, both their briefcases waiting on the ground beside Ben's canvas army dispatch case filled with his archival tools.

Kate was looking at her feet, her hair hanging in front of her face.

And Ben reached over and tucked one side of it back behind her ear.

She looked up at him and smiled a watery, self-conscious smile. "I think I'll call my mother."

"I probably would if I were you."

"You want to come with me?"

"You want me to?"

"You were Graham's best man. You're almost the only person I know who even remembers him. My parents never even got a chance to meet him."

"Well. I'm ready when you are."

They walked up the narrow brick steps and in through the side door. That end of the old house was deserted, fortunately. No one in the hall, or the reading room, or the lounge. And no one behind the reception desk. There were plenty of noises coming from the other end of the hall, from the sitting room and the dining room and the kitchen beyond—talking and laughing, glasses and cutlery clinking and clattering, doors being opened and shut—as Thanksgiving dinner was set out and eaten.

Kate could walk into the small wood-paneled phone booth without anyone watching—while Ben stepped across the hall into the book-lined reading room.

He ignored the game tables with chess sets and checkers and jigsaw puzzles laid out, and looked at the shelves of books—the shelf on the Smokies and North Carolina—watching the phone booth out the corner of his eye.

He was just telling himself that she'd been in there a lot longer than he would've expected—when the door opened and Kate walked out and stood in the middle of the hall.

There were tears streaming down her face. But she didn't walk any closer to him. She stood with her fists clenched at her sides and stared at him like she couldn't have made herself look at anything else. "It's Graham's eye."

"What?"

"Graham's eye. Cut out of him as soon as he died, pulled right out of the socket and stuffed in a bottle of preserving fluid!"

Ben walked over to her, pulled her against him, and wrapped his arms around her. The side of Kate's face was lying against his chest, and she was sobbing, her arms still tight against her sides.

Ben smoothed her hair with his right hand, over and over, letting his fingers feel the silkiness of it and follow the shape of her head.

Then Kate pulled her arms up and wrapped them around his waist. They stood there rocking back and forth. Till a waiter in a white coat appeared carrying a bill toward the cash register.

He took one look at Ben's face and turned around.

"Why? Why would anyone do it?" Kate had stopped crying on Ben's chest, but didn't move, her wet cheek on a wet patch on his shirt, his blood beating hot against her skin.

"I don't know, Kit. I don't know. Except sick things happen in a war."

"I *want* to know. I want to know who did it and I want to know why!"

"I would too, if I were you."

"I'm sorry. I don't usually make a fool of myself in quite this way. And I need a Kleenex." She was pushing herself away from him, trying to smile and looking embarrassed.

"Take my handkerchief."

"Thanks. Years go by and I don't cry."

Ben watched her blow her nose and wipe her face and push the handkerchief into her jacket pocket. "So what do you want to do about this? And what can I do to help?"

The publisher and author would love to hear your comments about this book. *Please contact us at:*
www.multnomah.net/sallywright

A CONSIDERABLE PART OF CUMBERLAND ISLAND (an eighteen-mile-long island roughly the size of Manhattan) *was* owned by Nathanael Greene and his wife Caty, and *was* sold gradually by their descendants in the 1800s—but no Greene in *Out of the Ruins* is based in any way on any person, living or dead, in that family.

Caty substantially helped Eli Whitney design and finance the cotton gin, and then lost more money than she could afford fighting his patent infringements. She did name the house she built on the south end of Cumberland Dungeness (after the hunting lodge Governor Oglethorpe had built on the island), but didn't live to see it burn after the Civil War.

Her children did nurse (and later bury) their father's friend, General Henry "Light-Horse Harry" Lee, the father of Robert E., who did come twice to visit the grave, much as it's described in the book. Henry Lee's gravestone is still in the Greene cemetery, but his remains were moved to the Lee Mausoleum at Washington and Lee University in Virginia in 1913.

The Greene land *was* bought by Robert Stafford, the son of the Greene's first overseer, who did have a common-law mulatto wife and several children he sent up north and provided for there with the fortune he'd made on Cumberland.

James J. Hill, the Canadian-born entrepreneur who settled in St. Paul, Minnesota, did build a successful railroad across America to the northwest coast without government concessions or subsidies (and is a person well worth reading about in *The Myth of the Robber Barons* by Burt Folsom, or in Albro Martin's full-length biography, *James J. Hill and the Opening of the Northwest*).

But James Hill never had a brother named Robert, or any other relation who owned Cumberland Island. James J. Hill built a house on Jekyll Island in a development started by friends, but the Hill connection to Cumberland, and the characters by that name in *Out of the Ruins,* are figments of my imagination.

Andrew Carnegie's brother, Thomas, bought most of Cumberland in 1881 and built a second Dungeness—a huge Victorian mansion that stands in ruins today after burning mysteriously in 1959 under a widespread cloud of rumors. If anyone now really *does* know how it burned, that person isn't talking.

None of the characters I describe is intended to suggest any living or dead Carnegie—but it has been the Carnegie heirs who've faced the difficulties, along with the many pleasures, of caring for Cumberland for a hundred and twenty years.

There was a sizable number of them too, by the middle of the twentieth century, for Thomas and his wife, Lucy (a very able and far-seeing matriarch who put the land in a long-lived trust), had nine children, and seemingly countless grandchildren and great-grandchildren—with differing lives and perspectives.

Some wanted to sell their parcels of Cumberland. Some

would rather have died, and consequently tried hard to talk the others into keeping theirs. The Candler family of Atlanta too, the founders of Coca Cola, had bought the north part of Cumberland in the 1920s. So with the island sliced into many more pieces, the real situation on Cumberland was more complicated than I've presented.

The National Park Service has come and stayed, of course. Cumberland's now a National Seashore. Though the collusion between a real estate man, a politician, the National Park Service and a developer brought in to scare the owners that I talk about in the book never took place in that way.

Aside from Greyfield Inn (which I describe as Whitfield in the book) with its three hundred acres of private land, most of Cumberland is owned by the federal government, or will be sometime in the not too distant future. Part of the island north of Greyfield is under the jurisdiction of the "Wilderness Act," which may mean (if a *proposed* Wilderness/Resource Plan for Cumberland is actually enforced) that the Carnegies, who own and operate Greyfield, and their handful of Greyfield guests won't be able to take wildlife tours across land they've cared for since 1881.

The ultimate fate of Greyfield itself is still uncertain. For the federal government did threaten in years past to condemn the land and take it over. So far it's postponed doing so. Though no one knows for how long.

There have been Carnegies who've fought that takeover, who've waged war with lawyers and media. And at least for now they've got Greyfield and a whole lot of breathtaking land.

But there are day-trippers on the south and north of the island now (44,000 in 1999), who tramp the woods and ogle the ruins, who come on the government boat and stay for a few hours. There aren't thousands a day yet. And there's limited camping. And they're more respectful than park tourists are many places. Some even have the good sense to look a little awed. So more people get to see what a Georgia sea island might've looked like before the modern age, and that may be a good thing.

Still, the issues of private ownership and government takeover remain. For all of us to study and consider.

One final note—all the nature illustrators and painters mentioned in the book are real people whose work is presented accurately, except that I took liberties with the artist who draws bones. I based my Jensen on a living one— Gendron Jensen, whose pencil drawings couldn't have been collected as early as 1961.

I couldn't have written *Out of the Ruins* without the help of many long-suffering experts in the areas I know nothing about. Dr. Robert Forney (pathologist), Dr. Julie Westerink (research scientist specializing in pneumonia) and Dr. Roger Wohlwend (general medicine) helped with medical matters. Kay Pritchard (Ph.D. psychologist) talked me through the personalities involved, particularly that of the murderer.

Dr. Rick Henninger (my horse's vet) discussed Journey's injuries and outcome (though my first horse lived through the track injury, as well as the years of starvation). Pat Salomon (who's taught me whatever I know about horses) researched horse events for me in Tryon, North Carolina.

Family friend, Rob Poole, suggested a Dyer boat. And Ted Jones, president of Dyer, talked to me at length, then sent me annotated photos to help me describe what I've never seen.

Mitty Ferguson, one of the owners of Greyfield Inn, helped with navigational questions, as well as life on the island. Bonnie Sovereign, administrator of the Amelia Island Museum of History, couldn't have been more helpful with my questions about Fernandina Beach and St. Mary's. (Unlike Mary Hill, I like St. Mary's a lot, and Fernandina too.)

Jeff Nelson, attorney at law, steered me through the legal maze, while Mary Boone, research librarian at Wood County Public Library, went out of her way to answer my weirdest questions. Linda Bridges at *National Review* provided archival information that helped a lot.

I'm an operatic illiterate, but our daughter is a mezzo much like Johanna, and she, Paul Dorgan and John Barthold provided needed information.

I pestered the staff at the Rhett House Inn in Beaufort, South Carolina (the house I use for Leah's shop in Beaufort), and at the John Rutledge House (another great inn, this time in Charleston), questioning them closely about all kinds of things, and was given substantial help. Angela Mack, curator of collections at the Gibbes Museum of Art in Charleston, made time to see me—and then gave me answers few people could have. Marilyn Harcharik, a long-time friend, fed and lodged us in Savannah, and helped with research too. Ann Allen in Tryon also let me photograph her home as a model for Daniel Henderson's.

I couldn't ask for better editors. Rod Morris at Multnomah is a very kind man and an excellent diagnostician. Joe Blades at Ballantine knows the mystery business as well as anyone, and couldn't be more pleasant to work with. My agent, Pam Strickler, listens patiently—then tells me what I need to hear.

But Hannah's story wouldn't have occurred to me if Reina Calderon hadn't described a bedridden MS sufferer from her church, "who still helps a lot of people in ways that might work in a mystery." I talked to her friend, and agreed, and then walked away telling myself never to complain again.

Like all the Ben Reese books, though, this one wouldn't exist without John Reed, retired archivist and ex–World War II scout, who still puts up with endless questions and gives me great ideas.

Enthrawling Mysteries in the Best Classic Style

PUBLISH & PERISH *Ben Reese mystery series #1*

A conservative professor dies of a heart attack moments after reporting an act of treachery, and Ben Reese's own life is on the line when he is called in to investigate.
ISBN 1-57673-067-0

PRIDE & PREDATOR *Ben Reese mystery series #2*

While investigating a man's death, American archivist and ex-WWII Scout Ben Reese is targeted by the murderer he seeks.
ISBN 1-57673-084-0

PURSUIT & PERSUASION *Ben Reese mystery series #3*

A Scottish professor dies of "natural causes" after writing a letter that makes it sound like murder.
ISBN 1-57673-416-1

www.letstalkfiction.com

A FREE
"BEHIND THE SCENES"
LOOK AT YOUR
FAVORITE
FICTION AUTHORS!

Let's Talk Fiction is a free, four-color mini-magazine created to give readers a "behind the scenes" look at Multnomah Publishers' favorite fiction authors. *Let's Talk Fiction* allows our authors to share a bit about themselves, giving readers an inside peek into their latest releases. Published in the fall, spring, and summer seasons, *Let's Talk Fiction* is filled with interactive contests, author contact information, and fun! To receive your free copy of *Let's Talk Fiction* get on-line at www.letstalkfiction.com. We'd love to hear from you!